ONE LAST LIE

A Novel

Rob Kaufman

For Chris

Without you, this book would not exist…
and neither would I.

1

The old man was dying, and the worst part was, he knew it.

He could feel it in his brittle bones, popping and cracking with every move. He tasted it in his mouth – the bitter phlegm sitting on his tongue. He could even see it through the viscous film caught between his quivering eyelids.

But the telltale sign of approaching death was the feeling of surrender that had crept into his aching body – complete resignation to his current existence and to the life he'd led. The fight was just about gone.

He pursed his lips, pushing back against the spoon Katy pressed to his mouth. He couldn't take his eyes off the thick braid of auburn hair hanging over her shoulder, moving like a pendulum, each swing bringing the broom of split ends closer to the bowl from which she scooped his oatmeal.

He refused to eat, trying to prove there was at least one thing over which he had control. Nothing tasted right anyway. Over the past thirty years food had lost its flavor, and his passion for the fine wines and nouveau cuisine he once sought was gone. He was now eating to live and wondered if it was worth the effort. As he approached his last days on earth, living had become secondary to discovering where his life had gone wrong and if, in fact, that day thirty years ago was the day he truly died.

"Jonathan!" Katy pulled the spoon from his mouth and tapped the uneaten oatmeal back into the yellow plastic bowl. "You can't go on like this. I don't want to have to threaten you with the feeding tube again."

Gently, she pushed the few wisps of white hair off his damp forehead, patting the mist of sweat with her apron. "I can see you smiling inside, Jonathan, under that sour grimace of yours. You can't fool me."

But he *was* fooling her. He wasn't smiling: not inside or out. Why *would* he smile? What inside this so-called "elite" retirement home could make him smile? The stench of urine wafting into his room from the littered hallway? The monotony of cries and moans from other residents, most strangers to him, some even younger than his 75 years, being hushed back into their rooms with gentle whispers? The crumpled white bed sheets, hardened and pilled by bleach and overuse? Were these the things Katy thought he was smiling about? *She must be crazier than I am.*

He looked at his pale, bony feet hanging off the side of the bed and longed for the security of his Westport, Connecticut home; a cozy, five-bedroom colonial where he'd lived in comfort until they wheeled him out on a stretcher almost five years ago. The sky was pure that day, an ocean of cerulean blue that seemed to go on forever. But mostly he remembered the leaves; the deepest of reds, painted by the heat of the sun and the frosty New England nights; bright yellows, sprayed with crisp and timeless autumn air. Others were almost fire-orange, with narrow veins displayed through their transparent skin, backlit by the intense sun. Bouncing on the stretcher as the paramedics carried him down the front porch steps, he held his chest, feeling the hard thumps of his failing heart and watching the leaves quiver in the frigid breeze. They dangled from the branches above him, holding on for dear life, seemingly aware that one strong wind could easily toss them into obscurity until they withered and died. At that moment he clutched the flannel bathrobe lapel into his fist, realizing he was hanging from the very same branch.

He waited until Katy carried away the oatmeal before he fell backward onto the mattress, his bare Achilles heels banging against the cold, metal bed railing. "I want to go home. I just want to go home. Why can't I go home? It's only a few miles from here. We can take a taxi –"

He heard a "tsk tsk" as Katy dried both hands on her apron and walked toward the bed. She sat next to him, her corpulence creating a valley that threatened to suck him in. He tried pulling himself up, but she grabbed his hand.

"Oh, Jonathan." She placed her other hand on top of the one she'd already swept up. He wondered how she could bear to touch his thin, age-spotted skin. "Oh, Jonathan," she repeated, her soft voice spilling puddles of sweetness all around him, like his mother, who could so easily lull him to sleep after a day of fighting with the world, a tough battle for an oversensitive ten year old.

"We've been through this so many times. Remember? Your home pays for this place – pays for me." He could barely feel the pad of her thumb wipe the tear from the side of his face. "Your house was sold years ago. This is your home now. It will be so much easier for you when you're able to accept that." She placed his hand back on his lap, stood straight up, and spread her arms to her sides, as though washing away the sadness.

"I'm going to do an extra special cleaning of your room today." She opened the pine closet door and rummaged inside. "And do you know why it'll be extra special?"

No... he didn't know, nor did he care. Just because he allowed her to wipe away an infrequent tear didn't mean she could treat him like a five year old. He lifted himself onto his elbows and sniffed.

"A surprise visitor's coming tomorrow."

Jonathan felt his chest tighten; behind his ribs, a hard thump, then another. "I don't know anyone. No one would visit me." The air rising from his throat was so arid he almost choked on the words. He squinted his eyes, glaring at her as she held the rag out in front of her and sprayed it with a foul-smelling mist. If that crap is something that attracts dust, he thought, she should use it for the inside of her head.

She jerked her head back as if she'd heard his thought, opening her mouth like a toad trying to catch a fly. Jonathan wasn't sure if she was laughing or asphyxiating from too much dust spray. She chortled and then pretended to get serious, "Oh, Jonathan Beckett, that's what *you* think. I'm sure plenty of people would visit if you weren't so grumpy."

He focused on her large bottom and the extra weight jiggling around her white scrub pants. They were tight, showing a lot more than he wanted to see.

"I do not want *anyone* coming into this room! Unless they're coming to wheel my dead body down to the morgue, no one comes in here!"

Nothing. Katy wasn't biting.

"Did you hear me?" Jonathan banged the mattress with the side of his fists.

Couldn't she understand that everyone he cared about, anyone he'd ever want to see was already dead or had been taken from him long ago? And with his own impending death so close, all he wanted was privacy – to spend those last precious moments on earth alone, recalling only memories that would make him smile.

Katy wiped a rag along the top of the television, a plume of dust erupting like volcano ash. She let out a cough. "Yes, I hear you." Another cough. "But this visit will be a happy one for you. I promise." She wiped her nose with her sleeve, sprayed more mist onto the cloth until it was damp, and stroked it along the top of the chest of drawers.

"Life is to be lived, Jonathan, and sitting in this room like a hermit is not living. You don't talk to your neighbors, you don't accept visitors, you barely talk to me." She waved her arm. "You don't even have any photographs in here. This is not living, Mr. Beckett. Not living at all." She unfolded and refolded the cloth, tucking it into the palm of her hand. Slowly turning toward him, she tried to force a smile. From the pained look on her face, Jonathan could sense she was uncertain whether or not to continue the diatribe. Her eyes focused on the wall behind him, avoiding his face. "This isn't living, Jonathan... it's dying."

The room was dark except for a few strips of light pushing through the slats of the vertical blinds. Every now and then Jonathan heard footsteps scurry past the closed door: maybe that thick-headed nurse Flo bringing pills to a resident she forgot to medicate; maybe lunatic Frank from the fifth floor sneaking behind the nurses' station, stealing cotton balls to put inside the imaginary spaceship he'd been building for years.

Or maybe it was all his imagination, just part of the barrage of sounds and visions that showed themselves nightly, invading his loneliness like a blast of arctic air and nearly taking his breath away. But it was always worth it, for when his breath returned, Philip came with it.

Tonight he ignored the chill and kept his eyes on the nearly invisible ceiling, focusing on imagined shapes: swirls and dots and circles floating amidst the darkness, falling then rising, then falling again. As always, Philip appeared through the shadows, his doe-like eyes a darker brown than they'd ever been before. His blonde hair glinted with golden highlights, feathery strands of amber sweeping across his forehead. A hint of stubble covered the lower half of his face, accentuating the glowing, silky skin.

They never spoke during these nightly visits; no need to. They stared at one another until Jonathan felt safe enough to drift off to sleep and dream of the life he'd once lived. But tonight, with eternity at the edge of each breath, Jonathan pushed a whisper from deep within his throat. "I'm coming," he mouthed, frightened by the meaning of his words, yet at the same time mesmerized by the thought that after so many years, he'd be whole again. "I'm coming."

He didn't wipe the tears from his face, nor did he struggle to pull the ends of the quilt out from beneath the mattress. Jonathan let his eyes close, took a deep breath, and replayed the part of his life he could remember – all the while, in the back of his mind, praying he'd be dead before Katy arrived with his surprise visitor.

2

"The girl was a square," Philip used the blade of his new sushi knife to push diced onions to the far end of the cutting board.

Jonathan leaned against the doorjamb leading into the kitchen, hiding his fists inside the pockets of his jeans. Fragments of onion were already sticking to the inside of the sink and tiny labels from avocado peels clung to terra cotta tile under Philip's left foot. Jonathan desperately wanted to start picking things up before the disorder got out of hand, but he knew better than to break Philip's momentum. Cooking was Philip's way of escaping the monotony of his CPA career – the daily influx of numbers and calculations that poured over him like a hot bowl of alphabet soup. Trying to tidy up while Philip prepared meals would be asking for trouble.

"A square, huh?" Jonathan perched on one of the metal stools in front of the island – the best place to stay out of Philip's way while keeping watch over the growing mess. "Was she dull? Boring? Did she dress like an old woman?"

Philip turned around to face him and leaned against the counter. He held the knife in the space between them and sketched a square. "No, I mean a *square*. You know, like a box with four corners. She was maybe five feet tall and about 250 pounds – literally a square." He turned back to the counter, grabbed an avocado, squeezed it and held it to his nose. Jonathan saw the furrow of Philip's eyebrows and immediately knew it wasn't good news. "Too freakin' ripe.

Jesus! As of today, we never buy another avocado from Balducci's." He tossed it into the open garbage container, grabbed another, squeezed it and pursed his lips. "I'm glad I bought extra."

Jonathan tried to keep him focused on the subject at hand – their impending dinner guest: a woman he'd never even heard of, until Philip mentioned a few minutes earlier that she was on her way from New York to eat dinner with them. He glanced at the stove's digital clock: 6:00. In fifteen minutes, the "square" would be ringing their doorbell.

"Are you kidding me? You hung out with a square all through college? How come I never heard about her?"

Philip sliced through the avocados with ease, his adept hands creating perfect halves to expose the pit. He held the pitted half in one hand and the knife in the other, tapping the pit with the long edge of the knife, wedging it deep enough to twist out the pit. They called this the "pit twist," but before Philip came along Jonathan didn't even know avocados had pits. He loved watching the pit twist, right up to the moment when Philip unhitched the pit from the knife by slamming it on the edge of the sink, splattering avocado gunk around the room.

"I actually met her at the Boston Common on the first nice day after the longest winter ever. Exams were driving me nuts and I had to get away from campus for a while. I spread a blanket and some books out on the grass, took my shirt off, and soaked in the sun."

The sweet smell of cilantro wafted through the air. Jonathan took a deep breath, and saliva filled his mouth. In a few minutes he'd be testing the guacamole.

"I fell asleep, and when I woke up a giant shadow loomed over me. It was Angela blocking the sun like the sail of a ship. At first I thought it was a dream."

Half-listening to Philip's story, Jonathan drummed his fingertips on the black granite. He wanted the kitchen cleaned before Angela arrived, but Philip was taking his time. Not good. He forced himself to take a deep, cleansing breath and marshal his mental forces. A mess in the kitchen did not mean the end of the world. It only meant discomfort: an "irritated state of being" as his therapist, Dr. Crowley called it.

The thought conjured up a mental image of Dr. Crowley, holding his pipe and pontificating at their final session together: "This irritated state of being is the root cause of your troubles, Jonathan." The doctor spoke with all the compassion of an executioner at the gallows. "And you'll need to work at keeping it under control for the rest of your life." Miffed because Jonathan had decided to end the expensive therapy, the doctor's words were a last-ditch attempt to convince Jonathan he should continue the sessions for the rest of his life. And with each sentence he spoke, Jonathan slumped deeper into the chair. *Maybe he's right... maybe just a few more sessions... maybe...*

Jonathan forced his spine straight and sat tall in the chair. He'd almost succumbed to the doctor's cunning logic, but a surge of strength – the same one that helped him originally decide to end therapy – warned him he must start handling the daily issues of life on his own. He leapt to his feet, slid on his sunglasses, and left the gaping doctor slouched in his vintage leather wingback chair.

Outside the office, Jonathan felt an emerging freedom that escalated with each step he took away from the doctor's frigid, air-conditioned room into the intense humidity of the mid-July day. The sun clawed through his tee shirt, heating his chest and working through his jeans – a sensation so opposite the arctic environment of Crowley's building that goose bumps covered his entire body. The warmth and sun enlivened him, exciting an optimism he rarely experienced. *This is a good omen.* The words rang in his head, *sunshine... not rain... a whole new day.* He pulled his shoulders back and strutted down Rices Lane, proud and ready for the fight ahead. And he knew it would be a fight – a constant battle against his "irritated state of being" and everything it entailed – such as today's obsessive thoughts of maintaining a spotless kitchen while Philip expressed himself as a cook.

Jonathan cleared his throat. "Okay, so this square is standing in front of you. Then what?"

Philip tossed the chopped garlic, onions, jalapeno and cilantro into the bowl of mashed avocado. He slid in a pile of diced tomatoes from the cutting board, gave the mixture a few good squeezes of lime juice, and stirred everything together with a whisk. "Well, she told me if I wasn't careful I'd get sunburned. I asked her jokingly if she was a doctor. She told me she was studying to be a nurse. Then I asked her if she wanted to sit with me. She hesitated at first, I guess because it was hard for her to squat, but somehow she made it down." He laughed and tossed his head back to push the hair from his eyes. "Anyway, we talked for like two more hours. About her dream of becoming a nurse, my dream of working for a Big 8 accounting firm and one day settling down and having a family with the love of my life."

Jonathan's eyes began to well up with tears. "The best laid plans..."

Philip dropped the whisk, its handle clanking against the metal bowl.

"You're telling me, Jonny." He shook his head slowly, grabbed the whisk and with deep strokes began remixing the ingredients. "Little did I know my sperm was useless."

Philip's mood change hovered in the air between them; a heavy fog holding fear and death. The mess created by his innuendo was much worse than the mess on the kitchen floor.

"That was before the cancer, Philip. Your sperm wasn't always dead. The radiation did it." Jonathan wasn't sure if these were the words Philip wanted to hear, but they were the only ones that came to mind. What were people supposed to say about cancer? He had no idea.

"You have testicular cancer," Dr. Jacobs had said, holding the papers in his hand while flipping through the pile of reports on his desk. "But this type can be very curable. I've seen cases where…"

"But he's only thirty-two," Jonathan interrupted. Philip squeezed his knee and when Jonathan looked up, he caught the deep red encircling Philip's eyelids: the first sign he was on the verge of tears.

"You know age has nothing to do with this, Jonny." Philip's voice trembled.

Jonathan knew his words didn't make sense, but the reference to age had less to do with the cancer than it did with the unimaginable thought that Philip could leave him.

Although the cancer was diagnosed and treated five years ago, it still felt like a bad dream from last night – doctors in scrub suits, CT scans, dark hospital corridors, sizzling fluorescent overhead lights, and trite expressions of sympathy from nine-to-five hospital workers.

The train rides to Grand Central Station were bathed in silence: Philip unable to discuss the prognosis, numb from the fear of an imminent death; Jonathan terrified of a life without Philip, the one person he'd given himself to and received ten-fold of love in return.

They went through the motions, week in and week out, after a while recognizing the taxi drivers who transported them from Grand Central to Sloan Kettering. On days when Philip felt too weak and nauseous from the radiation treatments to get on a train, they'd make last minute reservations at a nearby hotel on Madison. Before every treatment, Philip asked Jonathan to drive the Beemer into the city, but Jonathan refused. He'd done the research and would rather have Philip suffer for an hour on the train than force him to endure two or three hours of traffic on the I-95 corridor. Jonathan brought every one of their activities down to a science, making sure Philip didn't face any more discomfort than absolutely necessary. Too weak to argue, Philip acquiesced and followed the schedule, knowing Jonathan had one goal in mind: to keep him alive.

Six months after treatment began, the cloud lifted. In an office with papers and folders now piled from floor to window, Dr. Jacobs declared Philip cancer-free.

"There are no signs of malignancy and all the blood tests are clean." Dr. Jacobs glanced at each of them and paused. "I haven't mentioned the sperm count, because I didn't know if it was relevant in your situation."

Jonathan clenched his teeth and took a deep breath, the noise from his mouth sounding like a blocked vacuum cleaner hose. He leaned forward and placed his hand on the edge of the doctor's desk, preparing to announce their relationship was not a "situation," but a lifelong commitment of love, just like a "normal" couple. Before he could explode, Philip touched his knee with a calming hand.

Dr. Jacobs studied the back of his hands for a moment, avoiding Jonathan's eyes. "If you were planning to have children, that won't be possible, I'm afraid. The radiation and other treatment drastically lowered your sperm count – your healthy sperm count, that is." Philip pulled in a breath and Jonathan instinctively reacted by grabbing Philip's hand. Looking at him would have been too painful for them both.

Before Philip's diagnosis, they'd talked about having a family. Philip did constant research on insemination, surrogates, and child-rearing; absorbing the information like a daddy-sponge and relating all the facts to Jonathan every night in bed. Philip's excitement quickly spread to Jonathan and they'd fantasize a child lying in bed between them. "We're using your sperm," Jonathan said one night. "The last thing we need is another Jonathan Beckett running around." He gently traced his finger along the blond wave of hair that fell on Philip's forehead. "But a little Phillip Stone would be perfect... just like you."

That once-cherished scenario crashed down on them as Dr. Jacobs leaned back in his chair and clasped his hands over his chest. "Yes, Philip, you're infertile, but you're cancer-free. Be happy with the compromise: you might have lost a dream, but you didn't lose your life."

But what is life without dreams, you idiot? Jonathan kept his mouth shut.

Dr. Jacobs continued, "It's been a privilege knowing you, Philip. I admire your strength." He finally looked at Jonathan and forced a smile. "And you too, Jonathan. I wish you both well and plan on seeing you in three months for your follow-up."

With that, he stood and reached for Philip's hand, but Jonathan already held it and wouldn't let go.

Since that day, neither of them mentioned having a family. And now was definitely not the time, Jonathan thought, as he looked at his watch: three minutes until their guest arrived. He decided to avoid the cancer conversation and get back to Angela.

"We have about three minutes until she gets here, Philip. Give me a quick rundown of what she's like so I have an idea how to talk to her."

Philip dipped a small tortilla chip in the guacamole and brought it to Jonathan's lips. Jonathan devoured it, letting the silky guacamole fill his mouth with a perfect blend of spices and chili heat.

"Exquisite, as usual!" Jonathan licked the salt from his lips and reached for another chip.

"Hands off!" Philip folded the guacamole into a serving dish, wiped the rim of the platter with precision, and placed it on the island. He opened the oven door to check the empanadas again. "I hope she eats pork," he whispered.

"From what you told me so far, it sounds like she'll eat anything." Jonathan eyed the guacamole. "Now hurry up, tell me more."

Philip glanced at the clock on the stove. It was now 6:15. "I wonder if she had a problem getting a cab. She took the 5:07 and should have arrived at Westport at six. I should've picked her up… it *is* rush hour."

"What?" asked Jonathan, "Why are you shaking your head?"

"Well, she's either late or it's like the old days when she would just change her mind and not show up." Philip rinsed his hands and peered out the kitchen window.

"This isn't a good sign." Jonathan threw Philip the dishtowel sitting on the island so he could dry his hands.

"Angela was the best and worst friend I had in those days. She'd help me study for midterms and finals. She invited me over for meals so I wouldn't eat frozen dinners every night. She got me hooked up in the mailroom at an accounting firm so I could make a few extra bucks. We had good times together and she helped me out a lot. But other times, she'd turn into someone else, like she wasn't Angela anymore."

Jonathan squirmed on the stool, uneasy with the tone of Philip's voice.

"Are you telling me we have Sybil coming over for dinner? How many personalities does she have?"

"Don't be an ass, Jonny. She had one personality... okay, two... alright, maybe three." Philip exposed his white teeth, displaying the unnerving grin Jonathan had fallen in love with the day they met twelve years earlier. "Sometimes she'd get depressed and angry – like the goodness of her soul had left, just flown away, and nastiness took its place." Philip moved the curtain away from the kitchen window, searching for signs of a taxi within the looming dusk. Other than the bulging hydrangea blooms and umbrella pines, the long, narrow driveway was empty. "I think it was the whole weight thing. When she sat alone and thought about it, she got angry. She didn't have a lot of friends; just her coworkers at the hospital, a couple of other nursing students and one or two people from her classes. Sometimes I'd be sitting with her and say the most innocuous thing and she'd start screaming – or crying. Her face would contort and she'd look at me with disgust."

"Like Regan from the Exorcist?" Jonathan asked, trying to lighten the mood.

"Not far from it. I almost expected to see her head twist three hundred and sixty degrees." Philip threw the dishtowel onto the island countertop and scanned the kitchen as though trying to think of any detail he might have forgotten. For him, work in the kitchen was done. For Jonathan, it was just beginning. He still had a mess to clean up, and disorder lurked in every nook and cranny.

"And when I told her I was gay? Don't even ask. She didn't speak to me for weeks. The next time I saw her after that, she must've gained twenty pounds. A friend of hers called and said Angela really liked me, you know, in *that* kind of way. And when she found out it was never going to happen, she kinda flipped. After awhile she learned to deal with it and we still hung out, but things were never really the same. I always felt she thought something was going to happen with us. Between that and her multiple personalities, I really couldn't deal with the situation any more. A few months before graduation, we gradually lost touch. And I haven't seen her since." Philip looked out the window again; headlights swept along the asphalt driveway, glints of stone sparkling from within the Belgium blocks. "Until tonight." He wiped his hands on his pants. "She's here."

Jumping off the stool, Jonathan stood next to the island and straightened the small stack of magazines sitting by the counter's edge. The whole conversation made his stomach feel glacial, frozen from the inside out, and he'd lost his appetite – for guacamole and for Angela.

"I don't trust her, Philip." Jonathan curled his fingers around a loop in Philip's jeans. "Fifteen years you don't hear a peep, and now, here she is out of the blue. I don't like it."

Philip turned and smiled; he was used to Jonathan's distrust of people. "Don't you worry your pretty little head about her," said Philip, kissing Jonathan's forehead. "She's harmless."

Jonathan pulled back. "You say that about everyone. I'm older than you and I've met more crazies. I don't trust this one."

"You're older than me?" Philip laughed, covering his mouth with his hand. "Are you kidding me? You're what, five years older than I am and suddenly you're Mister Man of the World? C'mon Jonny, give me some credit, will you please?" He straightened the collar on Jonathan's green Polo shirt, rubbed his hand along Jonathan's well-defined pecs and winked. "You have the biggest, most beautiful blue eyes..."

Jonathan held back a smile. "Don't start the bullshit, Philip. I'm just telling you..."

"I know, Jonny, I know. Yeah, you're right, it's been fifteen years. But we've all changed. When she called, she really did sound like a different person. I'm hoping she's now only the good Angela, and left the evil one back in Boston."

Just like Philip, Jonathan thought, *always searching for the good in people. Even in a psycho-killer.* He took another deep breath and entwined his fingers within Philip's.

"If she shows one sign of lunacy, I'll drive a wooden stake through her heart and throw her out on the lawn." He looked at the pots, pans, utensils and avocado peels strewn about the kitchen. "After I have her help me clean this mess."

Philip pulled Jonathan's wrist toward him and twisted him around, slapping his butt as he walked out of the kitchen and through the foyer toward the front door. The doorbell didn't even ring before Jonathan heard the door open and a scream, as though from the devil herself, echoed past the foyer, through the kitchen, and straight into Jonathan's head.

<u>3</u>

While Philip greeted his guest and her shrieks of excitement settled into murmurs and giggles, Jonathan braced himself against the sink with his back toward the faucet. He pressed both hands flat against the black granite, fingers wrapped around its rounded edges, and waited for the giant creature to fill the doorway and spew fire from her mouth. He glanced around the kitchen, feeling perspiration mist over the back of his neck, embarrassed by the chunks of avocado stuck to the chrome backsplash and the endless array of cooking utensils on every inch of counter space.

When Philip walked into the kitchen, arm in arm with Angela, Jonathan's mouth dropped open and he suppressed a groan. The woman was stunning. According to Jonathan's on-the-spot calculations, she weighed no more than 110 pounds and had the figure of a runway model – too short in stature to walk the platform, but gorgeous enough to have her unblemished face on the cover of *Elle*. Her black hair was swept back and pulled tight, twisted elegantly into a French braid that reached mid-spine. She wore a hint of eyeliner that accentuated her blue eyes, a sweep of rose blush slightly coloring both cheeks, and subtle pink lipstick that brought out the sensuous curve of her lips. Jonathan was far from a fashion guru, but her understated clothing had to be designer-made. She wore a beige blazer over a white silk and lace teddy. Both blazer and teddy flowed seamlessly over a black linen skirt with a hem just below her knees, accentuating thin, shapely calves. If there was one name Jonathan knew, it was Prada, and he had no doubt her black shiny pumps were screaming the name as she slowly approached him.

This couldn't be Angela. This couldn't be The Square.

Before Jonathan could back away, she ran to him, flung both arms around his neck and pulled him close. He kept both arms at his sides and searched Philip's face for some kind of assistance, or at least reassurance this *was* Angela. Philip shrugged and tightened his lips, also apparently at a loss for words.

"So you're the one who finally got Philip," she said in his ear, loud enough to simulate conversation, yet soft enough to remain a whisper. "Congratulations." She gave him a gentle squeeze, wrapped her hands around his biceps and let his arms slide down through her hands. She grabbed his wrists and stepped back. "My, you *are* hot!" Her voice was now loud enough for Philip to hear. "You were right, Philip. Those lashes are to die for!"

Philip shrugged again, not much help to either of them.

"You look like you were expecting someone else." She puffed out her cheeks, lifted her arms so they hung way out to her sides, and slowly clomped backwards, side to side toward Philip. "Someone who walks like this maybe?" She was doing a perfect imitation of the person Jonathan expected to trudge through the door.

He forced a laugh. *Was it acceptable to laugh with someone who was ridiculing herself?* He wasn't sure of anything except his rising level of discomfort. He pasted a smile on his face, watching her move back to Philip's side. *She's a little strange*, he was thinking, when out of the blue her puffed out face displayed a glimpse of what she must have looked like all those years ago. For a fraction of a second the smile in her eyes changed into a sorrowful grimace; the corners of her mouth turned down, and her self-ridicule transformed into a challenge: *no one can laugh at me now.* It was as though she'd coughed up remnants of a person she despised and was asking Jonathan if he despised her, too.

Before he had a chance to react, the beautiful woman returned, her hand grabbing Philip's shoulder, her lean body pushing against his side. "I can't wait to catch up with both of you. But first, how 'bout a Double G and T?"

Philip gave her a peck on the cheek and practically skipped into the wet bar area, a short hallway that led into the expansive living room. He lifted the glass-paned door of the cherry wood cabinet that held nearly every kind of liquor imaginable. Although neither of them drank often (one or two martinis and they'd usually find themselves slurring over one another), they kept a fully stocked cabinet for get-togethers and impromptu parties. "Grey Goose and Tonic." Philip held up a three-quarter full bottle of the vodka and a tumbler he'd filled with ice. "Double G is Grey Goose and T is tonic," he informed Jonathan as he returned to the kitchen.

Jonathan rolled his eyes. "Duh," was all he could think of to say. He was still trying to feel out the situation. Who was this girl and why was she here? No doubt she had an attractive flair about her, an élan of sophistication combined with apparent zeal for her new, thinner life. His uneasiness in new social situations was a given – both he and Philip had accepted it years ago. Philip blamed it on some deep-seated insecurity; Jonathan blamed it on the simple fact that people were strange and couldn't be trusted. He'd gradually learned to accept their current circle of friends. But when a new face entered his life, Jonathan would always step back and wait for the newbie to prove himself.

Tonight's new face had been thrust upon him without sufficient warning – his internal uneasiness attested that fact. To make matters worse, this newbie arose unannounced from Philip's past and was someone Jonathan had no clue existed before tonight. Feeling the sweat on his palms, he recognized the absurd direction in which his thoughts were heading and decided to stop them in their tracks.

"Give me a Double G and T, too." He blurted, and then smiled at Philip's surprised expression.

"You sure?" Philip headed toward the wet bar. "You know how you get sometimes…"

"What's this?" said Angela, "Do we have a lightweight among us?"

"*Two* lightweights," Philip said before Jonathan had the chance. "I'm not the partier I used to be, Angie." He grabbed two tumblers from the cabinet. "And since I've been working so hard at preparing our meal, I'll have one, too." He set the glasses on the counter next to Angela's. "And I mean only one."

"Oh, Philip, I'm disappointed in you." Angela rubbed her palm against his back and gently caressed between his broad shoulders. "But I have to admit, since I lost all that fat, I'm kind of a lightweight, too."

Jonathan felt a sense of relief. Finally, someone mentioned the word *fat*.

Philip mixed their drinks like a scientist in a lab, carefully measuring each ounce of vodka with his eyes. After placing the lime wedge atop Angela's Double G and T, he spun around and set it in her open hand.

"Speaking of fat, you must tell us what you did to lose all that weight. I mean, you look unbelievable. There's no way I would have…"

Jonathan crept ever so slowly toward his drink. "Let's discuss this on the deck," he interrupted, feeling the need to douse his discomfort with liquor before heading into the fat zone. "I want to get some fresh air before the mosquitoes start their dive bombing exercises."

As they walked through the living room on their way to the deck, Angela stopped, leaned against the baby grand and gazed at the ceiling as though she were wishing on stars. Jonathan was about to ask if she was okay, when she took a sip of her drink.

"This cathedral ceiling is absolutely beautiful," she half whispered, "and that crown molding is to die for. Not too ornate, not too simple. Just right." She studied the room, stretching her neck to see past the Georgian-style pocket door leading into the formal dining room. "These colors fit you guys to a tee… mocha walls, maple and cherry, brown suede, everything… everything is just gorgeous. It's like the perfect mix of casual chic and classic. I love it." She took another sip of her drink and swallowed slowly. "This must be Jonathan's doing." She looked at Jonathan and raised her left eyebrow. "Philip was never into décor."

Jonathan lifted his glass to his lips, glad Angela liked his taste, but a bit uncomfortable about the compliment. "Thanks," he half-whispered into his Double G and T before taking a huge gulp.

"Hey, wait a minute!" Philip interjected, "I had some say in the décor!"

Angela softly patted his cheek. "I'm sure you did." she winked at Jonathan. "I remember your apartment at BU. Bare walls, a consistently unmade bed, two pairs of jeans hanging in the closet, and a dead plant sitting atop an upside down milk crate."

"Yeah," Jonathan added, "that's pretty much the way I found him."

Philip laughed. "You're full of shit." He turned to Angela. "And you're full of it too. My apartment wasn't that bad." He took a sip of drink and pretended to be thinking of the past. "I remember having three pairs of jeans in the closet!"

Philip wrapped his arm around her shoulder and guided her toward the French doors that ran along the back wall of the living room. When he slid open the door leading to the two-tier deck, a wave of humidity drifted inside, carrying the scent of jasmine and honeysuckle.

"It's almost seven o'clock, I thought it would've cooled off by now," Philip said, closing the door once they were all outside. "We're way too used to air conditioning, Jonny. We definitely have to get out more."

The pinkish hue created by the setting sun filtered through the spaces between the leaves of the giant maples, casting a soft crimson haze that hovered inches above the thick expanse of manicured grass. The three of them walked to the deck railing and looked out over the burgeoning backyard flora.

A thicket of forsythia rimmed the edges of the acre lot, their bright yellow flowers clinging to the branches that stood almost six feet high. Billowy andromeda overlapped the forsythia with spidery, ecru-colored tendrils hanging motionless in the heavy air.

This hedgerow, along with the maple and ash trees, ornamental grasses, and other precisely ordered plants and flowers, helped create a natural boundary from the rest of the world. Along with the stitching of copper-lantern-shaped garden lights threading through the boundary, the back yard resembled a mini-village.

Angela stood between the two men, the three of them silent, absorbing the stillness of the approaching dusk. Jonathan felt an intense hush pervade his being – an air of understanding that somehow pulled them together in a way that would remain forever. *Strange to feel this way about someone I don't even know*, he thought.

At that moment, Angela broke the silence. "This is like a photograph, guys, it's just surreal back here. But where's the dog?"

"What dog?" asked Philip.

"You must have a dog. I mean, two gorgeous men, a beautiful house in Westport, the best cars too, I'm sure. Only two things are missing: the white picket fence and the dog."

"Ha," Philip said, glancing at Jonathan, "I wanted the fence, but Jonathan said no to that. He walked over to Jonathan and grabbed his hand. "And as far as the dog goes, Mister 'No poop in my backyard' here said no to that also."

"Okay, okay, I didn't mean to bring up any sore subjects." Angela sauntered across the deck and studied each piece of furniture carefully before sprawling onto a lounge chair. "Let's just sit and catch up a little. I never get quiet like this in the city."

Philip gasped. "I forgot the appetizers. Let me just..." He placed his glass on the stone-topped table and turned toward the door.

"None for me," Angela said, patting her stomach, "That was my first rule when I finally decided to lose the weight. No appetizers and no desserts... entrée only. And since most of the time appetizers and desserts were my entrée, I pretty much starved at the beginning."

Philip turned to Jonathan with a look that needed no words.

"I don't need the guacamole now." Jonathan said, "We can wait until dinner."

"Please, boys, not on my account. You eat as you always eat. No special treatment. It makes me feel uncomfortable when people hold back because of me."

Philip picked up his glass and tapped Jonathan's stomach. "Some of us could use a little of Angela's discipline, couldn't we?" He made a dash toward the lounge chair before Jonathan could slap his backside.

"Ignore him, please" Jonathan said. "No, really how did you lose all that weight?"

Angela exhaled into her glass, letting the coolness of the ice reach her face. She looked away from them both into the darkening sky to the west. "Okay… here's the short version of a very long story. On my thirtieth birthday, I sat in my studio apartment on 16th Street eating an entire birthday cake by myself. To this day, I don't know where the realization came from, but all at once I knew I had three choices: Remain an unhappy, unhealthy, fat nurse without a social life, or *any life* for that matter, and die from a heart attack; or I could kill myself and just get the whole thing over with – and honestly, that was so tempting; or I could actually try to make a life for myself. I must've cried and yelled at myself for more than five hours before I finally decided on the third option. I actually threw the cake out the window. It's a good thing it was three in the morning or an innocent passerby might've been slammed with chocolate icing."

"I've been slammed with worse," Philip said, "Jonathan and I were eating some split pea soup for dinner one night at the kitchen island…"

"Don't go there…" Jonathan sighed.

"And he wasn't feeling too good to begin with…"

"I said, don't go there."

"Oh, now you have to go there, Philip!" Angela leaned over the arm of the lounge chair, her French braid dangling over her shoulder like a bungee cord.

"Before I knew it, my white tee shirt was green with his vomit!"

"That is so nasty!" Angela said, covering her mouth.

"I told you not to go there." Jonathan smugly took a sip of his drink.

"Although," Angela started, "when I was a nurse, I'd have someone vomit on me practically every day. It was like I was a puke target – patients waited just for me to enter into their rooms before they'd heave their load and try to hit me dead center."

The three of them groaned in unison. Jonathan told himself this was not pleasant pre-dinner conversation and figured he'd better put an end to it before all Philip's hard work was put to waste.

"What do you mean *when* you were a nurse?" he asked.

"Well, right now I'm a nurse manager at New York Presbyterian. I make sure all patients in specific areas are attended to. I recruit staff, work on increasing nurse retention, and basically spend my nights doing paperwork."

"But I remember how much you wanted to be a nurse," Philip said, with a tinge of sadness in his voice. "You talked about wanting to take care of people, holding their hands, saving their lives, blah, blah, blah. Remember?"

"Yeah, I remember. But honestly, for me it got old very fast."

Jonathan was surprised at the harshness of her tone, although he realized being a nurse, especially in Manhattan, must take its toll sooner before later.

Angela took a sip of her drink, the sky now reflecting a pink hue on her face. She smiled and shook her head. "And once I lost the weight, it seemed the execs noticed I had a brain too. After a few classes and some great recommendations, I now make a lot more money and get to manage puke instead of clean it up."

"Okay," Jonathan said. "So we're back to *that* again." He walked to the French doors and slid one open. "Let's eat now before we get into any other bodily functions."

Angela jumped up from the chair, ran to Jonathan, and stood in front of him holding up her glass. "Time for another one of these anyway. And by the way, what do you do Mr. Jonathan?"

"I'm a writer."

"Wow, a creative guy! I always thought Philip would go for a numbers guy like himself." She swirled the remaining ice in her glass. "What do you write? Books? Magazine Articles? Advertisements? TV Shows?"

Jonathan gestured with his arm for her to go inside. "Yes. All the above."

"You have to tell me everything you've written. I want to read all of it." She walked past the piano, through the living room, and into the kitchen as though she'd been living in the house for years. "You might even end up writing a book about why I'm here," she called back to him from the kitchen.

Jonathan stopped moving mid-step. He felt a weak throb in his chest. *I knew it was too good to be true.* He swung around, about to ask Philip if he'd heard what Angela said, but was stopped before he had the chance.

Philip smiled. "I heard. Just stay calm and take that sour look off your face. I'm sure it's not as bad as what your imagination is stirring up." He kissed Jonathan on the cheek and started into the kitchen after Angela. He paused mid-stride and called back, "She's great, right?"

Philip didn't wait for an answer. A few seconds later the oven door slammed and he called, "Dinner's ready!"

Thinking about Philip's question, Jonathan had decided it was too soon to make up his mind.

4

The mind chatter wouldn't cease, and the pit of Tommy's stomach began to burn. Angela's voice was inside his head and her words from their telephone conversation only moments earlier reverberated like a booming bass from the speakers of a souped-up '62 Chevy.

"You're smothering me, Tommy. I need room to breathe," she'd said. Through the telephone he could hear her shoes clacking on the floor and the echo of voices around her. Damn it! She was actually in Grand Central Station making good on her promise to escape to Connecticut.

"I don't mean to, Angie. I just wanna spend more time with you. I like being with you for Christ's sake. Don't you get that?"

"I get it," she said curtly. "And I have to go. We'll talk tomorrow."

He waited for her to continue, but there was silence. She'd hung up.

Tommy stared at the phone in his hand, wanting to smash it against the cubicle wall. Instead he slammed it into the cradle and banged his fists on the desk. He swiveled his chair around the tiny stall where he spent his days, stood up, and glanced over the partition. The office was empty – not a soul, not even the cleaning people. He listened carefully: nothing but the whirr of a computer a few spaces down.

He walked to the wall of windows lining the west side of the giant room. From the thirtieth story, the floor-to-ceiling glass showed the entire expanse of Manhattan below him. The Hudson River twisted and turned along its jagged shoreline, heading south from the mouth of New York Harbor and north past the George Washington Bridge. The setting sun spread dust through clouds as thin as paper, slicing the light and layering intense reds and simmering pinks onto everything it touched. A Circle Line Ferry puttered silently downriver, offering tourists and native New Yorkers a new perspective of Manhattan. A few sailboats darted through the channel, lucky, he imagined, to be going nowhere in style. If his mind wasn't so consumed with dire thoughts, he might've been able to appreciate the view.

He rubbed his eyes and looked at his watch: 7:07. What is she doing now? Why wouldn't she let me go with her? Who the hell is Philip and what is she *really* doing in Connecticut?

He kicked a recycled paper bin into the middle of the hallway, sending paper up to the ceiling and fluttering into the cubicles. Chunks of shredded paper settled as far away as the main hallway.

He stared at the mess he'd just made, his left eyelid twitching. This had happened the way it always did: Something would get under his skin, incessant thoughts took over, and before he knew it there'd be a mess – a hole punched in a wall, his dirty shoeprint on a taxi door, or blood splatters dotting his clothes after a bar brawl that started over a meaningless glance from an overfriendly patron.

Up until this moment, the new combination of Zoloft and Clozapine seemed to be making a difference. This was the first episode in three months, but now he was even more enraged by the fact that his medication didn't kick in when he needed it most.

Maybe he should boost the dosage. He'd ask Angela her opinion if she wasn't running off to some guy's house in Connecticut. What the hell was she doing out there, anyway? They were all fucking snobs, for God's sake.

"What the hell happened here?" Karen Martin stood before him, the tip of one red high heel pump buried in a pile of paper. He stared at her legs, following the sheer, silk stockings leading to a black Dior pencil skirt. The fabric hugged her slim frame, showing curves and shapes he'd never seen during working hours. She always wore asexual dresses or dull pantsuits, the exact opposite of what she had on now. He blushed at the twitch in his groin.

She looked at the paper scattered around the room and rolled her eyes. After a deep breath and a look at the ceiling as though asking God for assistance, she put both hands on her hips and stood over him. "What's this mess all about, Tommy?"

He shook his head to clear the thoughts about Angela, and then sank to his knees and began scraping the paper into piles.

"Hey, Karen. Sorry about this. I was trying to finish the numbers for Davis and Company and there was one page I couldn't find." This sounded reasonable, and since she didn't interrupt, he kept talking. "I searched through all my folders and still couldn't find it, so I figured I threw it out. Anyway, to make a long story short, I've been going through the garbage."

Karen had started tapping her toe on the papers. She glanced up and down the length of the mess, pursed her lips, and puffed out a breath.

"Jesus, Tommy. Just make sure it's cleaned up, okay?" She turned and walked toward her office. "I don't have time to discuss this now. I'm just here to pick up a brief on my way to Lincoln Center."

He continued to gather papers and shove them back into the recycle bin, forcing himself not to watch her walk away. Breathing a sigh of relief, he mentally patted himself on the back for keeping everything under control.

But her facial expression told him she was skeptical. He'd exploded a few times before, the most recent a little over three months ago. He went off during a meeting while the client was in the room, but Karen wasn't there – she didn't know the details. She heard about it third hand and wouldn't even listen to his side of the story.

She'd called him into her office two days after the event.

"Tommy, you know I like you. I really do. You're a nice guy and good at your job. The problem is, we have no tolerance for outbursts like the one you had the other day."

Tommy shifted in his chair and tried to speak, but she held up her hand.

"Please don't explain. I've heard detailed accounts from other employees, as well as the client." Rustling the papers in front of her, she grabbed a sheet and began fanning her face with it. "And I read the explanation you submitted to Human Resources. I'm sorry, but this just doesn't cut it."

She tossed the paper back onto the desk and swiveled her chair toward the window. Tommy saw his own reflection next to hers in the window – stringy blonde bangs sweeping his brow; the dark circles beneath his eyes, probably from overwork and over-worry; the fat knot of his tie dangling too low over his shirt to be professional enough for Karen. He was a mess, inside and out. He knew it and was very much aware of the fact that Karen, the woman who held his future in her hands, knew it too. He caught her gaze in the reflection and immediately shut his eyes.

She swiveled back, placed her elbows on the oversized mahogany desk, and clasped her hands. "This is strange, Tommy. You're usually so quiet and even-tempered. You don't look like the type of person who'd behave this way. And more than once, too. Looks can be deceiving, I guess." She intertwined her fingers, sliding them back and forth against each other. "So, the long and short of it is, I'm asking you to sign up for an Anger Management course. That's the only way I can justify keeping you with the firm."

Tommy still didn't look up. He felt her staring at the top of his head. She was full of shit; she didn't like *him*, she liked the work he pumped out... the long hours researching cases... the weekends typing up contracts... the extra time he'd put in writing dispute and deposition summaries when no one else would. She was a goddamn user. He wouldn't look up, but he had to say something.

"Thank you," he whispered. "I appreciate this."

"Tommy, don't thank me. Just use the course to get your anger under control. Who knows? Maybe you'll figure out some other things that might be bothering you."

Thoughts of jumping over the desk and strangling her with his tie forced him to reposition himself in the chair. He needed more meds... and fast.

"Okay." Tommy's voice trembled. "Will do." He stood, glanced at Karen one last time, and walked into the hallway. Heads bobbed from inside cubicles; faces wearing curious expressions, trying to figure out what had happened. Tommy kept his head down, maintaining a steady pace until he reached his desk. He grabbed his leather bag and searched frantically for the bottle of Xanax. Throwing two pills into his mouth, he washed them down with a long swig of a warm Coke that had been sitting on his desk all day.

"Goddamn piece of shit," he muttered. "Goddamn piece of shit," he repeated until he felt the medicine kick in and the tightness fade from the pit of his stomach.

And here he was again, 7:30 at night, cleaning papers off the floor like a scavenger, feeling the same tightness in his gut he'd felt three months earlier. In the end, he had no one to blame for tonight's fiasco but this son-of-a-bitch Philip – some shitbag from Connecticut Angela just had to see. He'd begged her to stay with him in the city, to go out for dinner, maybe hit a movie, and then do the sex thing he'd been looking forward to for weeks. But she rejected him again, muttered something about visiting her old friend Philip in Connecticut. Now, thanks to this fucker Philip, he'd been humiliated instead of enjoying an evening with the woman of his dreams.

Without pause, he scooped papers in his arms, threw them into the container, then scooped up more. When he finally stopped, he stood and rested against the bin to catch his breath. He noticed Karen's office was dark. She'd snuck out while his head was buried in the recycle bin.

He'd just finished placing the lid back on the bin when he heard the vacuum cleaner down the hall. Just in time. He ran to his desk, shut down his computer, grabbed his bag, and looped the strap around his shoulder. Looking at his desk phone, he thought again about calling Angela. *Smothering,* she'd said.

"Screw you!" he said to no one, and was out the door.

Two hours later, Tommy glanced up and down the street, unable to say for sure where he was. Other than the fact that he'd been thrown out of Brodsky's bar on 16th Street and remembered walking south on 9th Avenue a short time ago, his location was a mystery to him. He looked upward and almost fell over when the streetlights wobbled above him, blotches of yellow fluorescence streaking across the night sky onto the pavement below. Mist hovered above the sidewalk in front of him, lurking like the cryptic fog in horror films. Tommy kicked at the vapor, half expecting a monster to lunge at him, wishing he could rip its face apart with his bare hands. Instead, he fell backwards, the strap of his shoulder bag slapping his face. He went down hard and the back of his head slammed into the pavement.

"Fuck!" he cried out. "Help!" He looked both ways, searching for help, but the sidewalk was empty. For a moment he saw people on the other side of the street, but they vanished in the mist. The world around him was spinning so fast, he couldn't distinguish reality from mind play, so he wasn't sure the people actually existed. His head hurt too much to attempt another scream, so he pressed his palms against his eyes and pushed his fingers into his scalp, slowly rocking his head back and forth.

"God *damn* it!" he shouted, but only loud enough for him to hear.

He dragged himself toward a tree that stood about seven feet away, scooted up the wrought iron grate around it, and squeezed his spine as far as it could go into one of the spaces. Trying to stop the dizziness, he tipped back his head in an attempt to focus on a branch... one branch... any branch. That helped for about ten seconds, and then a wave rose inside his stomach and forced out the vodka he'd been drinking. He spewed a liquored volcano into the bushes surrounding the tree. Relief, for another ten seconds, until a second wave hit. Then a third. And finally, the last.

Beads of perspiration and humidity hung on his forehead. He wiped them with his forearm, which didn't do much good since every pore of his body was oozing sweat. His throat burned from the acidic saliva lining his esophagus. He coughed, inhaled, and swallowed hard, to no avail. The burning continued... all the way down his throat and deep into his solar plexus... the anger working its way back down to where it started.

He stumbled to his feet and rummaged in his bag for the cell phone. Squinting in the dim light, he pressed the CONTACTS key – and there she was, first in line: Angela. The sound of her voice would calm him. He'd be able to go home and forget this day ever happened. *For God's sake, give me some room, Tommy. You're smothering me!* Ignoring her voice in his head, he pressed the key and held the phone to his ear.

He stopped breathing the second she picked up.

"Angie... Angie... I'm sorry to call... I know you're in Connecticut... I know you're with that guy... I just wanted to..."

"Hold on, please." He heard her hand covering the phone with a scratching noise on the mouthpiece that vibrated something sharp inside him. His body shook and he started to worry he'd throw up before she came back. He took a deep breath and leaned against the tree.

"Ang? Are you there?" His voice quivered from fear, desperation, and the vomit residue stuck to the back of his tongue.

"Gentlemen, I'll be right back," he heard her say. "And only one more double G and T for me!" He heard her heels clack against the floor and waited for her to speak, to give him her full attention.

"Why the *fuck* are you calling me?" Her voice was a loud whisper. "I told you to give me some God damn space, Tommy." The deep echo of her sigh created static.

Tommy's mouth hung wide open. He wasn't ready for those words, that tone, and the sound of something that resembled, but only if he dared to admit it, hatred.

"I'm... I'm...." He stammered, running one hand through his hair. "I said I was sorry. I just needed to hear your voice. This day has really sucked and I thought..."

"Jesus, Tommy. That's the problem. You *don't* think." She took a deep breath, the way she always did when she got angry with him. "We'll talk about this tomorrow. Please let me enjoy my evening."

"Okay, I promise, I won't bother you again." He shoved his hand into the front pocket of his chinos and fingered a few coins. Calling her was the right thing to do. He could feel it. The sound of her voice, no matter what words she spoke, had calmed him. He smiled. "As long as I can talk to you tomorrow, it'll get me through the night. I'm sorry I bothered you. I love you."

Silence.

"I love you, Ang." Tommy waited. Nothing. He held the phone out in front of him: CALL ENDED. "She hung up! The bitch hung up on me!"

He glanced around wildly, searching for someone to hear him, to tell him what had just happened – on the phone and inside his soul. But no one was in sight, no one to put out the raging fire within his gut. He held onto a scream that caused stinging tears to teeter on his eyelids knowing that if he'd opened his mouth and let out the scream, it would have cracked the earth beneath his feet.

<u>5</u>

Philip watched Angela walk into the living room. She gave him a smile and a wave, then rolled her eyes at the cell phone.

He returned her wave and leaned back into the soft velour pillow lining the back of the dining room chair. It was still difficult for him to believe this was the same girl he knew in college. The woman standing in his home was so unlike the Angela from BU that at times during the evening he couldn't help wondering if she was an imposter. But once in awhile he'd see her eyes change, a glimmer of sadness from long ago creeping through her new exterior. In his imagination the puffiness of her forehead would reappear; the flaps of loose skin that used to cover her neck re-emerged like a rooster's wattle. And then he'd know she was real, and the guilt of abandoning her fifteen years ago sent a cold shiver up his spine.

Jonathan walked up behind him and whispered in his ear. "What's going on? You look like you're in a daze."

Making sure Angela's back was still toward them, Philip turned to Jonathan and gently kissed his mouth. "I am in a daze. I'm in a love daze. With you!"

Jonathan rolled his eyes and sat in the chair next to Philip. "You're so full of shit." He looked at Angela, then quickly back to Philip. "So what's up with her? Who's she talking to? Why is she here? Are you going to ask her already? I really do like her. I can't help it. But what's she up to?"

Philip placed his index finger over Jonathan's lips. "Shhhh. Stop asking so many questions for God's sake. I can't remember them all. Now go get another G&T for our guest, please. It looks like she's annoyed at whoever is on the phone and will definitely want her drink when she gets back."

Jonathan heaved a sigh and grabbed Angela's empty glass off the table. "Okay," he whispered, "but can we get to it? I still have an article due tomorrow and I'm only halfway through. And look at this table. There are enough dirty dishes to fill up the dishwasher three times. We can't entertain your ex 'whatever she is' all night. Plus…"

"I'll clean up, Jonny, don't let it worry you."

"Actually, that *is* what worries me." Jonathan smiled back. He kissed Philip's cheek as he stood. "That's why I'll be helping."

Philip shook his head as Jonathan walked away. He put his elbows on the table, rubbed his eyes, and kept his hands over his face, allowing the sensation of happiness to run through him. He was still amazed at his good luck – finding someone with whom to share the rest of his life. He and Jonathan were polar opposites in many ways, but those differences made them compatible and created a strong attraction the day they met at his twenty-fifth birthday party.

"I told you not to go to any trouble, Max. I don't need a party."

Max poured Margarita mix into the blender, barely paying attention to the amount of liquid flowing into the glass jar.

"Oh, stop it, Philip. It's just a few people. You're a quarter of a century old today *and* one of my best friends. Plus, it's the perfect way for you to meet Luc."

Philip leaned against the marbled kitchen counter and crossed his arms. "Max, you know I don't like to be set up. Especially on my birthday. It feels so obvious."

"Obvious, shmobvious, Philip. Luc is the one, I'm telling you. When I saw his sculptures at his show in Manhattan, I thought of you right away. I know how you like the creative type. I'm telling you, he is *it*." Max poured the blended Margarita into a martini glass and passed it to Philip. "Would you like a cherry?"

"No. This is great, thanks." Philip used his top lip to pull some of the iced Margarita into his mouth. He tasted the faint orange flavor of cointreau in the back of his throat and smiled. "Perfect, Maxi." He took another sip. "But I'm wondering why Mr. Frenchy is the one for me, and not for you."

Philip knew the reason, but gave Max the opportunity to explain.

"He's a little too foreign for me," Max responded, cleaning up the spills around the blender. "You know me. I like my men American, through and through."

Philip smiled and took another sip of his Margarita. For now he'd let Max think he believed the "country of origin" explanation, when the truth was, it was more an issue of age than ethnicity. Six months earlier when Max turned forty-five, he made a rule not to date anyone older than thirty. "It'll keep me young!" he announced on the night of his own birthday party, surrounded by fifty of his closest friends. They all cheered him on, clinking their glasses to his new code of misconduct – none of them expecting him not to have a date for six full months. Philip loved Max like the older brother he'd never had and couldn't muster the nerve to tell him that if he truly wanted any kind of relationship, he'd have to break his new rule – it just wasn't working in his favor.

"So, can you tell me who's coming?" Philip asked, breaking the awkward silence.

"The usual," said Max, repositioning the glass vase of tulips he'd placed on the buffet table that separated the dining room from the living room. "I kept it small and intimate, just for you. Soft music, high end wine, and eight filet mignons grilled to perfection by yours truly."

"And what time are they arriving?"

Max glanced at his watch. "Well I told Marina and Wayne to come at seven, knowing they'll show up at six-thirty." Philip nodded his head and smiled. "Ahhh, yes, he's your boss. You already know how over-punctual he is."

Philip continued to nod, refusing to say anything that could get him into trouble. "And then there's Taylor and Jacob. Couple of the year." Max rolled his eyes. "I told them six, hoping they'll show up by seven." He tapped his watch as though making sure it was still working. "But if they're fighting, I have no idea when they'll actually get here."

"And Luc? What time is he getting here?"

"I sent a car to pick him up so he wouldn't have to take the train. The taxis at the station can never find this house anyway. I swear to Jesus, I don't know what it is with those cabbies. You'd think I lived in the boonies of Tennessee."

Philip walked across the kitchen toward the dining room.

"So that means he'll be here at *what* time?" Philip asked, pushing for some sort of definitive answer.

"Within the half hour, I'd say. I wanted the three of us to spend a little time together." He shuffled his slippered feet across the kitchen floor and into the hallway that led to his bedroom. "But first I wanted some private time with you before everyone showed up, so I could give you your gift." Max was now shouting from his bedroom at the other end of the house. "The sun should be off the deck by the time everyone gets here." Silence. And then the sound of boxes sliding. "But who knew it would be so cool in June?"

"Who knew?" Philip echoed in his mind. He turned toward the dining room table and shook his head. It was classic Max, set with majestic elegance that looked like a scene from Martha Stewart's Living magazine. Solid, chocolate-brown silk covered the rectangular maple table – an embroidered silk fabric running along its rim. In the center sat a large crystal vase perfectly clustered with white, pink and violet rose blossoms, with petals of the same colors lying randomly from end to end of the silk cloth. Two white tapered candles, each in a hand-blown crystal holder, sat on either side of the vase, bringing symmetry to a table setting that only Max could accomplish.

Eight place settings with Max's finest bone china and silver lined the edges of the table. Counting one setting on each end and three settings on each of the longer sides, Philip wondered who the eighth setting was for. He knew Max would occupy the head of the table and, as guest of honor, he'd sit at the other end.

"Who's the eighth person?" Philip called, strolling back into the kitchen.

"What?" Max screamed from the bedroom, still skidding boxes along the closet floor.

"Who's number eight tonight?" Philip shouted back.

He looked out the kitchen window and for a full five seconds felt almost paralyzed. Walking up the extended driveway toward the house was a man almost six feet tall, with dark, wavy hair that fell down his forehead to the rim of his Armani sunglasses. His dark blue polo shirt showed off a muscular body, a v-shaped torso Philip himself had worked so hard to achieve. His slim waist and long legs were covered in sand-colored chinos that fell the perfect length to the top of his loafers. Philip couldn't take his eyes off the man, watching his every move as he walked up the middle of the two walls of rose bushes that led to the front door.

Philip placed his drink on the countertop and ran down the hall into Max's bedroom. The doorbell rang.

"Holy shit, Maxi, I think you're right!" He found Max on his hands and knees inside the humongous walk-in closet. "This guy could definitely be the one!"

"I could've sworn to holy Jesus I put it in here and now I can't find it." Max said, rummaging through cartons and throwing shoes across the closet.

Philip bent down, grabbed Max by the hand, and pulled him up. "Don't worry about that, Max! You've already gotten me my present and he's at the door."

"What are you talking about?" Max asked, slapping his hands against his trousers.

"Luc! He's at the door." The doorbell rang. Philip pulled Max harder, almost making the both of them fall onto the bedroom floor. "Hurry up. C'mon!"

"Shhhh… calm down, Philip." Max tried to compose himself by sliding his hands through his gelled hair and smoothing down his eyebrows. "I know. He's very hot. But he's got nothing on you."

Together they walked down the hallway and into the marble-floored entryway. The sound of their heels on the tile, clacking in unison, made Philip smile. They were both anxious, each for their own reasons, and it gave Philip a feeling of warmth to realize how much Max cared about him. Max turned to Philip, straightened his shirt collar, stood on his tiptoes, and gently kissed Philip's cheek.

"Remember, you're the better part of this deal. And it's your birthday. So even though these French hotties always think they have the upper hand, be sure to listen to your heart."

Max turned the doorknob and pulled. Philip could feel his heart pumping, hard and steady, on the verge of jumping out of his chest.

When the door opened, Max let out a nervous laugh.

"Oh, Jonathan!" he breathed, sounding to Philip like a sigh of relief. "It's you." Max turned to Philip. "It's not *him*, Philip, it's Jonathan."

"Jonathan who?" Philip asked softly, extending his hand.

"Beckett," Jonathan half-whispered, taking off his sunglasses. He handed Max a bottle of wine and hugged him, not taking his eyes off Philip. He then reached out his hand to accept Philip's. "And you must be Philip."

When their hands touched, Philip was captivated by the softness of his skin and the firmness of a grip that sent a tingle through his body. He clung to Jonathan's hand with an intuitive urge to never let go.

Max cleared his throat and pulled their hands apart.

"Philip, this is Jonathan. I told you he was coming, didn't I?" He led them both into the kitchen and placed the wine bottle on the cooktop. "He just moved to Westport from Manhattan. He's a friend of a friend of a friend of my mother's who asked if I could introduce him to, well, you know, people 'like us.'"

Philip picked up his Margarita and took a big swallow. "Would you like a drink?" he asked Jonathan. "Max is the best Margarita maker in town."

"Sure." Jonathan nodded.

Max didn't move. "Even though Jonathan's over 30, I let him escort me out for dinner one night..."

"Thirty and a half," said Jonathan.

"*Over* thirty," Max repeated, "Even so, we went out for dinner. He's a writer, very intelligent, and I thought he'd fit in well with all of us. I also thought he'd be *my* date..." He shot a side-glance to Philip and winked, "...at least for tonight."

Philip knew where Max was going and forced himself out of the spell in which he'd been floating since he saw Jonathan walk up the driveway. "I got it Max. Whatever you want."

Jonathan smiled at him. Philip caught it and smiled back. Max noticed the exchange and again ran his hands through his hair.

"Philip, Luc is coming. Remember Luc?" Max said. "Does the name ring a bell?"

"Who's Luc?" Jonathan tapped the cap of the blender in an attempt to get Max to mix another Margarita.

"He's Philip's date for tonight. I set them up." Max grabbed the tequila and poured it into the blender. "And it looks like I might've made a boo boo. I don't know *why* I never considered the two of you..."

Philip cupped Max's neck and pulled him close. "Don't worry, Maxi. All will be fine."

The doorbell rang and the three men looked at one another without moving.

Jonathan turned and started to walk down the hallway toward the front door. "I'll get the door," he put one hand in his pocket, "and Max, please mix up that Margarita, *pronto*. I have a feeling I'm going to need it."

Although Max was kind enough to sit Luc next to him and Jonathan next to Philip, Luc did not easily surrender what was originally offered. He used all his sexual ammunition to catch his prey. There was no denying Luc's dark brown eyes, lascivious accent, and exquisite European features were alluring, but Philip knew deep inside they didn't compare to the sensations he felt sitting next to Jonathan – the comfort and security dancing silently between the two of them. Not to mention the spark of sexual excitement that ran through him whenever their knees touched beneath the table or Jonathan brushed his arm. Luc was sexy, no doubt about it. But Jonathan was so much more. This was the clichéd epitome of love at first sight.

They decided to fight Luc off together, ignoring his intimate stares and sexual innuendos throughout dinner, finally confronting him when he ambushed Philip on the deck.

"Happy birthday, Philip," Luc whispered in his ear while cupping his right butt cheek. "What you say I take you to my apartment for your special birthday present?"

At first Philip thought it was Jonathan's hand grabbing his ass, but once he heard Luc's voice, he laughed at himself. From the moment he and Jonathan met, there'd been no flirtatious smiles or batting of the eyes; no looking one another up and down trying to figure out who would take which role when they hit the sack. What they felt for one another was more wonderment than anything else – deep curiosity about who this person was, and could he be as beautiful on the inside and he was on the outside.

Philip gently removed Luc's hand, turned around, and let the arm drop. He was about to tell him off when he realized it wasn't Luc's fault. Luc was primed by Max to expect something that wasn't going to happen. And, if Jonathan hadn't shown up tonight, he'd be in Luc's apartment right now, preparing for his first European sexual encounter.

"Everything all right?" Jonathan called from the doorway. "Philip? You okay?"

"Everything's good, Jonathan," he answered, still staring at Luc. "Luc, I'm sorry, but it just isn't going to happen." He backed toward the door until he could feel Jonathan's warmth on his back. "But thanks for the offer – and thank you for coming."

A drop of sweat rolled down Philip's back. It was over. Thank God!

"It's over," Jonathan said, "Thank God."

Philip shot a look at Jonathan. "Holy shit! Can you read minds, too?"

Jonathan handed Philip a drink. "Only on special occasions."

They didn't sleep together until their fifth date. The wait was a mutual decision, both of them knowing this relationship was different and shouldn't be treated lightly.

"And how many others *have* you had?" Philip asked at dinner one night. Jonathan brought the napkin to his mouth and looked up to the ceiling as though counting endlessly. He then lifted his wine glass and gently clinked it against Philip's. "*Others?*" He took a sip of wine. "Since I met you, I realize there have never been others."

Philip snorted, then laughed.

"Oh, boy, you really are a writer. So cool and collected. And you always find just the right words, don't you?"

Jonathan chuckled. "Not always, but usually." He grasped the stem of his wine glass, staring at the white tablecloth as though it held the answers to life's deepest questions. "But don't let these first few dates fool you. If you haven't noticed, I have a slightly obsessive, sort of neurotic, definitively Type A personality. There's plenty about me to love, but also a lot to contend with." He clasped his hands beneath the table and looked at Philip awaiting a response. "There, it's out. Now you know."

"You don't hide it as well as you think." Philip leaned back in his chair. "But I'm thinking that's part of your charm. That... and your great butt, of course."

"So I've been told," smirked Jonathan.

Philip smiled back and peered deep into Jonathan's eyes. This would be the night they'd be together, he felt it, and by the look on Jonathan's face, he knew the feeling was mutual. He waved to the waiter and signaled for the bill.

"I think it's time to leave now," he said, his voice holding the most subtle tremble.

"I thought you'd never ask," Jonathan was already standing and pushing his chair up to the table.

"Where did *you* go, my dear friend?" asked a voice from somewhere in the distance.

Still sitting at the dining room table, Philip rubbed his eyes and shook his head. Angela stood next to him, touching his hair with her fingertips.

"Just thinking," he said, reluctantly coming back to the present. "I was remembering, actually."

"Remembering what?" she twirled his blonde locks around her index finger. "When we were going to school?"

"No, back to when I first met Jonathan. My twenty-fifth birthday."

"Oh." Her fingers stopped moving. She edged backward and sat in her chair. "You really love him, huh?"

"Yes."

"That sounds definitive. No ifs, ands or buts about it?"

"None," he said, grabbing her hand in both of his. He turned around to look toward the kitchen. "But don't tell Jonathan. I don't want him to think he has the upper hand."

"I'm sure he's already on to you." She pulled her hand away. "It's been, what, ten, eleven years you've been together?"

"Twelve," he said.

Angela gently touched his nose with the tip of her finger. "Honestly, I've seen people together less than two years who don't look as happy as you… or who get along as well as the two of you. What's your secret?"

"What's this about secrets?" Jonathan placed a full glass in front of Angela and pointed to her cell phone. "Everything okay?"

Angela took a sip of her G&T and pursed her lips. "Yum!" She picked up her phone and clicked the ringer to vibrate. "Yes, everything's okay. Just work calling me, as usual."

"Oh, that sucks. I thought it might've been your boyfriend."

"Jonathan!" Philip lightly slapped his hand. "Don't insinuate for God's sake. If she wants us to know about a boyfriend, she'll tell us." He looked at Angela. "So, do you have a boyfriend?"

Angela sat down next to Philip. She leaned her head to one side and looked down at the table. This was the saddest she'd looked all night. He shouldn't have asked her the question.

"No. There's no boyfriend," she said, picking lightly at the tablecloth with her long, rose-colored fingernails. "I might look different on the outside, but I don't feel it on the inside. I'm working with my shrink on that."

Jonathan sat down on the other side of Philip and gave him a slight side kick on his ankle. Philip kicked him back and then turned toward Angela, hoping his movement would deflect any detection of their childish foot fighting.

"I'm sorry, Angie. I shouldn't have pried." He looked at Jonathan then back to Angela. "It's his fault. He brings it out in me."

Another side kick.

Angela's grimace turned to a smile. "No, please, don't even think about it. You can ask me anything you want, especially since I have such big question for you."

Philip braced for another kick, but it didn't come. The playing had stopped. Jonathan's way of saying, "I told you so."

6

Something was different about tonight: very different. He could smell it through the bleach mopped over the hallway floor; feel it in the moist spaces between the tenuous skin of his fingers. An invisible tension hung in the air, adrift until something or someone shook it loose.

He'd awakened a few moments earlier by what he thought was the door creaking. A nurse? An aide? Another nursing home denizen? A doctor?

Jonathan looked at the clock: 12:37.

"Shit." He felt the usual dryness in the back of his throat. Sooner or later he'd have to pull his arm out from under the blanket and grope around the bedside table for the cup of water. "Shit."

He could see the outline of the door, light from the hallway trying to push in through the edges. He squinted, attempting to see if anyone had entered the room and was hiding in silence, waiting for the right moment to attack.

"Hello?" He noted the tremble in his voice, not so much from fear as from old age. For a split second, that shakiness made him wish that someone *was* hiding in the darkness – someone who'd spring from the shadows and smother him with a pillow. That would bring him to the place he wanted to be, so much sooner than life's normal course of events.

He tried to swallow, the dryness like splintered wood against the sides of his throat. Reaching for the cup of water, he cleared his throat.

"If you're going to get me, do it now," he whispered.

Nothing. He took a sip of water from the cup. It hurt going down, his throat still parched. By the third sip, his throat felt better and the search in the darkness for a possible attacker had ceased. He realized he was alone. Again. As he'd been every night for the past thirty years. As he'd be every night until he took his last breath.

He still couldn't understand the unusual feeling crawling around inside him. It wasn't a sensation of impending doom, but more the inexplicable excitement of something so unlike anything he'd ever experienced, it induced both fear and wonder.

He clenched his fingers into a fist when he realized this was the same sort of feeling he'd had the night Angela invaded their lives. Although the meal was uneventful and Angela seemed likeable enough, the hair on the back of his neck wouldn't lie flat from the moment he met her. His instincts told him something was up, but he didn't put his finger on it until the three of them were sitting at the dining room table enjoying their last drink of the evening. He smiled into the darkness, remembering the way he and Philip had playfully kicked one another under the table. He inhaled deeply, wracked with the pain of missing Philip's touch.

"As you know," Angela announced, "We're the same age, Philip and I. Which means I'm approaching my forties."

The moment she uttered the words, Jonathan knew where this was going, but he held himself back, biting his lip to make sure no words escaped. He leaned his elbow onto the dining room table and moved forward so he'd have a better view of her and also be able to see Philip's reaction.

She rubbed her index finger along the condensation on her glass, fidgeting in her chair while sneaking peeks at both of them. Why wouldn't she just spit it out already?

"I want to have a child," she blurted out. "It's all I've ever really wanted, and now I'm finally ready to do it." She glanced at Philip, to Jonathan, and back to her glass. "I have no significant other in my life and the way things look, I may never find one. When I thought back to all the men I've known in my life, there's only one who stands out." She pointed to Philip. "Intelligent, logical, fun, social and of course, extremely handsome. You have every characteristic I'd like to pass on to my child."

She took a small sip of her G&T and placed it on the table. It seemed to give her the courage she needed to offer eye contact. After a few more seconds of silence, she continued. "And then of course, I remembered how back in college you would talk about having a family... wanting a son who you could teach to play ball. Bringing up children who would..."

She stopped talking when she noticed Philip's eyes getting watery. Jonathan rubbed the back of Philip's neck with one hand and held onto his arm with the other.

"What is it? Why are you getting so upset? If the answer is no, I'll totally understand, I just thought..."

"I'm sterile." Philip choked on his words. "Testicular cancer. Five years ago. I can't have children." He looked at Jonathan. "Ever."

About to lay into her for showing up out of nowhere after fifteen years and asking for sperm like it was a $10 donation for Save the Children, Jonathan cut himself off when the tears fell down Angela's face. She appeared sincerely distraught, although he wasn't sure whether it was for Philip or herself. Did her only hope of sperm donation suddenly crash and burn? Would she have to go back to her list of potential daddies and settle for second best? Or did she actually feel sorry for Philip? Watching the mascara smear down her face, Jonathan knew this wasn't the time to challenge her.

Angela took Philip's hands, still crying.

"I am so, sorry, Philip. I had no idea you'd gone through such a thing." She glanced at Jonathan, her sorrowful expression soothing his anger. "And I'm sorry to you also, Jonathan." She struggled for words, grabbing a tissue from purse. "I feel like such an idiot... and feel so bad... and don't know what to say."

"Shhh," Philip touched her head and let his fingers tread down her braid. "No worries, Angie. It's alright." He turned to look out onto the deck. His voice was shaky. "It's Karma, you know. Remember how you helped get me into that cryo bank in Boston? All those sperm donations I made to help pay my tuition?"

She nodded, holding the tissue to her nose.

"I gave it away to strangers, and now when I need it the most..."

Rubbing Philip's back, Jonathan cut in. "Stop, Philip. We've talked about this before. It's not 'Karma'. It's not 'Irony'. It is what it is and that's *all* it is."

Angela blew her nose into the tissue and sniffed. "And how are you now? Are you okay?"

"A-ok," Jonathan said. "He's one hundred percent healthy and cancer-free for five years."

"Thank God," she whispered, stuffing the tissue back into her purse. "I wish I'd known. I work with some top-notch oncologists. Who was your physician?"

"Jacobs at Sloan," Jonathan answered.

"One of the best," she said. "That's good. I have some friends at Sloan Kettering if you ever need anything. And I mean *anything.*"

Five minutes before, Jonathan was ready to pull Angela to the front door by her hair. But now, he'd opened up a bit and sensed her sincerity. The hair on the back of his neck settled a little and he could feel himself breathing deeper.

Jonathan drummed his fingers on the table and stood up. "Well, I have an article due tomorrow morning by eleven. So I'm going to hit the computer."

"And I have to get going," Angela responded, leaping from her chair. "It's getting late. Can you call me a cab?"

"Cab my ass," Philip said, "I'm driving you to the station. Let's check the train schedule, and if we have time I'll show you some of Westport."

Angela walked over to Jonathan, caressed his face and, wrapped her arms around him. Hugging him tightly, almost squeezing, she whispered in his ear. "Thank you for tonight and for taking care of him."

Jonathan hugged her back and kissed her on the cheek. "You're welcome for both." He looked at Philip, then back to Angela. "I don't say this very often, but I like you and would love for you to come visit again."

"He's right. He never says that. So you must be special," Philip said.

She squeezed him again. "I definitely will," she said.

Three minutes later, Jonathan watched from his office as the Beemer's headlights backed out of the driveway and lit up the street. Seconds later, they were gone.

More than two hours passed before the headlights swung into the driveway. Jonathan waited to hear the car door shut before sauntering to the front door. He leaned against the wall, waiting for it to open. When it finally did, he didn't say a word.

"Hey, babe," Philip said, closing the door behind him. When he saw Jonathan's expression, he stopped. "I know, I took a long time. But we did some more catching up, I showed her downtown, we had to wait for the next train, blah, blah, blah."

"I figured," Jonathan said, scolding himself for worrying. "That's why I didn't call your cell. I didn't want to be like my grandmother used to be." He kissed Philip's cheek and started walking back to his office.

"Are you kidding me? You are your grandmother!" Philip smacked Jonathan's ass and followed him down the hallway.

"Ha. Well if it wasn't for my grandmother, I wouldn't be here now, would I?" said Jonathan, falling into his desk chair.

"No, you wouldn't, and I say a prayer to her in heaven every single day for having a grandson like you." Philip laughed and plopped down on the suede love seat, facing Jonathan. He was silent, just staring at Jonathan as though waiting for a response. But there wasn't one. Jonathan continued typing. "And speaking of sons," Philip started.

Jonathan clicked "save" and spun his chair around. "Yes, go ahead. Get whatever it is off your mind." He crossed his arms. "I'm waiting. Speaking of sons…"

"Speaking of sons," Philip started again, "Remember when we used to talk about having one. You and I? And then the whole cancer thing happened?"

Jonathan nodded.

"I know we always spoke about using my sperm, since you didn't want another Jonathan Beckett running around the planet. But I'm thinking you were just kidding about that, right?"

Jonathan leaned forward and gestured for Philip to continue.

"Well, I for one would love to have another Jonathan running around this planet. I'd love to play with him, help him grow up, take him to art shows, get him really cool presents, and love him as much as I love you."

"Sounds like your drive to the train station involved a lot more than just catching up on old times. Did she actually have the nerve to ask if *I* would be the one to donate?"

Philip raised his hand. "Stop. No. It was me. I brought it up."

"Why? What would make you think…" Jonathan rubbed his head with both hands, as though trying to unscramble the words floating inside his brain. "We wanted your baby, not mine. I'm a mess, you know that. Why would we want to bring another neurotic, OCD kid into the world? And with Angela for God's sake. We don't even really know her. I don't get it."

Philip walked to Jonathan and fell to his knees. He looked up at Jonathan, his face holding a sympathetic smile. "First of all, you don't have OCD. You just like things clean. And you're not neurotic – you just worry a little more than most people." He rubbed Jonathan's legs. "I don't know why you always make yourself sound crazy. Unless it's some kind of excuse."

"An excuse for what? Why would I want to think I'm crazy?"

Philip kept his eyes on Jonathan's. "If you think you're crazy, then you never have to do anything that really means something."

Jonathan shivered as though tiny spiders were crawling up his arms and legs. He tensed, unsure how to respond or even if he could. Philip's words hit a nerve and his reaction was more paralysis than anger.

"Think about it," Philip continued, "Whenever you talk about writing a novel, you say you can't because then the world would know how crazy you are. Or when we discuss the kinds of articles you write, you say you like to keep them light and generic so readers won't sense your neuroses. Honestly, I think that's bullshit. You're playing it way too safe. It holds you back in lots of ways, and that hurts me because I think you're squelching your potential."

Jonathan found the strength to move and rolled his chair back, away from Philip.

"And what does this have to do with giving sperm to a total stranger?"

"First of all, she's *not* a total stranger. And second, it's the fact that you keep saying you wouldn't want to have a child because he, or she, would be neurotic and obsessive. You are neither. I think it's just another way of you holding yourself back."

Forcing himself to breathe, Jonathan stood and walked to the window. The lights lining the driveway lit up the hydrangeas from beneath, an explosion of blossoms illuminated from the inside out. A chipmunk scurried from one side of the path to the other, its tiny shadow following at first, then leading the way as it disappeared into the tall grass.

"And what does Angela think about the whole thing?"

Philip, now sitting on the floor, leaned back and used his arms as support.

"If you hadn't noticed, she thinks you're wonderful. And when I brought up the idea to her, she started to cry."

"Why? Because she has to settle for second best?"

"Don't do that, Jonny. It's not fair, to her or you."

Jonathan turned around and leaned against the chair rail. "I'm not agreeing to anything, but let's think about this logically for a minute. A girl you haven't seen in fifteen years shows up and asks you for sperm. A girl, by the way, who kind of went bonkers when you told her you were gay. And the two of you really haven't spoken since then. And now, because she's getting older and you're sterile, you want *me* to give her *my* sperm." Jonathan sat down on the floor in front of Philip so their knees touched. "Now, placing all that weirdness aside for a second, have you considered any of the legal ramifications?"

Philip drew circles with his finger on Jonathan's knee.

"Jonny, I haven't considered anything yet, other than bringing it up to you. First things first, ya know? And the first thing is to decide whether or not this makes any kind of sense. If it does, we talk more about it. Then, if it still does, we talk to G. She knows the law inside and out. And if she doesn't know the nitty gritty about sperm donation, she'll recommend someone who does. But first, it's you and I who have to decide if there's something here we want to get involved with." He brushed the wisps of hair falling in front of Jonathan's eyes. "No decisions have been made. Only points of discussion. Okay?"

"Okay." Jonathan pulled Philip's hand to his mouth and kissed the soft, padded skin of his palm, right below his thumb. "Okay. Now if I can get my mind back into it, I have an article to finish."

"S'il vous plaît continuer. Je suis désolé pour vous ennuyer," said Philip walking to the door.

"You're never bothering me. And cut the French crap. It reminds me of Luc."

"Mi dispiace, mi amor."

"Okay, now you're just showing off. Go take a shower or something."

Philip grabbed the door sash and swung around. "I vill be vaiting for vous, how you say, in zee bedwoom," he ran out of the room and down the hall.

Jonathan shook his head and rolled his chair back to the computer. Scrolling up to the top of the article, he stared at the headline: Data Security Specialists: A Day in the Life.

"Holy shit, this *is* dull."

Although it was just a whisper, inside his head it sounded like a scream.

Two days later, on a polished maple table surrounded by the faint smell of old paper emanating from the tomes of law books, Jonathan and Philip tapped their fingers in unison. The meeting room was elaborately decorated: mahogany built-ins held ancient books that seemed to breathe decades of jurisprudence, and the large window bordered with sepia festoons, held thick, wooden panes that split the glass into twelve small squares. All of it served to increase Jonathan's feeling of claustrophobia.

"G's done pretty good for herself, huh?" Philip traced his fingers along the spines of the law books.

Jonathan stood, walked to the window, and stared at the brilliant blue sky and enormous white clouds silently floating like huge cities of cotton. He grabbed the ridge attached to the bottom half of the casement window, lifted it up and inhaled deeply.

"Yeah, she definitely has. I can't believe she made partner and we didn't even know. We don't keep up enough with our friends." He turned to Philip. "You already know that, right?"

"One thing at a time, Jonny. Let's discuss the baby thing with her and then we can talk about what horrible friends we are."

Jonathan smiled, allowing Philip's soothing voice and logic to calm his nerves. He tapped the glass of the window, pointing toward Long Island Sound.

"I think I can see the Montauk Lighthouse from here. We should go back there before the summer's over. Let's look at our calendars and…"

"And you'll take me along, right?" G interrupted. "I need a vacation too, you know!"

"G!" Phillip jumped up, grabbed her, and pulled her close. "You look so hot!" He gently fondled the tight bun on top of her head. "And professional, too."

She pecked him on the lips. "You look better than ever, as usual." She threw her legal pad and cell phone onto the table and glanced at Jonathan. "Are you going to come over here to give me a proper greeting?"

Jonathan walked over, kissed her cheek and hugged her. It felt good to see her familiar face and warm smile among such cold surroundings.

"Congrats on the partnership," he said, holding her at arm's length to get a better look. "We're so proud of you."

"Thank you." She sat in one of the cushy leather chairs along the table and placed her notepad in front of her.

"It's still a bit strange seeing my name at the top of the letterhead and on the office signs. But I have to tell you, it also feels good."

Philip and Jonathan sat down across from her.

"You definitely deserve it," Philip said. "And by the look of that suit, it seems you also got a raise."

She brushed her hand along the notched lapels of her slim beige suit jacket; the black silk cami beneath it showing just enough flesh to stimulate curiosity.

"Armani," she said. "But I still look for sales. Some things are just inherent, I guess. Can't let a good deal go by. Just like my mother."

Jonathan touched the arm of her jacket, remembering G's mother, who'd died of breast cancer almost two years earlier. G was a spitting image of her mom, with the roundest of blue eyes, their color enhanced by a subtle shade of bronze eye shadow and deep brown eyeliner. A slight hint of crow's feet extended from the corner of her eyes, no doubt caused by late hours, hard work, and lack of sleep. With her hair pulled back from her face, Jonathan saw a beauty in her he'd never noticed before; a graceful profile, almost angelic, like that of a ballerina he'd seen in a portrait at the Met. The ballerina's photo had been surrounded by fog, giving the young dancer a spiritual quality. For a split second, Jonathan felt the same way about G and the real reason he and Philip were visiting her. Suddenly the idea of having a child felt surreal.

"To the subject at hand," G announced. "First we'll talk from a legal perspective, then I'll give my thoughts from a personal point of view, okay?

Both men nodded.

"I researched your issue, and I have to say it's more complex than you might think. States handle sperm donation differently. Some statutes give great weight to the interests of the progeny. And others do not."

Jonathan raised his hand as though a student in class.

"Yes, Jonathan?" she responded like a teacher, smiling at his wide-eyed innocence.

"You're talking statutes and progeny. We're kind of ignorant about this whole thing, so legalese isn't going to work. Can you dumb it down for us, please?"

"Got it," G looked toward the ceiling as though trying to translate her legal thoughts into laymen's terms. "What I'm about to go over with you only pertains to a situation in which something might go amiss between you and Angela. Right now, the three of you are getting along great. If all goes as planned, Jonathan's sperm will be implanted into Angela, a healthy baby will be born, and Angela will have custody of the child with the two of you acting as guardians with very open visitation rights. Am I correct so far?"

Again they shook their head in unison.

"Great. So let's say something goes wrong. For instance, let's say you disagree with how she's raising the child and get into a fight with her. She could try to prohibit visitation. Or suppose she loses her job and wants you to increase child support. That's where things can get complicated, especially when it comes to sperm donation cases. Are you with me?"

"So far, so good." Jonathan answered for both of them.

"Now, certain mothers have been inseminated with donor sperm and later brought the donor to court for one reason or the other. Previous trial outcomes show that although states differ in their opinions, most courts rule in favor of the child – the offspring of the plaintiff. So, back to the example of Angela losing her job and bringing you to court for more child support. If the court decided more money was needed for child's health and well-being, they would rule in favor of an increase in child support. The offspring takes precedence, not the disagreements between parties. As a matter of fact, in a recent ruling in Pennsylvania, the court imposed a statute regarding child support by a donor. They declared parents are liable for the support of their children who are unemancipated and 18 years or younger. In your case, legally speaking, Jonathan would be considered the parent. It doesn't matter whether the child is living with him or not. The fact that he donated sperm makes him the parent. Period. So let's take the subject of child support first."

"But we've already discussed child support and definitely plan on providing it," Jonathan said. "We figured we'd agree on a monthly amount with Angela. I mean, it *would* be our child and we'd want to help him, or her, have a great life. That's the way it should be, right?"

G looked at Philip, who was nodding in agreement.

"Okay, we'd have to draw up papers stating the minimum and maximum amount of support. But I'll say it again: what's on paper doesn't always prove out in court." G stood and walked to the other end of the table. She placed her fists on the polished mahogany. "You see, although you're writing and signing a document with the mother of the child, you're not constructing the agreement with the child. That means some courts would say your documents don't constitute a written agreement, since the child never had a say in the matter at hand." She looked at Jonathan, then Philip. "Does that make sense?"

"Yes," said Philip. "Perfect sense. But that's one of the main reasons we wanted to agree to provide support now. Then, if by some crazy turn of circumstances this goes off track, we won't be caught off guard. We'll have already agreed to the support issue. And we're doing well, financially, so we can keep little Jonny, or Joany, comfortable." He clasped his hands and hugged the back of his head. "Now, what about parental rights? How often can we see him?" He smiled at Jonathan. "Sorry… or her?"

G sat down and rested her chin on her hands. "For now, let's assume it'll be a he. The subject of parental rights make this even more complicated. For instance, do you want to sign a consent agreeing to give up all parental rights, which implies you won't make any decisions regarding his upbringing, or do you *want* to be involved in how he's raised?"

Jonathan leaned forward. "We'd definitely like visitation rights so we can see him, have him spend weekends with us, bring him on trips, to the museums, baseball games, stuff like that. I can't say it would be a daily kind of thing. We'd want to make sure he isn't being abused or neglected in any way, of course. Do we have to decide that now?"

G pointed to her pad at the other end of the table. "Philip, can you slide that down here, please?"

When the pad reached her, she pulled reading glasses from her breast pocket and let them rest on the edge of her nose. After flipping through about a dozen pages, she read:

"First off, in many states, true sperm donors are only those men whose sperm are inseminated through a licensed physician. So if you plan on informally donating your sperm, which I advise against, you probably won't be protected when it comes to paternity and visitation rights. Giving your sperm to a physician and letting the doctor give it to the mother can mean the difference between being considered a sperm donor and a parent. But again, the line of the law is muddled. There are so many gray areas." She pushed the glasses further up her nose and frowned. "Connecticut doesn't have hard and fast rules about these issues… yet. However, the more detailed your written and signed contracts, the more likely you can have the financial and personal relationship with your child that you'd like. Jason Deitrich is our assistant reproductive legal expert. He's in a meeting right now, but if you two decide you want to do this, he'll be the one to walk you through the steps." She removed her glasses and looked at them. "With me behind him every step of the way."

Philip and Jonathan glanced at each other and then back to G. She waited for a response. Nothing.

She leaned forward. "Okay, now for my personal take on this. You know I love you guys and want only the best for you in every way. If you want, and I mean *really* want a child without as many legal issues as I've already posed, you might want to consider surrogacy. That will allow us to work up specific legal documents."

"I know," Jonathan said. He pulled himself up from the chair and walked to the window. The clouds had flattened a bit, with silvery gray lining their bottoms. Ominous. "Then the child would be ours."

"Well that defeats the purpose, doesn't it G?" Philip asked. "We were doing this not only for us, but for Angela, too. She wants to be a mom and I don't think we want to be full time dads." He caught Jonathan's subtle nod. "We'd like to bring another one of us into the world, make sure he's taken care of, and spend lots of time enjoying and loving him. But I don't think we have the time, patience, or aptitude to do it all day, every day." He looked at Jonathan. "Do you agree, Jonny?"

"Totally," said Jonathan, turning away from the window and looking back toward them. "I lack the patience... Philip the aptitude."

Philip turned to G. "You see what I put up with, G?"

"And you love it," she replied, looking at her watch. "I have another meeting in five minutes, but let me add one more thing. I would get to know Angela a lot better before making any sort of decision. Philip, I know you were great friends in college, but a lot of time has passed since then. You might want to have a little background investigation done first. If all is clear, you should spend time with her. Get to know her better. Basically, you need to feel one hundred percent comfortable before having a child with her. Agreements are great to have and they're crucial to the process. But in the end, it's the *people* who make the difference between a wonderfully civil partnership and a horrific, unsettling mess."

G scribbled a note onto her pad, tore the page in half, and walked to the window where Jonathan stood. She handed him the slip of paper and kissed his cheek. "Here's the name and number of the P.I. we use. He's trustworthy, thorough, and doesn't overcharge. Please use him and let me know what he finds out."

She held her arms out to Philip.

"Love you, Love," he said, hugging her tightly. "And thank you so much for this info."

"It's my pleasure." At the door, she flipped her eyeglasses closed and slid them back into her breast pocket. "You can use this room until 11:30, if you want. And please, e-mail me an invite for dinner. It's been way too long."

She closed the door behind her, leaving Jonathan and Philip in a rare silence. Philip sat at the head of the long table. Jonathan slid the notepaper into his trouser pocket and sat at the other end.

Slouching in his chair, feigning exhaustion from the information they'd received, Jonathan uttered the only sound he could think of: "Hmmmm…"

"Hmmmm… back," Philip replied.

"Do you still want to do this?" Jonathan asked.

"Yes, I do. And you?"

"I do," replied Jonathan. "As long as we're one hundred percent comfortable with Angela." Jonathan's voice held both excitement and fear.

"Okay, then. You call the P.I. and get things rolling. I'll call Angela and set up a date to hang out again. We might go into New York so we can see where and how she lives. I could use a five-star meal anyway. I say Remi on Fifty Third. It's been too long since I had real Tuscan food."

"That works for me." Jonathan walked toward Philip, who met him in the middle of the room. "So we've made a decision?"

Philip touched his hand. "Yes, Remi on Fifty Third."

"No, Dumbo. I meant about having a child."

"I know what you meant. And yes, we've definitely made a decision. At least a phase one decision."

"Let's hope it's the right one." Jonathan said, getting up to look out the window again. The grayness of the clouds had darkened and wind currents blew strands of black vapor across the sky. "If I were superstitious, I'd say these clouds are telling us something."

He felt the warmth of Philip's hand on the back of his neck. "You're not superstitious, you're paranoid." Philip laughed.

"Is there a difference?" asked Jonathan.

"You tell me," Philip quipped.

Jonathan shrugged his shoulders, wishing he knew the answer.

The memory of that day in G's office sent a chill through his body, making him yearn for the plump feather comforter he and Philip used to lie beneath. He tugged at the sheets, cursing Katy again for tucking them under the mattress so securely; cursing himself for ever agreeing to have a child with Angela. If only he'd listened to the silent caution between G's words, Jonathan thought. If only he'd paid attention to the blackening clouds that drifted past the window that day; the first ominous sign of the darkness to come.

"If only," Jonathan cried, knowing his words were thirty years too late.

$\underline{7}$

"Shit!" Angela clung to the railing and tried to maneuver around Tommy, whose prostrate body was sprawled across the top steps of her brownstone. His head was buried in the corner where the cement landing met the front door; his legs dangled down the steps, crooked and bent, like a marionette whose strings had been cut.

He hadn't moved since she'd reached the steps and she cursed him under her breath. He'd better not be dead. The last thing she needed was a night of police questioning and medical examiners. She had to be at work by seven o'clock in the morning and was already working on only five hours sleep, if she was lucky.

She leaned over him to make sure he was breathing, but jerked backward when he snorted and turned on his side.

"You drunken shit." She kept her voice down, not wanting to wake him and get involved in an inebriated argument. But inside, her fury burned like a fire. She looked up and down the steps, then inside the glass door, for something to smash over his head. She could call it an accident; say she thought he was a homeless person who snuck up behind her as she tried to enter the building. She walked back to the sidewalk, still looking for a weapon, but there was nothing. God damn it.

She decided to try and sneak around him and raised her foot across his shoulder. Missing it by less than an inch, she let out a brief sigh of relief, until the heel of her other foot caught on the arm of his suit jacket. "Shit!" another whisper, but this one not muted enough.

"Ang," he gurgled. "Is that you? Angela?"

She reached into her purse and frantically searched for her keys. "Fuck, where are those fucking keys?"

His gurgling continued, every utterance fueling the fire in her belly. "Angela, it's me." He pushed himself up and leaned against the stone balustrade, rubbing his hands over his eyes. "I was waiting for you. What time is it?"

Ignoring him, she pushed the key into the lock and looked up to see Tommy's reflection in the glass door. One of the bulbs in the outdoor sconce was broken, but the remaining ones provided enough light for her to see him standing behind her, staring at her, eyes half closed. She took a deep breath, left the key in the lock cylinder, and turned around.

"Tommy, it's almost midnight. *Not* a good time." She darted her eyes up and down the street, checking to see if anyone was coming. "I'm tired and you're drunk... and extremely pathetic. If I were you, I'd turn around, stumble down those steps, and crawl back to your shit hole of an apartment."

"But..."

Before he could take his next breath, Angela flexed both hands and pushed him backward down the steps. The concrete platform at the bottom of the balustrade broke his fall, but not before he banged his forehead against the sidewalk. Still on his butt, he dabbed his forehead with the palm of his hand.

"I'm bleeding," he looked up at Angela, standing at the top of the steps with her arms crossed. "I'm fucking bleeding."

"Well so am I," she shot back. "It's that time of the month. I guess that sucks for both of us."

As he tried to stand, Angela looked him up and down. His gelled hair was sticking up in the strangest spots; his suit pants now had a fist-sized hole at the knee and a drop of blood had fallen onto his white collar. To her surprise, she realized she was turned on. She watched him struggle to his feet and when he finally did, she gestured with her finger for him to come closer.

"What?" He murmured, distrust and fear in his voice.

"Come here," she muttered, looking up to the neighboring apartments, checking for possible voyeurs. "You're turning me on."

He stopped at the bottom step, blotted his cut with the sleeve of his suit jacket, and leaned his elbow against the balustrade.

"Are you serious? You throw me down the stairs, make me bleed, and then tell me I'm turning you on?" He looked around, as if trying to find witnesses. "You're nuts, Angie."

"Nuts about you. Now get over here." She rubbed her left breast until the impression of her nipple showed through her lace teddy.

"Wait," Tommy started, "Before I do, tell me what's up with this Philip guy. And why are you getting home so late?"

She pinched her nipple and grinned flirtatiously, her eyes burning into his. "Why, are you jealous?"

Tommy walked up a few steps and stopped. "Should I be?" He pressed his tie against his shirt, top to bottom, trying in vain to flatten it.

"Maybe. We have to see what you got first."

"You know what I got." A few more steps up. "I don't want to compete with some rich fat cat from Connecticut. I want to be the only one you want."

She could smell the liquor on his breath, the sweat beneath his jacket. Rubbing her nipple harder, she closed her eyes, letting the heat in her chest drip down her belly and spread into her crotch. She opened her eyes, grabbed Tommy's tie, and brought his face inches from hers. His tongue reached for her lips, she leaned back just enough so he could feel the warmth of her breath on his mouth.

"I said, let me see what you have first." She shut her eyes again, this time forming images of Philip in her mind's eye; the soft hair she'd run her fingers through only hours earlier; those thick lashes that swept across dark chocolate eyes; the stubble he'd brushed against her face as he kissed her cheek at the train station. They were all within her as she touched Tommy's tongue with hers, devouring it like nothing else on earth existed. She opened her mouth and let him in, groaning and swaying her hips as his mouth seemed to pull the strength from her legs, the air from her lungs.

She tilted her head back, her eyes still closed, and took a breath. "Take me," she whispered, now unfastening the waistband of her skirt. "Take me now," she moaned, grabbing his hand and sliding it down into her panties. His fingers, first cupping her wet mound, quickly separated, his middle finger searching for the spot that would bring her close, but not completely, to where she wanted to be.

"Ang," he whispered.

Not wanting him to speak, she covered her mouth with his. For the smallest piece of a second, she knew that if she'd heard his voice, the images would vanish and she wouldn't be able to find her way back. She grabbed his buttocks and pulled him close, forcing both his middle and ring fingers deeper inside her. Eyes still closed and her breath trembling and shallow, she placed a hand on each of his shoulders, undulating up and down, waves of heat and chills rippling through her body with each movement.

"Oh, God." The voice seemed to come from far away. "Get a room for God's sake," the voice said again. She turned her head and let her eyes part slightly to see a man and woman walking their dog past the brownstone. A thin smile cut across her face as she wrapped her left leg around Tommy's waist, opening herself up wider for him.

"Fuck off," she heard. This time she knew the voice came from her, although again it sounded like it came from blocks away.

The subtle scent of Philip's cologne had clung to her teddy and she inhaled deeply. Armani. She knew it the moment she'd hugged him at his front door and had made sure to have enough contact with his skin to take the scent home with her, for a moment exactly like this. With one last push downward onto his fingers, she clutched his neck, holding on for dear life as her body shuddered top to bottom, the moisture from within flowing down the one leg that was barely keeping her balance. Her mind was empty, dizzy from the intense arousal and sexual flood tide she was experiencing. She'd felt nothing like this in years and wanted it to last forever. But it didn't. It couldn't. He wouldn't allow it.

"Babe?"

The voice was all too familiar. She kept her eyes closed; trying to ignore any sound or smell that might pull her from the pleasure too soon; allowing the sensations to permeate into every last cell of her body, until they faded into the outside air, leaving her exhausted and, for some obscure reason, enraged.

"Babe?" He nudged his mouth into the curve of her neck, darting his tongue into the soft skin. "Let's go inside and finish this," he whispered.

She rolled her eyes and let her leg slide down his, both feet now firmly on the ground. "I did finish," she said. "Now go home, it's late."

He stopped licking her neck and took a step back.

"Please don't tell me you're serious."

"As a heart attack," she said, grabbing her blazer. She forced herself to kiss his cheek. "I'm sorry. It's been a long day. We'll finish you up over the weekend, okay?"

Twisting the key in the door, she wouldn't turn around, nor would she buckle under and let him in. She wanted to savor what she'd just experienced, alone. As she opened the door, the reflection in the glass showed him holding the same stance, in the same spot she'd left him seconds before. She closed the door behind her, looked at the staircase before her that led to her apartment, and sighed.

"Shit," she whispered. She turned around to see Tommy staring at her like an old, pathetic dog that had just been scolded. She forced a smile and blew a kiss through the glass. That was all he needed. His scowl softened, his hand raised, and he gave her the slightest of waves. "Good night," she mouthed and started her climb to the third floor, shaking her head every step of the way.

The echo of her clacking heels on the stone steps of the brownstone was the only sound that could be heard. The smell of burnt steak wafted through the hallway, as it always did on Thursday nights, the product of the tenant in apartment 1G. Angela and her best friend, June, who lived in 2F had a long-time bet regarding 1G: Angela was convinced he was a pre-op transsexual; June felt strongly he was simply a very effeminate man. But Angela, citing recent articles, as well as her extensive medical education, was certain all signs pointed to a woman on the verge of having *the* operation to become a man. This had been a bone of gratifying contention between the two of them for almost four years, neither getting close enough to 1G to see for themselves what the truth might be. And, in their heart of hearts, neither of them really wanted to know.

Thinking of her tiny one-bedroom apartment two flights up, she almost gagged. Compared to the bright openness of Philip and Jonathan's home, she felt like a trapped goldfish – slowly dying, swimming around a tiny bowl; bumping into the same filmy walls day after day.

She looked around the foyer, the same lobby she'd entered every day for the past ten plus years, since moving from Boston to New York. When she first arrived in Manhattan, she didn't care where she lived. She was in New York City, had secured a job as a nurse at Mt. Sinai, and was ready to begin a new life. Her main goal was to leave her baggage behind and create a new existence. Finding the "perfect" living arrangements had always been far down on her list of priorities – until the first time she visited Chelsea. Just seeing the people who walked the streets gave her a sudden understanding that *where* she lived would affect *how* she lived.

Considering her size at the time, she felt the culture and open-mindedness of this neighborhood would be beneficial – a place where she could show people *who* she was before they judged her based on appearance. As she strolled up 5th Avenue, a new confidence emerged. She felt self-assured enough to stop and talk with artisans selling their goods; the pervasive self-consciousness that usually hung around her neck had vanished. She'd smile at people, they'd smile back. Not the center of attention anymore because of her weight: she was now one of the crowd, and the emotional load of her obesity seemed to lift with every step she took.

Only two hours into her apartment search, Marge the realtor led her to the brownstone onto 16th Street. From the moment she set her eyes on the building, Angela knew she'd found her new home. Getting up the three flights of stairs was excruciating. Each step depleted her body of much needed oxygen, and by the time they reached the third floor she had to lean against the wall to catch her breath. Her leg muscles hurt and stabbing pains ran across her lower back.

"Are you okay?" Marge asked, touching her arm. "Maybe this isn't the place for you."

Too breathless to speak, Angela nodded, trying to ignore the pounding in her chest. A few seconds later, she pushed herself from the wall and forced a smile.

"This is perfect exercise for losing weight," she said, pointing to the apartment door. "Let's see what the apartment looks like."

When they reached the door, Marge unlatched the three security locks and gestured for Angela to enter.

Although the apartment was empty, its old-world charm enveloped Angela immediately and she wrapped her arms around herself. The high ceilings gave her a sense of freedom, a new appreciation of space she'd been missing in the small hotel room she'd called home for the past week. The original hardwood floors gave off a scent that permeated her senses. She closed her eyes, trying to imagine the people who'd walked these floors decades ago. White crown moldings gave the rooms a feeling of elegance, gracefully flaring out and then disappearing into the pearl-like tone of the walls. As she moved through the arched doorway leading to the bedroom, a beam of sunlight streaming through the large window encapsulated her, warming her from the inside out. Turning to the left, she noticed the black and white hex tile of the bathroom floor that flowed into a vintage pedestal sink and a shower stall big enough for three people.

"I'll take it," she said, leaning against the bedroom wall. "It's perfect."

Marge threw her PDA in her pocketbook and came running in. "But what about the stairs? Maybe we should find a place with an elevator? *I* even had a problem and I'm…" She cut herself off. "I'm just saying."

"I know what you're saying." The edge in Angela's voice forced Marge to look down at the floor. Angela forced another smile. "Please, just get the paperwork ready. This place is perfect."

And it was perfect, until tonight. Now she'd seen what real money could buy – space, land, beauty, and room to breathe. The trip to Connecticut opened her eyes in so many ways, creating a catalyst for change and the need for a different life. The apartment that once seemed luxurious was now a prison cell; a place from which she needed to escape as soon as possible. She knew she could make it happen, she was just uncertain about the timing.

By the time she reached the second floor landing, a wave of exhaustion came over her. She plopped down on the top step to rest for a few minutes before climbing to the third floor. Looking over the expanse of the stairway, she breathed deeply, trying to ignore the smell of meat and aged plaster, imagining herself in a house like Philip's. Every morning, coffee in hand, she'd stroll through the huge French doors onto the teak deck, breathing in the fresh New England air, watching baby bunnies follow their mother into a row of perfectly landscaped bushes.

She propped her head on her hands and stared into the empty space before her, seeing nothing but the French doors – doors that would be her entrance into a world she deserved to be part of, but had always been denied. She decided she'd keep the doors in her mind's eye whenever she climbed these foul stone steps or unlocked her creaky apartment door or puttered in her midget-sized kitchen. Just as she'd visualized herself as thin, minute-to-minute, day after day, she'd envision those doors as her own: the scent of their cherry stain, the strength of their wood, the ease of their glide. She knew, then and there, at that moment, it was time to shake the fishbowl from the counter and let it smash on the floor.

"Psssst!" The sound jolted her; her thoughts instantly evaporating into thin air. "Angie... what the hell? What's wrong?"

Angela turned to see June peeking through her partially opened door.

Forcing strength back into her legs, Angela stood, dragged herself toward June, and leaned against the wall next to her apartment.

"Hey," Angela said, still foggy from the mass of thoughts just knocked from her head. "Nothing's wrong. I'm just beat."

June opened the door wider and checked the hallway to see if anyone was lurking. Angela looked her up and down, shaking her head. June wore the same plaid, flannel bathrobe they'd been arguing over for years. Angela begged her to throw it out. "If these are the type of clothes you *think* you deserve," she'd said countless times, "they're the only type of clothes you'll ever have." June would agree, promise to discard the robe, and show up months later wrapped within its tatters.

"That thing is like a ragged security blanket... the kind of crap babies don't give up until they're teenagers," Angela said, pointing to June's robe. "No matter how tired it gets, even if it's a tiny shred, you won't let it go. How many times do I have to tell you, June, if..."

"I know," June interrupted. "If I think this is all I deserve, it's all I'll ever have." She tightened the shredded belt around her thin waist. "Can you let me have one vice, Angie?" Stepping further into the hallway, she pointed to the landing. "At least I'm not sitting in the middle of a hall like some vagrant, staring into space at twelve thirty at night." She leaned her back against the door jam, bunched up the dirty blonde, straw-like hair dropping onto her shoulders, and tucked the wad into the collar of her robe. "And what the hell is with that boyfriend of yours? I had to step over him to get into the building. I thought you two were done."

Angela bit her bottom lip. "We *are* done." She thought about his hands, his fingers, and the amazing pleasure he'd just helped her experience. "Almost." She smiled.

June crossed her arms and wiped the remaining strings of hair from her eyes. "Yeah. That's the way it always is with you two." She rolled her eyes. "More importantly, what happened in Connecticut tonight? You wanna come in and tell me about it? What did he say? Is he going to do it? Did you..."

Angela placed her index finger on June's lips. "Shhhh. Too many questions. And it's way too late. I'll see you at work in the morning and tell you all about it."

June stamped her foot like a toddler. "Damn it, Angie. I've been waiting all night to hear about it. I couldn't sleep. And now you're just going to go to bed? That's not fair."

Angela clomped toward the stairs and giggled. "Life's not fair, my friend." She stopped short and turned around. "But I will tell you one thing that might help settle you in for the night."

"What?" June waited with her mouth hanging open.

"If I were you, I'd get on the Internet and start checking out the responsibilities of being a godmother... Aunt June."

With that, she twirled around and walked down the hallway to the stairs, not looking back or waiting for a response. She had a long night of planning and fantasizing ahead of her and didn't want to waste her remaining strength on getting into the details with June. Soon enough she'd need June's help, and that would be the time for nitty-gritty. But for tonight, she'd keep things as they were, leaving June with a reason to believe that sometime in the near future there'd be some kind of meaning in her life – a meaning she'd never find on her own.

8

June tightened the flannel belt around her waist, stopping right before her pain threshold. She slammed the door shut, staggered to the sofa, and fell into it, slouching deep into the horizontal crevasse separating the top velour cushions from the bottom. She stared at the pill bottles on the coffee table in front of her and winced as they appeared to stare back, challenging her to a battle of wills. She turned away, knowing if there was such a battle, she'd lose.

At times like this, June missed her home so intensely she'd hug herself and imagine her mother's arms wrapped around her. She closed her eyes and tried to recreate her favorite memory: sitting on the patio of their small country house in Wrightsville, the sweet smell of Georgia Cherokee Rose wafting through the humidity as they sipped ice cold glasses of sweet tea. In separate rockers, only inches apart, she and Momma swayed in unison, the only sound the hum of the ceiling fan, its blades pushing through the dense, stagnant air.

Even more than their conversation, she missed the shared silence; the long hot days on the patio gazing into the depths of the Wisteria vines while thinking isolated thoughts; Saturday nights in the kitchen, both of them too busy baking cakes for the next day's Church gathering to utter any word other than the occasional "thank you" or "excuse me"; early mornings with rain pattering on the tin roof, both of them lying in their rooms, knowing the other was awake and they'd soon meet in the sitting room for morning coffee.

The things she missed so passionately were also what drove her to leave and head for New York. Back then, the silence grated on her – the grinding of repressed emotions struggling to break free, pushed back by guilt, fear, and insecurity.

Maybe it was her brittle hair or tiny nose. Maybe it was her oversized teeth that never grew completely together. Whatever the reason, she'd spent her life trying to be invisible, which was hard to do in a small town like Wrightsville. And that's when the light bulb went on: What better place to get lost than the most populated city in the country?

And now, almost three years later, June slumped on the sofa staring down the pill bottles, wondering if she should swallow all of them and then dial 911. That would show Angela. She stretched her leg and gently placed her foot on the glass coffee table, her sciatica making its entrance as expected, an inseparable companion to anxiety and sleeplessness.

Like a monkey, she grabbed the amber vial of Vicodin with her toes and dropped it into her lap. She shook it and felt a sense of relief, the weight telling her she had enough to get through another few days. Twisting the label-less vial with her fingers, she examined her palm through the other side. This was the bottle Angela gave her a few weeks earlier, along with the unchanged dialogue that accompanied every delivery.

"I'm here for you," Angela had said, holding the vial up to June's face and shaking the Vicodin inside with her thumb and forefinger. "As you are for me, right?"

June nodded, wanting nothing more than a pill to cool the hot poker in her lower back that had been stabbing at her for two days. "Definitely," she said, almost a whisper. "Whatever you need."

With the door closed, they stood in the storage closet on the seventh floor of the hospital, the buzzing fluorescent ceiling lights sending a chill down the back of June's neck. She was about to grab the pills from Angela when she noticed the slightest change in her friend's expression, a combination of kindness and malevolence that made her uncertain what her next move should be. She froze, waiting for Angela to say something.

"That's great to know," Angela finally replied, handing June the vial. "Because there's something coming up I might need your help with." Angela turned and slowly moved toward the door. She turned back to June, the shadow cast from the lights above making her eyes look frightfully black. "I'm glad we became friends, June. I really am." Another smile. "And please say hi to your mom the next time you speak with her."

Still nodding, June pushed the vial into the pocket of her scrubs, regretting the pain in her back, her move up north, and the unspoken deal she'd just made.

A few months later, on a frigid February night, ten-inch icicles hung from the fire escape ladder and glistened sparkles of light into June's living room window.

Angela sat close beside her on the sofa, bundled up in an afghan blanket. Without warning, she swiped a pill vial off the coffee table.

"Remember that day in the storage room, June? The day we kind of made an oath to help each other?"

June nodded, a twinge of panic stirring in her groin. Since that day, Angela had been supplying her with the medication she needed, never saying a word about where it came from. The automated dispenser at work made it virtually impossible for her to be stealing meds from the hospital. In fact, the nursing staff continually griped about the complexity of security: passwords, PIN numbers, med codes. So unless Angela was a technological genius, she had to be getting the pills from outside the hospital. June finally decided her source was one of the slimy characters she'd seen Angela bring to her apartment, drunk and fumbling up the stairs, one hand on the banister and the other up her skirt. This conclusion only added to June's anxiety. She worried that one day she'd take a pill without any potency, or worse, swallow a pill laced with a lethal substance.

But this night, with Angela sitting so close to her, a different kind of anxiety arose. Somewhere inside she knew Angela wasn't paying attention to the television and the topic of conversation was about to turn to how she would pay for her addiction.

"I've been thinking." Angela hit the remote's mute button without taking her eyes off the screen.

"Uh oh." June laughed nervously, shoving a handful of popcorn into her mouth. She wrapped her robe more tightly around her, grabbed the crocheted blanket lying on top of the sofa, and threw it over her legs, the cold suddenly penetrating her thin bones. She had a sudden thought of her mother, wondering what Mom was doing at that moment: baking pies, reading a book by the wood-burning stove? Was she thinking of June as June so often thought of her? Waiting for the words to come out of Angela's mouth, June wanted nothing more than to once again share that comforting silence with her mother.

"I've been thinking about having a baby." Angela turned to June. "And I need your help."

June took the warm Budweiser from the side table and slugged a mouthful. The scratching effervescence felt good going down.

"I might not be a woman of the world, Angie, but I do know you need a *man* to help you have a baby." She looked down to her lap. "I'm not equipped to help you with something like that," she said, giggling at her own joke.

Angela's change of expression caused a sharp tremble deep within June's solar plexus. It was as though another face appeared on Angela's body: a countenance with narrow, beady eyes, a bulb-shaped protuberance of a nose, a slit for a mouth, and fat, red cheeks. June wondered if this was what Angela looked like before she lost weight. Although the face frightened her, for a moment she felt a stab of relief that Angela too had been homely most of her life. For the first time since they met, June felt as though they were on an even playing field.

"You stupid shit!" Angela spewed.

June envisioned flames flaring from Angela's nostrils. She curled the blanket deeper into her fists. The playing field was no longer even.

"Do you think this is a fucking joke? Is my life a fucking joke to you?" Angela reached behind her head and seized a pill bottle from the built-in bookshelf. Her scowl turned more threatening as she rattled the vial with a punishing shake.

"After all I've done for you, this is the God damn thanks I get?" She looked at the bottle in her hand. "One word to hospital security and they'll take you out in handcuffs. You know that, right? And don't think you can blame anything on me. My tracks are covered. I've made sure of that, you little shit."

June's face froze. It was just a joke, for God's sake, and now her job was being threatened. She couldn't bring herself to look up again and see the anger on Angela's face. But she didn't need to. She heard the fury in Angela's breathing, like a bull in the ring, stamping its hoof and puffing out air through oversized nostrils. Something wasn't right here. Angela was like a time bomb on the verge of exploding and June was sitting directly in her path. Not a good place to be.

She picked at the label on the beer bottle with her thumbnail, her thoughts fleeing to her bathroom medicine cabinet and her Klonopin on the top shelf. She tried not to take those too often, letting a Xanax, or two, or three, get her through an episode. Tonight she'd need something a lot stronger to keep her anxiety at bay.

"Angela, I'm sorry." Her voice fluttered. "I didn't mean anything by it. I was just kidding around." A piece of the beer bottle label peeled off and fell into her lap. She twirled it between her thumb and forefinger. "You never mentioned it before, so I didn't know how important this was to you. I'm sorry."

Angela's face changed like a werewolf turning back into a human being. The air of evil seemed to dissipate and fall between the slats of the wood floor.

"Well, it *is* important, June." She placed the vial back onto the bookshelf. "Especially because I'm going to be hitting the big 4-0 soon. If I want a child, I really have to do it now."

June knew this was a perfect time to ingratiate herself; she needed Angela as much as Angela appeared to need her. She grabbed Angela's hand. "How can I help?"

"Well, since there's no one special in my life right now, it looks like marriage any time soon is a far-fetched fantasy." She cut June off with a wave of her hand. "And don't even *mention* Tommy's name. The last person in the world I'd marry is *him*." She pushed the hair from her eyes. "So anyway, I've been thinking back to all the boyfriends I had, trying to figure out who might have the best genes. You know, someone I'd want to use as a sperm donor. And really, only one guy stands out."

June let the label fall into one of the openings of her blanket and gave Angela a "Well... who is it?" look.

"I had this boyfriend in college, Philip. Handsome, smart, sweet, and just an all-around good guy. I did some digging and found out he lives in Connecticut, an hour from here by train."

"That's great!" June feigned excitement, Klonopin still at the forefront of her thoughts. "So, do you think he'd do it?"

"Well, that's only one part of the problem," Angela gazed out the window behind June. "The other problem is, he's gay."

June pulled her head back, confused and waiting for Angela to continue. But she didn't and June was panicked that she'd say the wrong thing or ask the wrong question. They sat in silence until Angela sighed.

"No, I didn't turn him gay, if that's what you're thinking."

June pulled the blanket closer. "Of course I wasn't thinking that! What's wrong with you?"

"He must have been gay all along and just came out later in life. Cause I have to tell you, the sex we used to have was unfreakin' believable. He was so…" She stopped herself and patted June's hand, as though acknowledging June's obvious lack of sexual experience. "Anyway, he's living with some guy, like I said, in Connecticut. Westport, I think."

June smiled, hoping what she was about to say would make Angela happy.

"That's not such a bad thing, if you think about it, Angie. Two gay guys who can't have their own kid probably want one, but can't find the right woman. What could be a better scenario than having a beauty like you come along and ask for a donation? You'd have a child and they'd be daddies. Everyone would be a winner!"

"My thoughts exactly," said Angela, fingering the remote buttons. "But they'll have to understand I'm the mother and the baby stays with me. I want to bring her up and take care of her. You know, have her full time. They can visit whenever they want to and take her to the park and stuff, but I want her to be mine."

This time June patted Angela's hand. "Wow, you have this all figured out, huh? That's a good thing. At least they'll know where you stand before you all agree to something." June grabbed a handful of popcorn and ate one kernel at a time. "So, let me ask again, how can I help?"

"Really, just for support," Angela said. "I might need you around when I'm getting the sperm ready for injecting, but I also think it's a good idea for me to have a witness around – someone who sees what we did and how we did it. You know, just in case."

The last "you know" made June uneasy. Something wasn't sitting right in the air between them and she wanted to find out what it was before she agreed to anything that could get her into more trouble. It took her awhile to get the words out, trying carefully not to fumble. "What's going on here, Angie? What do you mean, 'just in case?' What aren't you telling me?" She attempted to keep a smile on her face, though her insides were tighter than harp strings. She awaited Angela's verbal explosion.

Angela wouldn't meet her eyes. "Nothing," she said casually. "There's absolutely nothing I'm not telling you. I'm just saying there are endless ways this could end up. And I can see possible legal issues, too. So we... I mean, I...need to be a little careful." She finally looked directly at June. "And of course, being my child's godmother, you should be involved from the very beginning."

A deep throb pushed through June's chest and into her throat. She couldn't believe what Angela had just said. June? A godmother? She was ecstatic and frightened and at that moment, unable to differentiate the two. Her anxiety mounted and she felt her mouth almost water for the Klonopin. She swallowed hard to push down the lump still climbing up her throat.

"Oh, Angie. Me? Are you sure?" Her voice quivered.

"Yes," Angela said, her hand on her shoulder, "I'm sure."

"I don't know what to say. It's an honor. I don't know how to thank you."

"There's nothing to say, June. As long as I know you're always there for me and the baby. That's all the thanks I need."

June leaned over and wrapped her arms around Angela's neck. "I'll be there for both of you. Always."

Since that night, they'd not spoken about it again, until Angela told June that very afternoon she'd be leaving work early to go to Connecticut. It was time to "put things in motion" Angela had said. "The clock's ticking!" was all June heard as Angela dashed down the hospital corridor toward the elevators.

June waved at Angela's back and wished her good luck, though she doubted Angela heard a word. The iPod's earphones were already in her ears as she pressed the elevator button again and again as though to make it arrive quicker. June waited for the elevators to show, hoping Angela would wave or acknowledge her before entering. But she bolted through the opening, leaving June alone in the middle of the corridor, alone, embarrassed and wondering if she'd be able to handle the requirements of godmotherhood.

And now Angela couldn't even find the common courtesy to tell her what had happened during the Connecticut excursion.

She took two Vicodin from the vial and placed them on her tongue. The bitterness caused her face to scrunch as she pressed them against the roof of her mouth. She quickly realized they were too big and sour to dissolve without liquid, so she grabbed the open bottle of Chardonnay from the refrigerator and took a swig. The fruitiness of the wine felt good against the bitterness of the medicine and she took another few gulps until both pills disappeared.

Within a few seconds it was obvious that the fighting within her head - whether or not to bring the bottle back to the living room - was futile. So she shut the lights, slouched back down into the couch, brought the bottle to her lips and closed her eyes. With another swallow, her mind began to wander: back to Mom and the solitude of a country patio, to the hum of the ceiling fan, to the brilliant white, puffy clouds that hung in the summer Georgian sky with promises of a future so different from the one she was living.

<u>9</u>

"C'mon, Angela, it's almost eight o'clock. I have to get to work!"

June squirmed her head, attempting to remove Angela's hands from in front of her eyes. Standing behind her, Angela carefully led June down the hallway toward her apartment.

"You've been waiting for the past three weeks to see how I've redecorated and now that the big reveal is here, you're rushing me?"

They stopped in front of Angela's apartment, the door wide open as though awaiting their appearance.

June inhaled deeply. "I can smell the fresh paint," she whispered. "I can even almost smell the color!"

"Are you ready?" asked Angela, loosening her grip.

"Yes!" June shouted. "Yes! Let me see already!"

Angela took her hands from June's face, gave her a slight push forward into the apartment and shut the door behind them.

"Well," Angela said quizzically, "Do you love it?"

June moved her head slowly from side to side then ceiling to floor. Her mouth was open, her eyes almost bulging from their sockets.

"I can't believe this is the same apartment, Angela. It's absolutely beautiful." June walked cautiously to the kitchen, set her pocketbook down on the small, glass bistro table and gently examined the granite countertop. "Just beautiful."

When she reached the center of the living room, she turned her entire body around and made a full circle trying to catch every new feature of the apartment.

"I love the brown wall color," June remarked.

"Mocha," Angela snapped.

"And the furniture… that wood… it's just so… what's the word?"

"Rich?" Angela smirked, proud of herself and her choices.

"Exactly!" June shouted.

"It's cherry." She pointed to the chenille loveseats sitting beside the zebrawood coffee table. "Real cherry, not that fake stuff."

June made her way to one of the loveseats and glanced at Angela, her expression bashfully asking permission to sit.

"Of course," Angela said, "Just be careful. That loveseats costs more than your monthly rent."

Ignoring Angela's impertinence, June sat down and leaned back.

"I feel like a queen in this loveseat." She turned toward the dining room and gazed at the new crown molding. "Angela, it looks like you had a professional interior decorator do this. Where did you get all the ideas for these colors... the upholstery... the silk window treatments?"

Angela walked to June and fell back onto the other loveseat. Fingering the wool throw blanket she'd draped over the back just that morning, she looked around the room and felt a jolt of anxiety. *Shit! Did I make this look* too *much like Philip and Jonathan's house? Did I overdo it?*

Philip and Jonathan's first visit to her apartment was only a few days away and she'd wanted to show Jonathan that the two of them had more in common than just the desire to have a child. Angela's new décor did not come close to her preferred style, but she felt it imperative that Jonathan feel they had similar tastes and that she, like him, had a penchant for the finer things in life. But now, as she listened to June's comments and took some time to examine the extent of the decorative changes, she wondered if she'd gone too far, if Jonathan would be able to figure out what she was up to and why she did what she did. *He's not* that *smart... is he?*

"Did you hear me, Angela?" June was now standing over Angela, a look of confusion cutting across her face. "Are you okay? What's going on in that head of yours?"

Starting to feel a bit flushed, Angela placed the palms of her hands upon her cheeks. She shook her head ever so slightly, trying to snap herself out of the funk the wave of anxiety had caused.

"Nothing. Yes. Everything's fine." Angela stood and walked to the kitchen. She reached into the dish rack, grabbed a few plates and placed them into the new cabinets. "Philip and Jonathan are coming to visit this weekend and I just want everything to be perfect."

June grabbed her pocketbook from the table and slung the strap over her shoulder.

"Well, you have nothing to worry about. This place *is* perfect. You did an amazing job and should be proud." She waited for Angela to smile before taking a few steps toward the door. "Do you think I'll be able to meet them? I mean, just a quick 'hello'?"

Angela stopped putting away the plates and flung the dish towel over her shoulder, its damask fringes settling on her chest.

"Really, June? I'm trying to make this the perfect visit for the two men who could possibly be the fathers of my child and all you're worried about is meeting them? Do you really think that's why they're coming here? To meet *you*? Do you think that meeting June Stokes is on their list as one of the first things to accomplish when they get here?"

June shook her head. "No. I don't." She raised her eyes to meet Angela's. "I just thought it would be nice. There's no reason to get so bent out of shape for God's sake." She turned to the door. "I have to go to work."

Angela waited for June to open the door before replying. She wanted her out of the way so she could put some finishing touches on the furnishings and wall hangings.

"I'm sorry, June. I'm just a little frazzled because…" She stopped mid-sentence, her apology a few seconds too late. June was already slamming the door behind her. "Fine," Angela whispered. "Be that way."

It wasn't until 3:30 that Angela finished hanging the last Ansel Adams on her bedroom wall and rewarded herself by flopping down on the bed. She angled her head on the pillow, studying the photo frame to make sure it was straight. *Perfect.*

A wave of fatigue crept inside of her. She turned on her side, slid off her shoes to the floor and cuddled a pillow beneath her head. Her eyes still open, she saw her reflection in the art deco landscape mirror she forgot to have the contractor hang in the bathroom. Too tired to move it now, she snuggled her pillow tighter and cupped her hands beneath her chin.

Her gaze traveled from her feet up to her smooth, slender legs, over the small hill of her thigh and past the gentle curve of her hip. For a moment she paused her inspection to admire the petiteness of her waistline, the shapeliness of her mid-section leading up to her full breasts. Moving her eyes to her face, she tried forcing a smile, but could only summon up a roguish smirk.

As she stared into her own eyes, the light around her began to fade, the periphery of the room slowly disappearing until all that remained was the outline of her head and body. With her eyes focused on the silhouette of her face, she watched in horror as her body began to increase in size, larger and larger, rounder and rounder, until she mirrored the image of her former self from decades earlier.

The beating of her heart grew louder, hammering hard against her chest the way it did when she held all those extra pounds. And then her face, like an inflating balloon, expanded into a pear-shaped mass. She started to panic. *Were these past few years a dream? Did I never lose the weight? Or am I dreaming right now?*

She closed her eyes, took a deep breath and hurled out the most sudden of prayers, demanding that when she opened her eyes she'd once again be shapely and beautiful. But her prayer went unanswered and the sight before her changed into something even more horrifying: she was no longer the woman lying on the bed. The person staring into the mirror was now her mother, exactly as Angela remembered her twenty five years before.

The surrounding space had changed too, back to the soiled walls and stained carpet that covered the floor of her mother's bedroom. The smell also materialized – a sour, oily malodor caused by bacteria, moldy food and the lack of bathing.

Now on the other side of the mirror, Angela stood facing her morbidly obese mother. Although she was a 15 year old miniature version of her mother, she was repulsed by the sight of this woman; her auburn-gray, matted hair sprawled across the pillow, the food-stained, terry cloth bathrobe once a bright white, now the color of coffee-stained teeth. And then there was the emptiness of her eyes, the colorless hue of someone gone mad years before yet unwilling to surrender that final thread of sanity.

"Angie, my baby," she groaned, reaching out her hand. "Take Mommy's hand, baby."

Never knowing what to expect, Angela shivered as she walked toward the bed with an extended hand. When she got close enough, her mother grabbed her hand and tucked it under her enormous face.

"Angie, Mommy's not feeling well tonight. So I'm not gonna have that chicken you're making for me. But I want *you* to have it. I want you to have the whole thing if you want."

Angela turned her head toward the television, the Six O'clock News blaring so loudly she could barely hear her mother. And that was fine with her. She'd rather hear about all the death and destruction going on in the world than listen to anything the crazy woman lying in front of her had to say.

Her mother fumbled behind her back for the television remote. Without looking at it, she pressed every button until the television was muted. "Can you look at me, Honey?" She waited. Angela kept her eyes on the silent TV screen. "Angie?" Her voice was beginning to swell.

She threw Angela's hand from her own so it smacked hard against Angela's chest.

"God damn it, Angela! Look at me when I'm talking to you!" Angela jumped back, her arms straight by her side like a soldier awaiting inspection. "You're just like your father, that piece of shit. Ignoring me until he needed something. Treating me like dirt until the day he left." She tried rolling onto her back but couldn't find the strength to match the effort. Her hollow eyes pierced into Angela's as her volume grew in intensity. "And it's your fault he left, you know. He could *deal* with *me*. He *loved me*. It was *you* he couldn't stand to look at. You know that, right?"

Angela didn't move. She didn't utter a sound. She was used to this kind of tirade, these violent speeches that had to be endured in silence in order to come out the other side as unscathed as possible. Angela knew her mother was sick. 'Schizophrenic' she'd once heard a doctor say while eavesdropping on her Aunt Margaret's telephone call. But knowing her mother was crazy didn't make the words less hurtful or the damage less acute.

Her mother softened her voice to an almost imperceptible level. "But your father hating you doesn't mean you're a bad person, my dearest. It just means that nobody gives a shit about you... or me for that matter. Those people laughing at us as we walk down the street? If you tripped and fell or got hit by a car, you think they'd give a shit?" Her breathing intensified as her volume crescendoed. "No. They would keep laughing, because that's the way people are. You need to fight for things in this world without a worry about what happens to others... because they don't care what happens to you. It's the only way to get what and where you want in life." Her throat gurgled and she swallowed hard. "Now, this is what..."

"Jennifer Jean!" a voice yelled from the bedroom door. Angela and her mother looked toward the sound. It was Angela's Aunt Margaret, home from work in the nick of time. "What ignorance are you spewing at your daughter?"

Angela's mother used all her energy to twist herself onto her back. "The truth, Margaret," she shouted. "I'm spewing the truth."

Margaret removed her sweater, revealing the nurse's uniform that would always provide Angela with a vague feeling of comfort. She walked to the other side of the bed and closely examined three of the prescription pill bottles.

"Did you take your medication today?" Silence. "Jenny! Did.You.Take.Your.Medication.Today?"

Jenny turned toward Angela, her expression blank, the color of her face almost identical to the shade of her robe.

"I don't remember," she replied.

"Is this what I have to come home to? I take care of people all day at the hospital and then I have to take care of my sister?" Margaret sighed and looked at Angela. "Honey, can you go get dinner ready? I'll be there in a minute."

Angela took one last look at her mother, walked out of the room and closed the door behind her. She entered the kitchen where a whole chicken sat in a roasting pan on the stovetop waiting to be put in the oven. But she didn't want to cook; she didn't want to eat; she didn't want to stand where she was or breathe the air she was breathing. Feeling faint, she sat down in one of the kitchen chairs and forced herself to take deep breaths. *One. Two. Three.* She could hear her mother yelling from the bedroom. *Four. Five. Six.* More yelling. *Seven. Eight. Nine.* The voice had softened, the shouting turned to mumbling. *Ten. Eleven. Twelve.*

Angela looked up when she heard the bedroom door open. Margaret closed the door behind her as gently as a mother trying not to wake her newborn. She sat down at the table next to Angela.

"You can't listen to her when she says things like that. You know that, right Angie?" Angela nodded. "She's got this problem, a mood disorder of sorts, and if she doesn't take her medication, she goes off the edge. It's a pity you have to see her like this. Such a pity."

Angela looked down at her plump fingers and started to pick at the worn away cuticle of her thumb.

"Will I be like that one day?" She picked harder at the cuticle. Margaret placed her hand over Angela's. "I feel it sometimes, you know. The anger, the rage, but I can keep it under control. It feels like black smoke, like a dark cloud of like, something evil, is trying to creep into my body. Into my veins." As she spoke, the cloud began to make an appearance, making it easy for her to hold back tears.

Margaret caressed her hand. "Some doctors I've spoken with say it could be genetic. Others say it's not. I don't know, Angie. I really don't. What I *do* know is that I think you're strong enough to control whatever creeps into your body. And I also think that you're strong enough to lose the weight you need to lose and *not* become the woman on the other side of that door."

Angela offered Margaret an obligatory smile and lifted herself up onto her feet. She knew her aunt was either lying or completely naïve. It was obvious she'd already become her mother and it was only a matter of time before she'd be lying in the same bed and taking the same pills as the woman they could both hear snoring from the next room.

Angela's eyes jolted open and her body jerked with such force that she fell off the side of the bed and landed on her back. Although her insides were frozen, she felt a sense of relief when she realized the ceiling she was looking at was the ceiling of her brownstone apartment. Her relief intensified when she turned to the mirror beside her and saw her reflection; she was still thin, still beautiful, still the opposite of the girl from the memory she'd just experienced.

Pushing past her fatigue, Angela stood up and made her way into kitchen, lifted her pocketbook off the counter and reached deep inside. She fumbled through the disorder until she found the bottle of Lithium.

"Thank Christ," she whispered, walking to the kitchen sink. She threw a pill in her mouth, turned on the kitchen faucet and bent her head beneath it so she could suck water from its spout.

Angela wiped her sleeve across her mouth. Her insides started to warm up a bit, the intensity of what she'd just experienced starting to fade. Yet she still felt the need to talk with someone, anyone who could understand what this memory did to her and how it made her feel.

She thought about calling Aunt Margaret, but she'd destroyed that relationship long ago. Then she thought about her mother, but speaking with her would also be impossible. She died the night of that last tirade while Angela and Aunt Margaret ate chicken and watched reruns of *The Honeymooners*. The Medical Examiner couldn't be certain if it was the medication overdose or massive stroke that killed her. And Angela never really cared.

Feeling her mood pick up, Angela grabbed her cell phone and speed dialed Tommy.

"Hey, Ang. What's up?" Tommy sounded surprised.

"Come over." she was almost whispering.

"Sure, after work. I just need to…"

"Now," she insisted. "I need you now."

A few seconds of silence.

"Ang, it's not even five o'clock yet. I can't go leave without…"

"It's now or never," she interrupted. "Come over, Tommy. It'll be well worth the risk."

A few more seconds of silence until she heard Tommy sigh.

"Alright. I'll be right over."

She hung up the phone and threw it onto the sofa.

In the back of her head somewhere she could hear her mother's voice, "You need to fight for things in this world without a worry about what happens to others… because they don't care what happens to you. It's the only way to get what and where you want in life."

Today there was no doubt in Angela's mind, she was definitely on her way.

<u>10</u>

The window's glass was cold against Jonathan's cheek, a sure sign autumn had reached the Northeast and the bitterness of winter was approaching. Sometimes he wished he could stop winter from arriving; raise his hand like a crossing guard and halt its attack; block the arctic air from moving in and baring the trees, graying the skies, and darkening his mood.

Jonathan rubbed the back of his hand against Philip's leg as the train passed through Greenwich station. "It's getting cold. I'm not sure I can deal with another winter."

"You say that every year." Philip laughed and turned a page of his New York magazine. "You talk about how you love the turning of the leaves and the fresh, chill of the fall air, and then you complain about winter at the same time." He closed the magazine, rolled it up, and slipped it into his coat pocket. "Why not just enjoy where you are instead of worrying about what's coming? You know, take advantage of the moment. Otherwise, you're just living in the future."

The train hit a bump and Jonathan held onto the seat in front of him as the car swerved to the left. He turned to Philip. "Where did you hear that? Oh, wait, don't tell me. You just read an article about 'living in the now. Another Deepak Chopra, special edition." He gazed out the window again.

"Maybe. What's the diff? It makes sense, doesn't it?"

"What's the '*diff*'? What the hell is a 'diff'?" Jonathan felt an anger creeping inside and wasn't sure where it was coming from. He let his head fall against the window again, hoping to block the advancing wrath.

Philip slapped Jonathan's thigh. "Jonny, look at me," he commanded in a loud whisper.

Jonathan obeyed, gazing into Philip's limpid brown eyes.

"What's wrong with you? You've been like this since you got up this morning. You're a freakin' grouch. What's going on?"

Jonathan watched the houses fly by, backyards filled with broken leaves waiting to be raked, piled high and jumped on by some spoiled Greenwich kid. Within seconds the landscape turned into the expanse of Long Island Sound, its contents still as glass, except for three or four boaters trying to extend their summer. The sudden glare of the sunlight on the water forced him to turn away and again look at Philip, who was still awaiting an answer.

"Sorry," he said, "I really don't know what it is. It's like hormonal or something. Maybe I have a chemical imbalance and it's coming out today. It should be in full force by the time we get to Angela's, and she'll then know I'm a nut."

Philip combed his hair away from his eyes with his fingers and laughed. "You've got an imbalance alright. I'm just not sure it's chemical."

"Ha." Jonathan wasn't biting.

"Is it Angela? Did you not want to see her today? We've been having a great time with her the last few months, haven't we?"

Jonathan picked a piece of lint off Philip's pea coat. He twirled it in his fingers. "No, it's not her at all. And we *have* had a great time. I don't know. Maybe it's the cold weather or something. Maybe it's just that it's so dreary outside and it's ruining our Saturday. Hopefully this will pass when we get to Grand Central and out of this shithole they call a train."

Philip smiled, sliding on his sunglasses and leaning his head back. "It's not ruining *my* Saturday. It's the same Saturday it was this morning, just a little rainier."

Jonathan snorted. "Okay, Deepak."

"Relax, Jonny. You're probably just a little nervous. You know, going to Angela's place for the first time, seeing where she lives and stuff. Realizing it could be where your son grows up."

Jonathan flinched and felt a flutter in his chest. He fell hard against the train wall.

"Holy shit, Philip. When you say it like *that*, it scares the shit out of me."

Philip looked around to make sure no one was watching, then leaned forward and gave Jonathan a quick peck on the cheek. He gazed around again: all clear.

"Jonny, you're not obligated in any way. I hope you know that. If you don't want to do this, then we don't do it. Period. You don't owe it to me and you definitely don't owe it to Angela. You have to do what feels right."

Jonathan sat up in his seat. He felt perspiration on the back of his neck when only moments before he was cursing the cold.

"Most of the time it feels right, especially when I think about it at night or when we're in the kitchen and I imagine a little kid asking us stupid questions about your cooking utensils or why a stove gets hot. It feels right when we're watching television and I see a small 'me' sitting between the two of us, or you throwing a football to him outside in the yard, like he's your own son. I'd love that for you... and for me." He gazed out the window. "But at times like this daylight knocks out fantasy and reality hits like a ton of bricks. I know it's something I have to get over. Otherwise, like you said, I'm living in the future."

Philip leaned back again, his eyes covered by his sunglasses, his pursed lips signaling an "I told you so" without saying a word.

"You're a shit," Jonathan said.

"Quiet," he replied, "Deepak would like to take a little nap now."

Walking up 5th Avenue, Jonathan felt his energy start to refresh; the chilly New York City air breathing life into him he hadn't felt all day. The walk felt good too, the first exercise both he and Philip had had all week, thanks to JSB's major accounting software glitch and three additional articles thrown on Jonathan by his largest client. He could have turned them down, and almost did, until he thought about their upcoming visit with Angela and the realization that if they did have a child, additional income would definitely help.

"We make a right here, on sixteenth," Philip said, gesturing with his hand.

After turning right, they slowed their pace, attempting to take in the entire area. They'd been in Chelsea many times, but this was different. Today they'd try to see it in a new light – deciding if it was a decent place for a child to grow up healthy and well-balanced. Jonathan observed the street with enthusiasm, like a judge gathering all the evidence before handing down his ruling. Everything looked different today: the people, buildings, the sidewalks marred with cracks branching in countless directions. Plastic garbage bags lined the sidewalks. Jonathan bit his bottom lip – so different from the garbage containers he and Philip placed neatly by their curb every Thursday. Half way up the block, they passed St. Francis Xavier High School where a group of teenage boys stood under the red canopy, huddled together telling secrets, the book bags strapped across their backs helping to create a fortress from the passersby.

Philip crouched by a lamppost and slowly turned his head side to side, like the Terminator scanning for Sarah Connor.

Jonathan grabbed Philip's shoulder. "What's wrong? Are you okay?"

"Fine," Philip said, still gazing around. "I'm just trying to see what this place looks like from a five-year old's perspective."

Jonathan rolled his eyes and put his hand back into his coat pocket. "You don't need to squat down to do that." He laughed.

"Oh, whattaya know, someone got their sense of humor back," Philip said, using Jonathan's arm to help him up.

"Yeah, and before it leaves again, can we just get to Angela's already?" He pointed up the street. "I think it's that brownstone on the left."

After pressing the button next to Angela's name, they waited for the buzzer that would allow them entrance to her building. Silence. Philip buzzed again while Jonathan peered through the door's window. Still silence, until they saw Angela running down the stairs toward them. She pulled open the door and threw her arms around Jonathan's neck.

"You didn't think I'd just buzz you in on your first visit here, did you?" She kissed his cheek and moved aside so he could step into the hallway. Philip followed and she lifted herself onto her toes to hug him. "I am *so* excited you guys are here. This is gonna be great."

Her bare feet didn't make a sound as she jumped onto the first stone step. "I'm at the top," she said. "Third floor." She smiled at Jonathan, who'd been searching for the elevator. "No elevator, Jonny. Just stairs." She moved her open palms up and down her body. "How do you think I came to look so svelte?" She laughed. "Now get your butts up here."

Jonathan looked at Philip. "You first."

"No prob. It's the best exercise we've had all week," Philip followed Angela, taking two steps at a time.

Jonathan moved slower in order to get a better flavor of the building. His first impression was one of comfort: the seasoned blend of early 1900's charm with flashes of contemporary art and architecture. This was definitely Chelsea at its finest.

Quiet and solid, the building oozed a sense of warmth, both in temperature and sensitivity. As he climbed the steps, he thought of how different this was from where he and Philip lived; the openness of their property opposed to the density of New York City, an intense concentration of so many people living in such a small part of the world. There were so many things about the city that he didn't like, but mostly it was the stimulation that overwhelmed him: the crowds, the hustle and bustle, piercing fire engine sirens that vibrated his spine. There was too much of it for him, too much of everything for him and it's what made Jonathan suddenly realize New York City was not the place for his child to grow up.

Halfway up the stairs to the third floor, he heard what sounded like a door open behind him. When he turned around, the door to 2F was ajar, movement barely visible through the opening. Knowing someone was watching him, he paused and tried to adjust his eyes to the dim lighting. . At that moment the door slammed shut and he heard the sound of a locking bolt.

"Weird," he whispered, restarting his climb.

Mozart's Piano Concerto No. 22 in E flat drifted down the hall, leading Jonathan into Angela's apartment like the scent of fine wine. Next to Vivaldi, Mozart was his favorite composer. He didn't know if he'd previously discussed his love of Mozart with Angela, or if their similar taste in music was just coincidence. If it was happenstance, then so was their uncanny similarity in décor selection – unmistakable once he entered the apartment and saw style and elegance almost identical to his own.

While decorating the Westport house, he'd tried to combine what he called Casual Chic with "Contemporary Classical. Philip teased him, saying the decorating styles opposed each other and he'd be going around in circles trying to get the house like he wanted. But from the moment they stepped inside their vacant house, Jonathan had a plan in mind, instinctively knowing which classic tones would catch the light and shadow in certain rooms, while other rooms needed softer, more mercurial hues. He chose functional furnishings with clean, horizontal shapes that blended metals, wood, and leather into a harmonious, non-obtrusive flow from one room to the next. In the end, it worked out exactly as he'd imagined and other than a few plants and paintings, they hadn't changed a thing for over five years.

And here he was, standing in Angela's apartment, taken aback by the amazing similarities in décor. The living room walls were painted the color of the café latte he'd drunk that morning, blending perfectly with the honey-colored accent wall leading into the bedroom. The furniture was almost undistinguishable from his own: tan chenille loveseats with rolled arms and saber legs placed on either side of a zebrawood coffee table. In the center of the table was a single white orchid flowing from a silver tube vase surrounded by platters of crudités, crackers and what appeared to be specialty cheeses from Grand Central Market. It looked like he'd set the table himself.

A sepia floor runner extended from the edge of the living room into the kitchen area. It was obvious the galley kitchen had been renovated since its pre war days, with new appliances, an Italian stone floor and backsplash and a granite countertop that served as a pass-through to the small, oval dining room table placed in front of the window. Silk curtains hung from a copper rod, their hem stopping less than half an inch from the polished wood floor, adding an intriguing element of depth to the entire room.

Jonathan strolled to the arched wall and peeked into the bedroom. He didn't want to appear excessively curious so he turned himself around, stood beneath the archway and shrugged his shoulders.

"Wow, this is great," he said, slipping off his coat. "It's beautiful."

Philip nodded. "I knew you'd say that, because the place looks like you decorated it!"

"Stop, boys!" Angela said. "This looks *nothing* like your house. I couldn't come close to that."

"No, really," Jonathan looked scanned the room again. "It does resemble our house. When did you have it done? Everything looks so new. I think I can even smell paint."

"Have it done?" Angela pulled her hair into a pony tail, twisted it into a bun and clipped it in place. "Sadly, I can't afford to 'have it done'. I did it myself." She walked back into the room and ironed the front of her shirt with her hands. "I redecorated about a year or so ago. But I did do some touch ups yesterday because I was having two very special visitors. That's why you smell paint. So do you honestly like it?"

"He loves it," Philip said. "Can't you tell? It's exactly his taste. And anyone with his taste is a-ok. Right, Jonny?"

Jonathan smiled and shook his head. "Not everyone. Your friend Jason from work has my taste and you know how I feel about him. He's one of the last…"

"Okay, let's not go there." Philip gave Angela a shrug. "Wanna give us a look around, Angie?"

Although the tour lasted less than four minutes, Jonathan was impressed with how Angela had made such small surroundings appear so unconstructed and hospitable. She had a great sense of working with space and the rooms appeared functional and accommodating enough for a child. But his mind wandered back to the city streets: the noise, throngs of people, the silky layer of soot that covered everything. His concern about nurturing a child in the city resurfaced like an itchy rash. He pasted a smile on his face, trying to disguise his thoughts.

He and Philip sat together on one of the loveseats, crudités and prosciutto-wrapped mozzarella beautifully presented on a black, tiled serving tray sitting in the middle of the coffee table. She brought a large pitcher of homemade iced tea from the kitchen, set it on a coaster next to the tray, and perched on the ottoman across from them.

"Now, what I figured we'd do today is walk around Chelsea a bit. You know, I'll just show you the area, some of the hidden gems, stuff like that. Then we can hang around, go out for dinner, or do whatever you want to do." She looked at Jonathan and pushed the tray of crudités closer to him. "There's a great art exhibit a few blocks away in SoHo. It's by this new artist who uses miniature doll parts on large canvases. Makes it look like people being sucked into outer space or something. I read about it in New York Magazine. It looked kinda cool."

Jonathan tightened his lips and raised his eyebrows in a "maybe" "maybe not" sort of way. His mind wasn't on artists or hidden gems. Nor was it on SoHo or outer space. He was consumed with how to tell Angela and Philip he couldn't go through with the sperm donation – not if his child would be raised in New York City. He imagined himself lying in bed at night, wondering what toxic fumes his son had breathed that day and what the side effects might be. Images of tiny, sandaled feet, soiled with the city's soot and grime shot through his head; a piteous street-child buried in the filth of the most merciless city in the world. He closed his eyes, attempting to rid the thoughts from his mind, but his mind wasn't hearing any of that.

Angela crossed her legs and shot Philip a bewildered look. She unfastened the top two buttons of her pink, cashmere sweater and clasped her hands on her knee.

"Okay, what's up with you?" she asked, darting glances at the two of them. "Something's not right here."

Jonathan looked at the appetizers. Philip peeked at Jonathan, then back to Angela.

"He's been a weirdo all day. Not sure what it is. He thinks he has a chemical imbalance." He grabbed Jonathan's neck, leaning him into his own shoulder. Kissing the top of Jonathan's head, he made a grumbling sound. "But he doesn't have a chemical imbalance. He's just moody today."

Angela smiled and laid her hand on Jonathan's knee. "We're all moody sometimes. It's part of the way things are. Don't even think about it. We don't have to do anything you don't want to. We can just sit around and watch television. I don't care."

Jonathan pulled himself away from Philip, sitting himself up straight. The piercing heat of tension was beginning to rumble in his gut and he knew if he didn't speak his mind or run out the door, he'd sink into a much darker frame of mind. He played with his fingers, exhaling loudly to break the awkward silence.

"What is it, Jonny?" Philip grabbed his hand. "What's the matter?"

"I can't do it," Jonathan blurted. "I can't."

"Can't do what?" asked Angela, now leaning forward, her head above the uneaten appetizers.

"Have a kid." It was all coming out now and with each word, Jonathan felt the heat in his stomach gradually extinguish.

The silence grew heavier, nothing but Jonathan's uneven breathing and the faint echo of water running through pipes filtering through the room. Angela removed her hand from

Jonathan's knee as Philip tightened his grip around his hands. Fearful of their facial expressions, Jonathan still hadn't looked up. His mind had raced, he'd thrown out his thoughts for all to hear and now all he wanted to do was run from the reaction.

"Shhh, it's okay, Babe. Don't sweat it. I told you that on the train. It is what it is. Calm down. We're okay with it."

Jonathan glanced up at Angela at the same moment she placed her hands atop theirs.

"It really is fine, Jonathan. You have to be comfortable with something like this. It's a big step and I totally understand." She stood up, walked to the window, and spread the sheer draperies further apart to let in more light. "Maybe it's not the right time for you. Maybe you don't think I'm the right woman. Maybe you just don't…"

"It's not that," Jonathan struggled out of his coat, his internal heat creating droplets of perspiration that soaked the back of his neck. "We really do want to have a child. And right now, I don't think there's anyone more perfect than you. The problem is…"

Angela leaned against the wall; eyes wide open, tensely anticipating the end of his sentence. Jonathan looked at Philip, who held the same expression.

"Shit, okay, the issue is with this place, this city." He rose, took a few steps toward Angela, then back toward the front door, and finally positioned himself against the granite counter that separated the kitchen from the living room. "No offense, Angela, but for me, New York is a great place to visit, but I wouldn't want to live here. And basically that means, I wouldn't want my child living here."

He looked across the room at Philip.

"So in essence," Philip said, "it's a geographic thing."

"Don't make me sound crazy, Philip. You know as well as I do, growing up in New England is a lot different than growing up in New York. The people are different, the environment is different. The *air* is different, for Christ's sake."

"No one's saying you're crazy, Jonathan." He leaned back on the sofa and blew out hard, his cheeks swelling like a balloon. "It's just that you come out and say you don't want a kid, without giving any kind of reason. If it's a location problem, then say it's a location problem. Maybe that's something we can work out. But don't just flat out say 'I don't want a kid,' how do you think that makes Angela feel?" They both looked at Angela, still leaning against the wall by the window, now with a wide grin on her face. "What?" Philip tilted his head, baffled by her untimely smile. "What's so funny?

She slid over to the small roll-top desk in the corner of the living room, pulled open the top drawer, and took out a sheet of paper. With both hands she dangled the paper out in front of her, arms at full length as she took slow steps toward Jonathan. He struggled to see the writing, but could only make out a strange looking blue logo resembling a butterfly. When she finally reached him, he gently took the paper from her hands.

"What is this?" Up close, he realized the butterfly looked more like the letter Y, part of the Yale New Haven Health System logo he'd seen on billboards along I-95. It was a letter, addressed to Angela and signed by the Human Resource Manager at Bridgeport Hospital.

"What is it?" Philip asked, walking toward Jonathan.

"It looks like a job acceptance letter," Jonathan said, looking at Angela.

She rolled her eyes and grabbed the letter.

"It says if I want a position as a Nurse Manager at Bridgeport Hospital, the job is mine." Neither Philip nor Jonathan uttered a word. They simply stared at her, waiting for what was coming next. "Well, it seems Jonathan and I are on the same wavelength... again." She smiled and swept the loose hair from Jonathan's forehead. "I was going to bring it up to you today, you know, the fact that I *also* don't think this city is a good place to bring up a child. So over the past month or so, I've been looking for jobs in Connecticut."

She turned her back to both of them, walked to the sofa, and flopped down. "Now don't get nervous. I know you guys haven't even made up your mind yet, and I'm not pushing you into anything. But my thought was, if I want to bring my child up in the right environment, why not move by his or her fathers? And even if you decide you *don't* want to go through with the whole thing, I knew a year ago it was time for me to leave this New York City craziness behind. And Connecticut's a good place to start anew, right? Especially with you guys living there."

Jonathan sat on one of the counter stools and hooked his heels on the stainless steel footrest. He felt his insides start to settle, like a warm shroud of calm encompassing his body. Staying silent, he let her continue.

"So I found this opening at Bridgeport Hospital and have actually been looking at homes in the Fairfield area. It's close to you and near the hospital. I got this letter two days ago and told them I'd need a few days to decide. That's why I thought today would be a perfect time to bring it up." She looked at Jonathan and smiled. "And when Jonathan started talking about location and his issues with New York, I figured why wait til later? And so I brought out the letter." Crossing her legs Indian-style, she leaned her elbows on her thighs. "And that's that. Now it's your turn."

After a few seconds, Jonathan sauntered toward Angela and fell into the opposite side of the sofa so he could look at her. He let out a sigh.

"This is scary, you know." He looked up at Philip, who had been checking out the view from the window and was now coming toward him. "We have the same taste in music, décor, and food – and now, while I'm freaking out about not wanting to bring up a kid in New York, you've already been planning to move to the country," he said, using his fingers to represent quotation marks. "If I didn't know better, I'd think you were psychic."

"Not psychic," she responded, "just a logical thinker with good taste. Like you, I guess."

Philip sat down beside Jonathan and rubbed his leg.

"Wow, the perfect parents. Just like June and Ward Cleaver," he joked. "Come to think of it, Jonny, you do have a little Ward going on in the eyebrow area."

Jonathan pushed Philip's hand away and turned to Angela. "Did you say I have good taste? Well you must have a lot better taste than I do because look who *I* get to spend my life with."

Angela leaned over, placed a mozzarella wrap between her teeth, and eked out a smile.

"Poor you," she said, shoving another wrap into her mouth, the smile never leaving her face.

<u>11</u>

If he had a rifle, he would've shot everyone on the street.

"Too many fucking people." Tommy shoved through a crowd of pedestrians waiting to cross Broadway, muttering under his breath. "Just too many fucking people." He said it over and over, like a mantra, standing on his toes to keep Angela and the two men within his sights.

"God damn faggots. What the hell is she doing with those two faggots?"

A nearby Asian woman shot him a look of contempt before taking another sip of her coffee. He realized his mumbling was no longer under his breath, but scowled at her anyway and pushed through the crowd, hoping to be first across the street when the light changed.

Jumping to see over the heads of the others, he saw the three of them make a left onto 46th Street, Angela in the middle, her arms tucked into the arms of each man. A searing poker pierced his belly, spreading heat throughout his body.

This isn't fair! This isn't fucking fair! It was his only day off this week and she promised to spend it with him. But she'd cancelled late last night when he called to finalize their plans. She said it was an emergency, but she couldn't discuss the details. That's when he decided to wait at the end of her street, all day if necessary, and discover the so-called "emergency" for himself.

When the two men walked up the steps of her brownstone at 2:37, he immediately knew who they were. One of them had to be Philip, the ex-boyfriend she brought up every time they had an argument.

"He knew how to treat me," she'd say, a quiver on the edge of her voice. "He knew how to touch me, how to talk to me when I felt sad." She'd let out a huff and wrap her arms around herself. "I just can't explain it, Tommy. It's something that comes naturally to some men."

"But he's a fag, Angela! I don't care how well he treated you back then. What the hell does that mean now?" He stuck both hands in his pants pockets and straightened his arms, leaning forward so she'd hear him better. "And of course he knew what to say to you. He knew what to say to *all* women because he's almost a woman himself, for God's sake!"

The argument would heat up from there, with Angela kicking him out and vowing never to speak to him again. After a dozen phone calls and messages left on her voicemail, she'd finally return his call and let him take her to dinner and woo her all over again.

But the last few arguments had been different, because she no longer talked about Philip in the past tense. He was back in her life, along with his fag boyfriend, and Tommy didn't understand why. When he asked for an explanation, she'd only say the men were "good friends." He didn't buy that for a minute. If he was ever going to find out the truth, he'd have to do it behind Angela's back.

And now here he was, following them all the way into Midtown Manhattan – his questions still unanswered. Before reaching 9th Avenue, they turned into Pomaire, his and Angela's favorite Chilean restaurant. The heat from the poker in his belly grew more intense, a fire so blistering he had to cover his mouth to hold back a scream. He walked past the restaurant, keeping his face buried in the lifted collar of his jacket. When he reached 9th Avenue, he leaned against the concrete blocks of the corner bank and waited.

The only sound he could hear was the hollow echo of his breath. It was as though the city's speakers had been turned off: fire trucks whizzed by him without making a sound; a mass of yellow cabs swarmed up the avenue in silence. All around him people's lips were moving but he couldn't hear their voices. He heard only his quivering exhalations, now fueled by the ire and frustration of being cast aside, yet again.

Way down, beneath the rage and fire, he knew this was crazy. Angela was just a woman, one of millions from which he could choose. And yet, from the moment he first saw her, he couldn't let her go. No one would take her from him. Especially a fag.

The sky grew darker by the minute; the shadow of silvery-gray clouds marching in from the Hudson adding an intensity to the autumn chill, forcing pedestrians to pick up the pace.

Tommy also walked faster, on his way back to Angela's, silently praying he'd get there before she arrived. He'd waited on the corner of Ninth and Forty Sixth for almost two hours, pacing back and forth, trying to decide what to do.

He thought about going into the restaurant and sitting at the bar, casually glancing around the room until he caught her eye. Then he'd walk over to her table, feigning surprise and delight. But he knew she'd see right through it and would shun him for weeks if he pulled an obvious stunt like that.

He then considered calling her and asking if he could join them. Once she said "yes," he'd walk around the block five or six times before finally entering the restaurant and pretending to be out of breath, as though he'd run from his uptown apartment to arrive just in time for appetizers. When he reached for his phone, his heart skipped a beat: If *she wanted me at dinner, she would have invited me.*

He threw his options back and forth for two hours before deciding the meeting had to take place on the street; pure coincidence, as it sometimes happened to the people he worked with. If it could happen to others, why couldn't it happen with Angela?

She can't blame me for that, right? I'm just walking on the street... it's a public place. She can't blame me for that. I'm allowed to walk on the street.

He decided it should take place near Angela's apartment building, since he knew sooner or later the threesome would end up there. He planned to make the meeting appear even more accidental by walking toward them when they met. But he wasn't sure how to choreograph that moment. What if they went to a movie or a museum and returned from a different direction? What if they took a cab and were dropped off right in front of the brownstone?

"Fuck, what-if." He slid his hands into his jacket pockets and tilted his head away from the invading wind. "I'll make it happen."

When he reached 16th Street, he walked past Angela's building and continued to 5th Avenue before turning around to look behind him. So far, no Angela. He rested against the street lamp, ignoring the grunts of people who had to walk around him. His insides trembled in anticipation, still uncertain what he'd say when their paths converged – and how Angela would react.

He looked at his watch: 9:35. *Jesus Christ! A three hour meal? What the hell are they talking about for three fucking hours. She never sits with me for...*

A heavy pounding beat against his ribcage when he saw a taxi turn onto 16th. The headlights of the car behind it beamed through the rear window, revealing three shadows in the back seat. He quickly stood up straight, swiped his hands along the sides of his head to push down any stray hairs, and began his brisk walk for the cab. As he marched toward the brownstone, second thoughts swirled inside his head. He swore to himself if it wasn't the three of them, he'd call the whole thing off and go to Brodsky's for a few shots. The potential damage this could cause to his relationship with Angela just wasn't worth it.

He quickened his pace, hoping to pass them before they exited the cab, but as he approached the brownstone, an older couple appeared out of nowhere and crept down the street in front of him. He could either cross the street, which was bumper to bumper with cars stuck at a red light, or push the old farts out of the way and hope no one would notice. About to make a decision, his legs froze when he saw Angela jump out of the cab and look directly at him. He tried to think of a way out, but his brain froze. Other than turning around and running like a madman, he was out of options.

He knew Philip immediately. *So fucking Connecticut. Blonde hair, WASPY face, fancy shmancy coat.*

"Hi!" Angela shouted, waving him down.

He looked behind him. *Is she talking to me?*

"Tommy!"

His legs were moving, his arm waved as though a puppeteer pulled the strings from somewhere in the blackness of the sky. As he approached them, Philip took a few steps forward and held out his hand. It took less than a second for Tommy to decide Philip's smile was forced, a mask to hide jealousy and anger that Angela had a male friend. But he was concealing it well. Tommy had to give him that much. He took Philip's gloved hand, the soft leather against his skin sending a chill up his arm.

"Philip, this is Tommy. He's a good friend of mine," Angela glanced at Tommy with a smile as forced as Philip's.

A good friend? What the hell was she talking about? Tommy continued shaking Philip's hand, though his eyes remained on Angela. If he was going to set them straight, let them know he was Angela's boyfriend, he'd have to speak now. But Angela's eyes forbade him.

"This is Jonathan, Philip's partner." He heard Angela's voice somewhere in the distance. "Jonathan, this is Tommy."

He took his eyes off Angela and unintentionally looked directly into Jonathan's piercing blue eyes. It was obvious now: they were mocking him; hiding frowns of disapproval behind false smiles and hand shaking.

"Nice to meet you." Tommy said. He pulled his stare away from Jonathan and turned back toward Philip. "I've heard a lot about you."

"Don't believe anything she told you!" Philip gave Angela a fake punch in the arm. "She's a liar!"

Angela tussled Philip's hair, then turned to Tommy, her smile wide.

"I've only said *nice* things, right Tommy?"

"Absolutely," he responded. "All good things." *I sound like a fucking retard. Jesus Christ.*

"We have to get to the train or we'll be waiting another hour before the next one comes." Jonathan held up his index finger, signaling the cab driver to wait. "Nice meeting you, Tommy." He tapped the side of Tommy's arm. "Angela!" He gave her a tight hug. "Wonderful time, as always. We'll call you during the week." He kissed her cheek and slid into the cab.

Philip grabbed Angela and held her close, rocking her back and forth. "Love being with you," he said.

Tommy looked at Angela's face, her eyes closed, her chin resting on Philip's shoulder as she hugged him back. It took all his strength not to pull Philip back by his hair and punch him in the face. When Angela's eyes opened, they were empty.

Jonathan's voice spilled out of the cab. "C'mon Philip, let's go!"

Philip gave Angela a peck on the mouth and turned to Tommy. "Hey, nice to meet you." He jumped in the cab, slammed the door, and waved as the vehicle pulled away.

Tommy stood unmoving, too frightened to spin around and face Angela. He waited for the cab to disappear before curling his hands into fists and swinging his arms by his sides. He took a few steps back and snuck a glimpse.

She leaned against the railing that overlooked the ground floor apartment. Her arms were crossed and she tapped her foot on the pavement, reminding him of the elementary school teachers who used to drag him to the Principal's office. *I'm not ten years old anymore,* he told himself.

"Do I even ask?" Angela reached down and slipped off her left shoe, then her right.

He leaned against the railing beside her so they were both facing the street. "Ask what?"

She kept her gaze on the sidewalk. "What the hell are you doing here?"

Tommy tightened his lips, determined to stick to his story. "What are you talking about? I was coming from the festival on 23rd and thought I'd pass by to see if you were home."

"I don't believe you." She stretched her toes on the pavement. "You just happen to be walking down my street at the exact time we're getting out of the cab? Give me a fucking break, Tommy. I'm not that stupid."

Stick to the story. Stick to the story. "I don't give a shit what you believe, Angela. It is what it is. I checked out the arts and crafts show in the park, which was a load of crap by the way, and came down your street to see if you wanted to grab a bite or some espresso." He kicked the toe of his shoe against the sidewalk. "Believe whatever you want to believe. Coincidences happen."

A full minute of silence passed between them before Angela turned and started walking up the steps.

"Okay, let's go upstairs."

Tommy's insides were shaking. "Wait a second, Angela. I have some questions."

She stopped midway up the steps and turned around. Lowering her shoulders in frustration, she sighed.

"Questions about what, Tommy?"

"The emergency you had to take care of today. What was it? If it was so freakin' important, why were you having dinner with those fags from Connecticut instead of with me like we planned?"

She looped her fingers through the straps of her shoes and swung them back and forth by her side. Smirking, she shook her head.

"How did you know we went out for dinner?"

SHIT!

Unable to respond, paralyzed by his blunder and sheer stupidity, Tommy simply stared at her. All those hours of thinking... all that time to prepare. For nothing. It took him only seconds to blast his plan to smithereens and drown any hope of negotiating with Angela. He tightened his fists and clenched his teeth, awaiting the wrath that would fall down upon him.

"Now stop asking questions and let's go upstairs. I want you inside me. Now."

Running up the stairs behind her, Tommy shook his head, realizing he'd never be able to figure her out. And maybe that was what kept him coming back.

12

"Twenty five hundred dollars a month?" Angela's voice quivered.

She held the document in front of her and let herself fall back against the wall. She then slid down until she was able to rest her elbows on her knees, looked around at the half-empty moving boxes scattered throughout the living room, and fought to hold back the tears.

"Well, we want to make sure everything's taken care of," said Jonathan, bending down, squeezing her knees.

Angela shook her head, tears clinging to her mascara. "It's too kind. It's too much." She struggled to push the words through her constricted throat. "I have a good job. I can take care of us. This is too generous of you." She peered up at Philip. "*Both* of you."

Jonathan pressed down against her knees and sprang up. "Well…" he cleared his throat, looked at Philip, then back down to Angela. "As you can see, unfortunately it comes with conditions." He backed up and darted his eyes around the room, almost as though he'd heard something and was searching for its source. "If it wasn't for our lawyer, G, who is also a good friend, we wouldn't even have you sign this. But she's a worry wart, very anal, like most lawyers, and wants to make sure we're protected. Just in case…"

Angela wiped her eyes with the back of her hands. "Do you have a pen?"

"For what?" Philip said.

"To sign this, silly!" She extended her arms, waving them back and forth in front of the piles of boxes. "I can't find anything in all these boxes. How am I supposed to find a pen?" Emotion lined the ragged edges of her voice and this time Philip bent down and grabbed her knees.

"Calm down, Angie. It's all okay. Everything is fine." He looked up at Jonathan and tightened his lips, almost forming a smile. He turned back to Angela. "You shouldn't sign this without having an attorney look at it. We want to make sure you're comfortable with everything. It's important that we're all on the same page with this so that there are no surprises down the line."

Angela placed the document on the oak floor and swept the hair from Philip's forehead. She let her finger follow his nose and down to his chin, where she pointed her nail into the shadow of his dimple.

"Let's see, I just moved my entire existence from New York City to Fairfield, Connecticut. Do you think I'd do that if I wasn't comfortable? I trust the two of you so deeply there's no reason for me to get an attorney."

Jonathan bent down beside the two of them. "You never know what can happen, Angela. You just never know. You can't sign this document without reading what we've put in there. It's important that you..."

Angela rolled her eyes and grabbed the document. "Okay, how 'bout this? You both go get us a pizza or something, and while you're gone I'll read it. When you come back, it'll either be signed or you'll find it shredded on the front porch." She laughed as she used Philip's shoulder to help her stand. "Like I said, I trust you guys and know you'd never want to hurt me."

Philip brushed the back of his hand along her cheek. "Well, we really think you should have an attorney read it. If you need one, I'm sure G knows another lawyer." Angela grabbed Philip's arm, then Jonathan's, turned them around, and pushed them toward the door. "Now, I don't like sausage, but I do like pepperoni. And make sure there's plenty of onion. And olives. I need my olives."

"Angela..." Jonathan started until he looked at Philip.

"It's no use," Philip said, "Let's just go."

"Smarter than I thought," Angela said, now pushing them onto the porch and down the wooden steps. "And don't forget the Diet Pepsi!"

As the soothing hum of the Beemer faded into the distance, Angela sat on the top porch step. The sky was typical November Sunday: a dark-silvery blanket holed with patches of bright blue.

The tree-lined street was quiet; eerily still; almost as if time had pulled up stakes and taken any sign of life with it.

She looked around her small front yard. *Not bad for a quarter acre.* The picket fence would need a new coat of white paint, but she'd wait until spring for that; the season was changing too quickly to start such an undertaking. The small porch grabbed onto something within her, pushing a vague childhood memory toward her mind's fringe: paint-chipped planks of wood, either gray or white, it was hard to tell, lined the empty porch, begging to be sanded and painted with a fresh coat of paint – another spring project. She crossed her arms and grabbed each shoulder, trying to warm herself and put a stop to the shivering thoughts creeping up her spine.

What did I get myself into? Holy shit!

A gust of wind skidded dead leaves across the empty street. She grabbed the sweater hanging on the porch post and threw it over her shoulders.

Stop it. Stop it. Stop it. Stop it.

The buzzing in her sweater pocket made her jump. She fished around the huge woolen pouch, found her cell phone, and glanced at the display. It was Tommy calling for the third time since ten o'clock that morning. Tossing the phone back into her pocket, she pulled the sweater around her, bracing herself against the wind that was getting gustier by the second.

Tommy was going to be a problem and she should've ended things with him once and for all. She'd had the opportunity – it was right in front of her that day in her apartment; the day before she moved when Tommy practically begged her to stay.

"I still don't understand this whole fucking thing, Angie." Tommy paced the floor, kicking boxes as he passed them. "One day you love me and we're going to move in together and the next thing I know, you're packing up to go live with those fags. And in Connecticut for Christ's sake! What the fuck is wrong with you?"

Angela closed the box flaps and fixed them closed with the tape dispenser, the friction creating a "shhhhhh" that echoed through the apartment. "First of all, Tommy, keep your voice down." Another "shhhhhh". "Second of all, I'm not moving in with Philip and Jonathan. I'm moving miles away. And third of all…"

"Say what you want, Angie. Just tell me *why*. I don't get it. Why are you moving? And why are you leaving me?"

Angela picked up the box and placed it atop the other three cartons piled against the wall. She crossed her arms, laid them on top of the box, and buried her face within them, her nose rubbing the acrid-smelling packing tape.

This could be the moment, she thought, the turning point, but only if she decided it would be. It was now or never: get rid of Tommy so she could start fresh without this crazy albatross hanging around her neck, or say something that would keep him around if she needed him, but far enough away to not destroy her plans.

She heard his breathing increase; laborious puffs of air coming out his nose. Knowing she had to make the decision quickly, she glanced up to get a look at his face before speaking. He had stopped pacing and was staring at her, waiting, still breathing heavily, a veiled expression of sorrow and disbelief poking through his rage.

A stab of empathy shot through her; a feeling she had not felt for years, since the days her weight had given others the perfect opportunity to snub and reject her at every turn. The expression on Tommy's face was identical to the devastation she felt with every rebuff; the swelling anger of unjustness; the primal, yet silent pleading for someone to look into her heart and see her pain. She wondered if she'd ever shown it the way Tommy was showing it now. If she had, she could slap herself across the face for allowing anyone to see what she was feeling; the same way she could slap Tommy for showing it now.

His pitiful expression and air of helplessness enabled her to make the decision. She bit her lip, knowing what she was about to say was a lie. But it didn't matter. Her future hung in the balance and no one was going to fuck with it.

"Tommy, we've been through this before. Don't you understand it's for both of us?" Angela slid her bare feet across the wood floor and stood in front of him. "I can't stand this city anymore. It's too crowded... too hot in the summer... too full of crime... too dirty.

I'm just waiting for *you* to see the same thing. Once you do, you'll come and be with me."

Tommy seized her hand. "You've said that before," he lowered his voice. "But why wasn't I involved in *anything*? You decide to move without talking to me about it. You buy a house, I wasn't involved at all. You're packing and don't even ask for my help." He shook his head. "Yeah, I'm a little fucked up Angie, I know that. That's why I'm taking the meds. But no matter how crazy I am, or how crazy you think I am, I know there's something not right here."

She placed a hand on each of his shoulders. "You're not fucked up." She pulled him toward her, pushing the back of his head until he let his forehead fall onto her shoulder. "I'm the one who's fucked up. I'm just used to being on my own and making all my own decisions. I should've involved you more, especially if you're going to move in with me one day. I promise that from now on you'll be involved a lot more. I just have to get through the move, settle in, and then we'll make all our future plans together, okay?"

Tommy didn't say a word. He slid his hands around her waist and buried his face in the crook of her neck. Angela looked up to the ceiling, hoping she'd made the right decision.

Sitting on the porch, immersed in her sweater, doubts about Tommy crept over her like ants on half-eaten candy. Between Philip, Jonathan, her new job, the house, and getting pregnant, she was overwhelmed and Tommy added yet another complication.

For now she'd have to deal with him one day at a time; one phone call at a time, until she was ready to let him go – for good.

The way her foot tapped incessantly on the porch step made her realize that her anxiety was reaching a new level. Angela knew how important it was for her to find a way to keep her nerves under control; this was no time for weakness. She couldn't bring herself to walk back inside the house, into the mess of boxes and chaos that would make her more anxious, so she grabbed the cell phone from her pocket and stared into the darkening sky, lost in thought, until she figured out who to call.

"It sucks here without you, Angie," said June. "It really does. There's like no one to talk to anymore. And work *really* sucks. The new woman who took your place is a bitch on wheels and…"

"June!" Angela shouted into the phone. "Could you close your mouth for one freakin' second?" She waited for silence. "I'm going crazy here. I called you for *support* for Christ's sake, not to hear you bitch."

Angela heard rustling on the other end of the phone and could tell June was taking a pill. She rolled her eyes. "I'm sorry for yelling," she started. "How are your meds? You have enough?"

"Yes, thanks." June said. "*More* than enough."

"Good, then take what you need and please calm down. I need you to be level headed."

Angela pictured June in her typical position: on her sofa, legs tucked beneath her and hanging off the sofa to her side, head resting against the wall. It was a stamped image in her mind, the way she knew she'd remember June long after their friendship ended, which, if Angela had her way, would be within the next few months.

She shook her head, suddenly perturbed by the fact that June was so frail and such a dullard. If only she was pretty and had a halfway decent personality, Angela could set her up with Tommy and kill two birds with one stone. But that wasn't going to be, and she silently cursed June who sat on the other end of the phone waiting to be told she could speak. The facts were clear: Tommy was a nut and June was close to being a nonexistent entity, which meant Angela would have to take the bull by the horns and cut her ties separately with each of them. *Shit!*

"You there, June?" Angela asked.

There was no response and Angela quickly realized she'd made a mistake by calling June. She would get no words of advice, no support. June didn't have it in her; she was a lost soul who couldn't help herself, let alone anyone else. After a few more seconds of quiet, Angie let out a sigh.

"June?"

"I'm sorry, Angie." June finally spoke. "It's just that I miss you. So tell me, what's going on there and why do you need support? Are there problems?"

The wind picked up and Angela buried her face into her sweater's extra-large sleeves. "Actually, things are okay. I'm just trying to handle a lot of shit at once and it's tough." She cleared her throat. "Anyway, I'm really calling because it looks like next weekend will be the weekend. So keep Saturday open."

"Oh, my God!" June shouted, her first ray of life since she answered the phone. "I can't believe it! This is great! And I get to meet Philip and Jonathan... *finally*."

"Yeah, great, but remember, this isn't a 'June meets the Boys' party. No hors d'oeuvres or fancy dinners. You're coming out here to help me get pregnant. That's it."

A few seconds of silence. "I've got it, Angie. You've said it a million times. I'm just excited. Can't I just be excited for you?"

Angela picked at the paint chips bending upward on the step below. She caught one under her nail, peeled it up, examined it and then flicked it into the grass. "Yes, you can be excited. I'm sorry. Like I said, I'm just overwhelmed with all this shit."

"What do you need me to bring? Anything from the hospital? Syringes? Cervical cup? Saline? What about tubing, it's always a good idea to..."

Angela tightened her lips to keep the verbal venom from escaping her mouth. "June, stop. Please." She took a deep breath. "I have everything under control and I have everything I need. I work in a hospital, too, remember? I don't need you to do a thing."

"Sure," said June, the melancholy dripping from her voice. "I just thought I could help. But if you don't want me to bring anything and you don't need me to do a thing, why do you want me there at all?"

June's question made Angela realize her impatience was jeopardizing her relationship with one of the only people she could trust. She shook her head at her own stupidity. She'd come this far and couldn't allow her personality flaws to destroy her future.

If the years of obesity had taught her one thing, it was how to keep true feelings hidden deep beneath the surface. Back then, it was easy to hide fear and anxiety beneath layers of fat and cellulite. Now, there was no place to hide her emotions other than beneath the cold, steel drum that guarded the pit of her stomach.

"I'm sorry... again, June. I don't know what's wrong with me. It's probably the Clomid. I started it a few days ago so I'd have a better chance of getting pregnant. The hormones are raging through me like shards of ice."

"Oh, Clomid can definitely do that to you. I worked in a fertility clinic for a few months when I started nursing. There were women on Clomid and some of the other fertility meds who would actually scream and yell at the television while waiting to see the specialist! It was like a loony bin in there sometimes."

Angela forced a smile. "Well, at least I know it's not just me. And by the way, I want you to know that I want you there as a friend, you know, moral support. Someone to be with me while I'm inseminating. And afterwards, of course. Sometimes I get a little scared thinking I'm going through this alone."

"You're not alone, Angie. Remember that. I'm always here for you no matter what." The tone of her voice became softer and Angela heard June bring the phone closer to her mouth. "Do you need me to come there now? I have a late shift, but I can switch with Rosa. She's always looking to work nights."

An SUV slowly rolled past the house, the first sign of life Angela had seen since coming outside. A small girl, about three years old pushed herself against her car seat trying to get closer to the window. She waved frantically at Angela until it was obvious her gestures would not be reciprocated. The movement of her hand slowed and an expression of bewilderment enveloped her face.

Angela rolled her eyes. "Kids," she whispered.

"What?" asked June. "Are there kids there?"

"No," Angela said. "No kids. Just talking to myself." She paused. "Look, I gotta go. There's no need to come out now. I'll call you mid-week and we'll set up plans for Saturday." She jumped up, not allowing herself to shiver. "Thanks again. Say 'hi' to everyone at the hospital. Bye."

Angela pressed the "END CALL" button before June had the chance to reply. She scurried into the house, found the legal document, and flipped to the last page. Grabbing a pen from her pocketbook, she leaned the papers against her thigh and signed her name. As she clicked the pen closed, she heard the Beemer pull into the driveway. She threw the pen back into her pocketbook, turned the last page over, and placed the document neatly onto the dining room table.

"Done!" Angela whispered.

The heat inside the house had turned her chills to perspiration. She fixed her hair into a pony tail, unwrapped her sweater, and through the dining room window watched the men carry the pizza up the front porch.

"Come in!" She shouted before Jonathan had a chance to ring the doorbell. "And don't even think about using that bell again," she said as she grabbed a pizza box from Philip's hand. "Mi casa, es su casa!"

13

Oversized Euonymus hedges lined with miniature lanterns blocked the view on both sides of the graveled driveway, reminding June of the elegant Georgia landscape she loved as a child. The only sounds she heard were the rock crunching beneath the tires and her own breath, quickening in anticipation of what was to come.

When the headlights swept along the last few inches of hedge, June gasped as she tried to take in the entire face of the house. The lush evergreen plantings, still green despite impending winter, graced the foreground of the home with raw beauty. Natural wood shingles surrounded by wheat-colored trim brought the immensity of the house down to a comfortable size, making June feel more welcome than overwhelmed. In the dusk, the yellow hue of inside lights reminded June of her mother's Georgian home and the intensity with which she missed it. Ironically, the warmth made her shiver and she held in her breath for a moment, blinking back sudden tears. "Oh, my God, Angie, this house is gorgeous!" June covered her mouth with her gloved hand, muffling her voice. "It's like a palace. I've never seen anything like it."

Angela shifted the Land Cruiser into Park and cut the engine and headlights. "I know." She leaned back in the seat and crossed her arms. "It really is a perfect house. And if you think the front is nice, you've *got* to see the backyard."

June felt a slight twinge in her stomach. She'd spent the entire train ride to Westport wondering what Angela's mood would be like. And so far, so good. Angela seemed relaxed and happy.

"I can't wait!" June said, now peering out the side window. "I've been wondering for so long what their house looks like."

"June," Angela huffed, "Please remember this isn't a museum tour. You're here to help me get pregnant."

June closed her eyes and nodded. She turned to Angela and waited for a return gaze. "You don't have to remind me. I know why we're here." She paused, choosing her words carefully. "I'm here to help you. Period. If you're going to be a bitch about it, take me to the station and I'll go back to the city right now."

June's heart was pounding. She'd never stood up to Angela before and had no idea why she was doing it now. But whatever the reason, this felt good and she wasn't going to let go. She hung onto her resistance like an overboard passenger to a lifeboat, even when Angela's eyes widened, her nostrils flared, and she started peeling off her gloves. June stared into the darkness of Angela's eyes, shaking inside, preparing to be swallowed by the two black holes.

Angela threw her gloves onto the dashboard. "Of all the times you decide to get angry and slap me back, you choose *tonight?*" She shook her head. "One of the most important nights of my life and you decide to turn mean? I can't..." Angela covered her eyes with her hands. "I just don't believe this."

June squinted with confusion and tried to get a better glimpse of Angela through the harsh shadows of dusk. Other than anger, she'd never seen Angela display emotion. "Angie?" June whispered into her own hand. There was silence. A sniff. More silence. "Angie? Are you crying?"

Angela turned and June caught the glint of a tear on her cheek. She almost gasped, the drama so foreign to her. In all the years she'd known Angela, not once had she witnessed softness. The realization that Angela was human created a sense of buoyancy within her.

"I'm sorry!" She stroked Angela's arm. "I didn't mean to get you upset. I know you're on edge because of…"

She stopped talking when the front door opened and Philip, known to her only by photographs, waved for them to come in.

"Shit!" Angela wiped her face and grabbed her gloves. As she pulled the handle to open the door, she tossed June a grimace. "Just know, June, if you fuck this up, you'll not only stop getting your meds, but I'll make sure your new boss knows enough shit about you to fire you on the spot."

Angela opened the door, grabbed her bag of supplies, and ran toward Philip's open arms, leaving June to fend for herself. June couldn't move, paralyzed by Angela's words and erratic behavior. She looked at Philip hugging Angela, his face so pure, his hand apparently waving for June to join them. *He seems so nice,* she thought, swallowing hard to push down the lump in her throat. *Why would he want her to have their child? Doesn't he know what she is?*

"Come inside," Philip shouted, both hands now in his pockets as he jumped up and down trying to keep warm. "It's freezing out here!"

June forced half a smile and waved back.

"Come on, June!" Angela's fake smile lit up the walkway. "We're not going in without you!"

"I'm coming," June said to herself. "I'm coming."

June stopped in amazement at the threshold of each room. She'd never seen such exquisite style and architecture. From the lacquered dark maple floor to the deep tray ceilings and high crown molding in every room, she found it hard to take in everything. She took a deep breath, picturing herself inside Willy Wonka's Candy Factory, a camera spinning around her as she whirled about.

But it wasn't just the home's beauty that struck her. Philip and Jonathan sealed the deal. She'd seen them in photographs and an occasional sneak peek as they climbed the stairs to Angela's apartment, but now she understood why Angela was so enamored by these two men. Their handsome New England features and their kindness made her wish they'd throw Angela out the front door and let her be the mother of their child.

They led her from room to room, pointing out items that held special meaning: Max's abstract painting of the two of them above the fireplace in the bedroom; the flawless glass bowl in the center of the dining room table – a gift from a friend they met on the island of Murano during their last Italy trip; the photo sitting atop Philip's desk – a shot taken of Angela, Jonathan and Philip on the day she moved into her home.

When they returned to the living room, June could only shake her head.

"Beautiful, isn't it, June?" Angela said, opening the stereo cabinet to search through the extensive CD collection.

June couldn't bring herself to look at Angela and shatter the moment. From the second she entered the house, June realized that Angela's apartment redecoration was purposely styled after Philip and Jonathan's home. Why would she do that? What sense does that make? Whatever Angela's reasons, June knew this wasn't the time to try to figure it out. She turned to Philip.

"You've done an awesome job here. Your home is exquisite."

"Thanks." Philip stuck his index finger into Jonathan's ribs. "Mostly his doing. He's the one who got *that* gene." Philip laughed and held up his hands in defense.

"No need to protect yourself," Jonathan said, grabbing Angela's hand and walking her to the suede loveseat. "I won't waste my time responding to that." He smiled at June. "You don't pay attention to him either, June. Come sit down."

June walked to a second loveseat opposite Jonathan and Angela and sat down, rubbing her fingertips along the delicate suede fabric. She closed her eyes, absorbing the warmth of the sofa, the room, the music, the people. This was a world she'd only read about in books or home decorating magazines. She didn't know when she'd be back and wanted to soak in every ounce of it.

"June, snap out of it." Angela looked up at Jonathan and let her head fall on his shoulder. "You'll have to excuse her, gentlemen. She doesn't get out much."

Hiding her irritation, June smiled along with Angela's laughter. Angela was being Angela, she supposed, but now there was a subtle difference; a kindness to her actions and words, even the sarcasm. June noticed this difference from the moment they entered the house, and now she understood why Philip and Jonathan were so taken with Angela: she was funny, nice, affectionate and, yes, charming – characteristics she hadn't seen Angela display in all the years they'd know one another. It seemed as though an imposter slipped into Angela's body the moment she crossed the door jamb into the main foyer – the alter ego of the vicious, conniving person June struggled with on a daily basis.

Why were these intelligent men so easily fooled? Yet, as she watched Angela's perpetual smile and constant stroking, physical and verbal, June realized the question was moot. Angela was good.

She was very good. June's instinct was to jump up and start screaming, "She's a bitch! She's crazy! She's acting! Don't believe her!" But if she dared utter a word against Angela, *she'd* appear crazy and would probably be escorted out the front door.

Philip flopped down beside June, spreading his arm along the back of the sofa so his hand fell only inches from the back of her neck. She felt herself tense up.

"Can I get you something to drink, June? We have both alcoholic and non-alcoholic beverages." He switched his gaze to Angela. "Although the non-alcoholic ones are really for Angela. Once she's pregnant, no more Double G and T's for her. She's lucky if we let her drink a Pepsi once a month."

Except for Handel playing softly in the background, the room was silent. Philip's comment brought the true reason behind this get-together to the forefront of the conversation and no one was sure what came next. June looked at Angela and dispensed a strained smile.

"This is weird, huh?" Angela tightened her grip around Jonathan's hand.

Jonathan placed his other hand around hers and smiled at Philip. "I've been saying that to Philip all day. It *is* weird. I mean, we've all talked about it at least a thousand times. But now that it's actually time to make this happen, it feels... well, strange."

"I keep telling him to loosen up." Philip smiled back at Jonathan. "Like I said, just put your stuff in the cup and give it to Angie. She's the professional. She knows what to do with it."

Angela rolled her eyes. "You make it sound so... *special*, Philip. Have you no shame?"

"He doesn't." Jonathan jumped in before Philip could open his mouth. "You should know that already, Angie." Jonathan smiled at June. "And I guess it's something you should learn about him too, June. He's a little rough around the edges."

June laughed quietly, holding her hand in front of her mouth. "From what I've heard, you're two of the most wonderful men on the planet." June and Angela exchanged glances. She could tell Angela was pleased with her comment, so she moved her hand from her mouth to her lap. "I've heard nothing but extreme praise." She turned to Philip, "about *both* of you. So I'm not going to believe any of this."

"I heard the slightest of a southern twang in there," said Jonathan. "Am I wrong?"

"You're absolutely right. I grew up in the south. Wrightsville, Georgia to be exact."

Philip scooted around and leaned his back against the arm of the sofa in order to get a full view of June.

"We love Georgia. Thought about moving down there once or twice, but decided we wouldn't be able to stand the humidity... or the bugs."

June smiled. "Yes, bugs can be a problem. Especially the palmettos. They're huge, and they crunch like pistachios when you step on them."

Philip turned to Jonathan. "Living, breathing pistachios that crunch. Now you see why we're not in Georgia." He turned back to June. "Why haven't we met you before?"

June looked to Angela and found nothing but a blank stare. She felt perspiration on her palms; fast thinking had never been her strong point.

"I work a lot," she started.

"*A lot!*" Angela chimed in.

"I'm never home. Always at the hospital, working my own shift or someone else's. It's not good for the social life, but it's definitely good for the bank account."

"I think I might've seen you looking out your door as we were climbing the stairs to Angela's apartment." Jonathan said. "It might even have been the first time we visited her. I'm not sure."

June rubbed her moist hands together. Jonathan was right. She'd been peeking out her door that day to get a glimpse of them, too afraid of Angela's reaction to even think about introducing herself.

"I'd just gotten home from an eighteen hour shift. I looked terrible and didn't want to put you through such a horror show."

Angela leapt up and placed a hand on each shapely hip.

"Okay everyone, are we here to learn about the history of June Stokes, or are we going to get pregnant?"

Philip stood, walked to Angela, and kissed her cheek.

"You're right. And I can't believe we're actually doing this. I think about fifteen years ago and how we've become two totally different people. And now we're going to be making a baby together!" He turned to Jonathan. "Well, you know, the two of you will be making a baby, but…"

"The three of us," Angela cried. "The three of us are going to be making a baby together."

Watching Angela hug Philip, June's thoughts raced. Something wasn't right in the way Angela held onto him; almost squeezing him, her face leaning against his shoulder with a look of contentment; an unintentional admission that she'd love to remain there for the rest of her life.

For a brief moment June shuddered at the enormity of the bathroom which was almost the size of her living room and kitchen combined. Light from the dimly lit sconces splashed through frosted glass and onto the shiny black granite countertop, where tiny specks of gold glinted from different angles. Again, she covered her mouth with her hand, gazing at the most beautiful slate floor she'd ever laid eyes on; gray-black stone that added additional elegance to the intensely modern room.

Angela threw her suede bag onto the countertop and looked at her reflection in the mirror. Using the index finger of each hand, she carefully wiped under each eye, trying to erase any sign of smudging mascara. She glanced at June and rolled her eyes.

"Get over it, June." She rummaged through her bag and pulled out a hairbrush. "It's a bathroom. Not the Taj Mahal. Please stop acting like such a hick. It's embarrassing."

June felt a tightening in her stomach. The Bitch was back.

"I know it's an important night for you Angela, so I won't be mean again. But if you don't mind, please try to be nice to me for the rest of the evening." She turned to leave the bathroom. "You don't need to kiss my ass like you do Philip and Jonathan's, but you can at least be civil." She walked out of the bathroom and dropped her pocketbook onto the bed. "*You're* the one who's embarrassing."

June heard Angela sigh, and then her heels clacked across the slate floor.

"You're right," Angela said. "I'm sorry. I'm totally uptight and I'm being nasty." June felt Angela's hand on her shoulder, but wouldn't turn around. "Please forgive me, okay? I need you tonight."

June finally turned around and looked at Angela, whose eyes were wide, her expression outwardly sincere. *She* is *good.*

"Okay. Apology accepted." June surrendered. "But I do have one last question."

"Anything. Go ahead."

"Why would you decorate your apartment to look exactly like this house?" June stiffened up as she awaited Angela's wrath.

Angela folded her arms across her chest. "What?"

June swallowed hard. "It's obvious you redecorated your place in the style of this house. The paint color, the furniture, the curtains. Even the sink faucets. Why would you do that?"

"First of all, I don't know what the hell you're talking about. I'd been considering redecorating for years. I just decided to do it now. And second of all, my place isn't like this house at all. My loveseats are tan and my living room coffee table isn't like their living room coffee table. Mine is zebrawood and theirs is maple or something. And third of all, I can't..."

June crossed her arms, same as Angela, and stood directly in front of her. "As usual, I'm not going to get a straight answer from you. So I'm not going to push it tonight. But I have to tell you, Angela, it's a little strange."

She almost fell backward from amazement as Angela wrapped her arms around her, squeezed tightly, and whispered, "Life is strange, June. But all that aside, I'm so glad you're here with me. This is awesome!"

With that, June dropped to the bed and lay on her side, already exhausted from a night that hadn't even truly begun. Angela returned to the bathroom and spewed forth the evening's rules like an instruction manual, forcing June to struggle to hear through the wall between them.

"Here's how it's going to happen. I'm not sure who will bring the sperm, but you take the cup and bring it to me. I'll go into the bathroom and load the syringe. Then I'll come out, lie on the bed, and you can prop some pillows under me. I'll then insert the syringe and dispense the sperm. I've practiced it about a thousand times, so I'm pretty good."

June rose from the bed and walked to the bathroom door. She leaned against the jamb and crossed her arms.

"So tell me, Angie, are you saying I came all the way out here with you to prop up pillows?"

Angela turned to June, her smile forced.

"June, like I've told you over and over, you're also here for moral support. Or are you upset because you really wanted to insert the syringe so you can get a good look at my…"

"Jesus, Angela. What's wrong with you?" June shook her head. "Of course I don't want to insert the syringe. I just thought I could help with the things I know best. Like adding saline to the sperm to minimize waste. Or getting the bubbles out of the syringe before insertion. You know… something that will really make me part of the potential conception."

Angela rubbed June's arm, her smile fading so quickly June could've sworn she heard it hit the floor.

"First of all, don't call this conception 'potential.' It *will* happen. It *has* to happen. And second, I'm not using saline, because there's too much dilution. I want this to be pure, unadulterated sperm." She slid her bare feet toward the mirror and leaned against the sink, her palms flat on the counter. "Now, after I get the sperm inside me, I'll be making myself cum. You might want to be in the bathroom for that."

A wave of dizziness made June's head spin. She slithered along the bathroom wall, stopped when she reached the corner, and slid down until her butt hit the floor. This whole thing had become stranger by the minute. When Angela first asked her to be a part of this, she'd been so flattered and excited she could barely wait for this day. But now, with Angela's erratic behavior at a whole new level, she felt like a caged bird searching for the tiniest of openings to fly away.

She tried to smooth the dry sprouts of hair falling onto her forehead. "What do you mean you'll be making yourself cum? What's that for?"

"Well," Angela dabbed cherry colored lipstick onto her bottom lip. "If you really knew what you say you know, you'd know an orgasm helps the cervix dip into the vaginal pool. That helps the sperm get sucked up faster and also helps speed up the sperms' movement." She pressed her lips together, smoothing the lipstick evenly over her mouth. Turning to June, she leaned against the sink and crossed her arms. "Now, my dear, if you can find the strength to rise, we'll get started." She reached out her hand and helped June stand. "Are you ready?"

June looked to the ceiling, her eyes searching for the God she'd long ago given up on. Finding nothing but the reflection of sconces floating in a sea of white, glossy paint, she almost started to sob. Instead, she looked into the mirror and saw the scrawny, pitiful girl she'd always been; a desiccated bushel of hair sitting atop the most ordinary of faces; pallid skin accentuated by dark circles under her eyes, and lips as thin as razors.

She used all her strength to hold herself up, realizing that someone like Angela, someone crazy, erratic and basically emotionless, was the only kind of person who would befriend her. If she wanted any contact with the outside world, she'd have to accept Angela's hatefulness as part of the package.

"Yes," she whimpered, "I'm ready." She walked into the bedroom, falling onto the bed next to her purse. As she dug through it, she felt Angela's judging eyes on the back of her head. "I'm ready," she mumbled again. "I just need a pill first."

The soft knock on the door made June jump. She sprang to her feet and almost leapt to the bedroom door, smiling timidly when Philip handed her the small plastic cup. Once again she felt the urge to scream: *Don't do this, Philip! It's a mistake! Can't you see?* But instead she turned to Angela who was lying on the bed and offered a smile. Angela smiled back, but only to Philip. She gave him a wave.

"This is it," he said through the partially opened door. He waved back and looked to the floor.

Sensing his uneasiness, June touched his hand. "If we need anything, we'll let you know. It shouldn't take long."

Philip tightened his mouth, creating a dimple beneath his left cheek. "Okay. We'll be in the living room when you're done." He gave Angela the thumbs up and smiled. "Good luck," he whispered.

June watched him walk down the hallway before she shut the door and turned around. Angela was already standing behind her, arm fully extended, waiting for the cup. Startled, June jerked backward, nearly dropping the contents of the cup down the front of her shirt.

"Jesus Christ, June!" Angela shrieked. "Give me that cup and go wait by the bed. I'm going to fill the syringe."

Cup in hand, Angela practically ran to the bathroom and slammed the door behind her. June sat on the bed. wiping the nervous perspiration from her forehead. *What would have happened if she dropped the sperm? What would Angela have done? What would Philip and Jonathan think of her?*

Noises from the bathroom stopped her worry in its tracks. It sounded as though a cleaning crew was in there: clanging metal, clinking glass, a sound similar to silverware being stacked away in a drawer. The ruckus continued for another minute or so before the room fell silent.

When the bathroom door opened, Angela held the syringe in her open palm like a doctor holding a heart about to be transplanted. It was as though she were in a trance, her face holding an expression so serene and tranquil June was suddenly convinced Angela *would* get pregnant tonight. She could see it in her eyes and sense it in the air between them.

"I'm ready," Angela said, almost floating toward the bed.

June ran to her side. "Here, let me help you." She grasped Angela's arm and assisted her onto the bed. Taking the pillow she'd plumped up earlier, she scooped it under Angela's hips so her bottom was raised and her pelvis canted. "There, I think you're all set."

"Thank you," Angela said, looking up at June, peacefulness still surrounding her like a vaporous cloud. "I'm glad you're here," she whispered.

"Me too," replied June, brushing back the wisps of hair from Angela's forehead. "Let me know if you need me for anything."

Gently patting Angela's arm, she rose from the bed and walked into the bathroom. Before she had the chance to see her mirrored reflection, she flicked off the lights, crouched down, and held her head in her hands. She was finally alone, exactly where she wanted to be, with nothing but darkness and the slap of her tears hitting the most beautiful slate floor she'd ever laid eyes on.

14

With barely three hours of sleep, Jonathan struggled to clear his eyes so he could see what all the noise was about. He finally focused on Katy, unloading brown paper grocery bags on the other side of the room. As if the racket from the other nursing home patients wasn't enough, it seemed Katy had joined the club to do everything she could to disturb his sleep. He cleared his throat but didn't utter a word, knowing the sound would force her to turn around.

"Well, well." Katy spun around, holding the most scrumptious-looking French crumb muffin Jonathan had seen in years. "You're finally awake, sleepyhead. It's almost ten o'clock." She placed the muffin on the table next to the television and walked over to the bed. With one hand she pulled the cord of the window blinds, with the other she lifted the afghan that clung to Jonathan's knobby knee.

He turned and looked out the window, his heart skipping a beat when he saw dark, heavy clouds blanketing the sky. Although he dreaded the arrival of Katy's surprise visitor, whenever he'd imagined the meeting it took place in a sun filled room that contained at least some semblance of joy. With rain pelting against the window, the room would seem even more depressing than usual. So much for the cheerful, radiant greeting he visualized.

As though she'd read his mind, Katy stood above him and smiled. "Not to worry, Jonathan. I brought two bouquets of flowers to help brighten the atmosphere in here." She returned to the muffin, set it on a paper plate, and brought it to Jonathan's bedside. "And I brought you something special for breakfast. Let's just clean you up a little first, get your hair nice and tidy, and then I'll find a glass of orange juice to go with your muffin."

Jonathan didn't know what to think. He was still confused about who wanted to visit him and why it seemed so important to Katy. Not a soul was left in his life he cared to see, let alone speak with, and that realization infuriated him. He was already agitated by the fact that he hadn't died in his sleep, and the long night had left him empty and more fractious than normal. Now, the anxiety swelling in his gut changed into a cold sense of dread that would infiltrate his nervous system. This kind of disquiet had plagued him since childhood, and here it was again today – no less intense than the fateful day almost thirty years earlier – the day Philip had been taken from him. On that morning, from the moment he opened his eyes and rolled over in bed to kiss Philip's shoulder, a silent nagging and jangling nerves told him life was about to change.

Jonathan snorted. Now he was too old for his life to change. He had nothing important to lose or gain. Katy was, as usual, making a mountain out of a molehill. Whoever was coming for a visit would probably be as bored with him – and he with them; passing the minutes watching television or wheeling around the corridors, feigning pleasure while smelling fresh urine and listening to the screams of demented patients.

It was time to put an end to this debacle before the combination of anxiety and irritation got the best of him.

"Katy," he snapped, hating the quaver in his voice, "Why the hell are you doing this to me?" He pulled himself up in the bed and she quickly puffed up the pillows behind. "I already told you, there's no one I want to see. Why can't you get that through your head?"

Katy sat down on the bed next to him and took his hand in both of hers. She rubbed his thin, cool skin gently with her thumb.

"Jonathan, I promise this will be the last time I ever bring a visitor to your room. It's just that…" A tear formed in the corner of her eye and trickled down her face.

This isn't good, he thought and tried to pull his hand away, but she grasped it tighter and held on. He heard a croaking noise, an utterance of desperation, and it wasn't until Katy looked at him with concern that he realized the sound came from somewhere deep within his throat.

Katy kept her eyes on his face and he felt anxiety turning to panic. He almost laughed aloud at the irony that the woman who'd taken such good care of him would now kill him by causing him to have a heart attack. *Breathe… breathe… breathe…*

"Can I be honest with you, Jonathan?" Katy's voice revealed the slightest hint of her Tennessee childhood.

He nodded, the tension once again climbing.

"I mean *really* honest," she said, again sweeping the hair from her eyes.

He nodded again, twiddling his fingers.

"I know you want to die." She took a deep breath and puffed out her cheeks, exhaling hard. "I've worked with many people like you, especially older men who've lost their wives or children and feel they have no reason to live. I can't say I know what you're going through, but I've seen it before – many times – and I can pretty much sense when a person's time is near."

She met his eyes and offered a feeble smile. Without expression, he nodded for her to continue.

"It hurts me when people die empty or alone." She wiped the tear crawling down her face with the back of her hand. "And it hurts me when people die without knowing the truth."

An invisible claw gripped Jonathan's abdomen, squeezing so hard he clutched his stomach and tried to pull it away. *What the hell is she talking about? What truth? That I'm dying alone? That I'm leaving a life that's been worthless for the last thirty years? What the fuck truth is she talking about?*

Pulsating rain hit the window like breaking waves against rock. Jonathan tried to pull himself forward, but his arms were too weak, his stomach still trembling from what she'd said. He fell back and took a deep breath.

He cleared his throat to stop the phlegm from muddling his voice. "You know nothing about me for Christ's sake. What truth could you possibly know?"

As his voice withered, Katy rose and took his shaving kit from the cabinet. After running water into the plastic basin, she turned and leaned against the table with her arms crossed, frowning at him.

"A woman called me last week who said she knew you. Said she'd known you many years ago and asked if it would be okay if she came for a visit." Katy brought the pan toward him and set it on the bedside table. "And before you go nutty on me again, Jonathan, it's not that woman Angela you've ranted about."

Jonathan closed his eyes. "Don't ever say that bitch's name again."

"I'm sorry." Katy walked to the bed and rubbed her fingers against the steel railing. "I apologize for bringing her up. I know you've never wanted to talk about who she is or what she did. All I know is I've heard you scream her name, or something that sounds like her name, whenever you have a nightmare. I've always wanted to ask what she did."

"Do not go any further with this, Katy. I'm warning you. Get off this subject right now." Jonathan squeezed the blanket with his bony fingers, wringing Angela's neck with each twist.

"I'm sorry again," she said, this apology less convincing than the first. She picked at the blanket with him, found a snag and pulled it with her fingernails. "I just want you to be happy, Jonathan. I'd just like to see something other than a scowl come from those lips of yours. I know you've got a lot more in your heart than the hatred you always show. There's sweetness in you... I know it better than I know myself. I've seen it when you stare out the window and daydream. I caught glimpses of it when I ask the questions about Philip you refuse to answer. You're a good man, Jonathan Beckett." She turned and shuffled back to the basin. "And that's why it's important you have your visit today."

"Who is it?" Jonathan snapped. "Who called you and wants to talk this truth bullshit?" He shut his eyes and took a deep breath. "Katy, listen to me, please. You said yourself I'm ready to die. You said I'm on my way out. Why would you do this to me... and *now* of all times?" His voice shook and his eyes welled up with water.

"I promised her I wouldn't tell you her name."

Jonathan grunted, his thoughts spinning recklessly. If only he had the strength to get out of bed and leave the room. "Jesus Christ, Katy. Who do you work for? Me or her? Whose money do you take every week? Mine or hers?"

Katy turned to Jonathan, anger showing behind her half-smile. "Please, Jonathan. I would hope that after all these years you'd know that you come first. Geez." She sighed and looked to the floor. "It's just that she made it sound so serious… as though what she has to tell you is so important and she didn't want you to shut down before you saw her. But I can see that's happening anyway. I just can't win with you can I?"

The rain had stopped, and the sudden silence helped calm Jonathan's nerves. He looked out the window at the silver-white clouds being torn apart by an invisible wind. The sky was clearing, splashes of blue growing larger with each second. Jonathan lifted his hand and rubbed his eyes with the palm of each hand. His fantasy of a room filled with sunlight as his visitor entered was about to be realized. He despised Katy for doing this, but couldn't help feeling a tinge of appreciation, for this was the first time in years he'd felt the excitement and anticipation of something new.

"Darn it!" Katy said to no one in particular. "We've been bickering for so long, you're not going to be ready." Her eyes moved from the razor to the muffin sitting beside Jonathan's bed, then back to the razor. "Okay, would you rather I shave you so you can look nice, or would you rather eat your muffin?"

Jonathan reached over and grabbed the muffin. As he was about to take a bite, someone tapped on the door. In unison, both he and Katy turned toward the sound. It took him a few seconds, but when he realized who was walking toward him, he dropped his muffin onto the bedspread and let out a moan. Electrified pin pricks worked their way up his spine and out every pore of his body.

15

There was something about genuine mahogany that made her feel comfortable, at home. Maybe it was its depth of color or the way its grain formed so naturally into straight, uniform patterns. Or perhaps it was the memory of those quiet evenings she'd spend at her father's wood-paneled Midtown law offices many years ago; during high school working endlessly on her algebra homework, and later, while studying for the bar exam, utilizing the endless tomes lining the majestic walls of the firm's library. Whatever it was about this special wood that typically put Marina at ease wasn't working tonight, even though it was now surrounding her – from the bar at which she sat to the dining tables filled with patrons.

"What is it, Marina?" Wayne took her hand that she'd been unconsciously rubbing against the sleeve of his blazer. He kneaded her palm with his thumb. "Why are you so tense? I thought you loved this place." He took a sip of his martini, tilted his head backward and closed his eyes; his expression that of a man in the midst of receiving the most gratifying massage of his lifetime. "Ahhhh. Perfect. Just what I needed." He nudged Marina's full martini glass along the bar so it sat directly in front of her. "Maybe you should start drinking yours a little faster. It might calm you down a bit."

Marina twisted around on the stool, turning away from the bar so she could look into Wayne's eyes.

"Philip and Jonathan are like brothers to me. I know Philip works for you and I know you like to keep that *business* part of the relationship intact. But to me, they are my brothers, my family. And I'm concerned."

Wayne took another swig and swirled the alcohol in his mouth for a few seconds before swallowing. "That's one of the reasons I wanted to have this dinner tonight. I wanted you to meet Angela for yourself and put your mind at ease. From what I've heard, she's a great girl." He looked at his watch and then up and down the bar. It was filling up. "And please, Marina, do *not* put Angela on the stand tonight. We're here to enjoy ourselves, have a nice dinner and meet the woman who is having their child." He looked at his watch again. "If they ever show up, that is."

Marina turned and took a sip of her drink. The liquid burned her throat and continued to sting as it made its way down to the empty pit of her stomach. She could feel the alcohol attempt to numb her veins and she tried to fight it. She wanted her faculties intact tonight in order to assess the full extent of the situation.

From the moment Wayne had informed her that Philip and Jonathan were planning on becoming fathers, Marina felt troubled. She didn't know from where this eerie sensation stemmed nor could she explain the frigid feelings that ran through her at the thought of some strange woman showing up out of nowhere and having Jonathan's child. And because she couldn't find the proper words to explain how she felt, Wayne would consistently accuse her of negative thinking and a "glass half empty" mentality. But tonight, Marina, like Wayne, was hoping that meeting Angela and seeing her together with Philip and Jonathan would eradicate her anxiety. "It has to," Wayne had said earlier that evening on the way to the restaurant, "we have no choice."

"Here they are," Wayne said, waving his arm to get their attention. He turned to Marina. "Don't worry. Keep calm. It'll all be fine." He gently tugged her chin with his thumb and forefinger and kissed her bottom lip. "And, by the way, they're like brothers to me, too."

Their table sat along the wall of windows through which they could see the Rippowam waterfront and the new Harbor Point high-rises jutting into the Stamford skyline. The sky was typical November, an early darkness that looked cold enough to touch, with wispy clouds infiltrating the black expanse – a distant auspice of warmer seasons to come.

Marina placed the silk napkin on her lap and went for her martini. She typically had no problem with social situations, proficient at small talk and knowing the precise moment to show her pearly whites. But tonight the unexplained tension held her back and for the first time in recent memory she was at a loss for words.

"You're beautiful," Angela said without hesitation. "And I love, I mean *love* that outfit."

"Thank you," Marina said as she set her martini glass on the table. "I was actually going to say the same thing to *you!*" She smiled and touched Angela's blouse. "I was looking at a top just like this online last night. And I'm glad I didn't order it because I definitely couldn't pull it off like you do. The v-neck works so well on you and those accordion pleats in back... they are... well, it just fits you perfectly. "

Marina hoped her lies were coming off as genuine. Just last week Wayne was telling her about the photos he'd seen of Angela, the svelte beauty with the perfect figure. But when Angela first walked into the restaurant with Philip and Jonathan, Marina was taken aback by her appearance. The puffiness of her face, the swelling of her stomach and calves – she looked a lot further along in her pregnancy than just a couple of months. Marina, unable to become pregnant herself, didn't know firsthand how large or small Angela *should* be at this point in the process. But she did know that although every woman doesn't carry a child the same way, the dozen or so friends she'd helped through pregnancy had not shown like this at only two months. *What's this girl eating?*

There was no doubt, however, that at one point Angela had been much more attractive than she was at this moment. Although her hair was held back into a ponytail with what looked like an office supply rubber band, Marina could see Angela's perfectly formed facial features. In addition, her makeup was flawless. A frosty blue eye shadow enhancing the intensity of her deep blue eyes, an orange-red lipstick that brought out the fairness of her unblemished, rose-colored cheeks. *This girl knows how to turn it on.* Marina glanced around the table. *And who, exactly, is she turning it on for?*

"Again, I'm sorry we were late," said Philip, holding his chin up with the menu. "Traffic on 95 was a mess."

"And of course," Jonathan added, "Philip had to get his hair *just right* before leaving the house. Angela, as usual, arrived at our home exactly on time. It was Philip's hairdo that wasn't cooperating."

Philip tapped Jonathan's head with his menu. "Let's not talk about hair, Jonny. If I told everyone how long your belt selection takes…"

"Boys… boys." Wayne interrupted. "We don't care about your hair, your belts or the traffic. You made it. We're all here and that's what matters." He lifted his empty martini glass and gestured to their waiter the need for a refill. "Let's get all these glasses filled again so I can make a toast."

The appetizers arrived and Marina took her first taste of lobster ceviche when she noticed Angela had nothing but beets on her plate.

"Beets? Is that all you're eating?" Marina asked, wiping the ceviche juice from her lips.

Angela smiled. "Well, I've read they're good for the baby. Plus they're supposedly marinated in honey and balsamic – one of my favorite dressings."

Marina had actually read the opposite about how beets affect pregnancy but did not want to ruffle any feathers. At least not yet. Wayne's words played loudly in the back of her head, *"Please do not put Angela on the stand tonight."*

"How *is* the pregnancy going? Is everyone healthy? Are you feeling okay?"

"Everyone's fine. Great. We're all healthy. Thanks for asking." She took a bite of a beet and washed it down with a sip of Pelligrino.

The tone of her voice made Marina's insides cringe. There was a peckish quality to her response, as though Marina had crossed a line by asking about the health of Angela and the baby. She could feel the hairs on the back of her neck stiffen and she brushed her hand across them.

"That's wonderful," she whispered into the din of the other restaurant patrons. *Another subject. Get onto another subject.* She looked at Philip and Jonathan. *The perfect subject.* "Philip and Jonny can't say enough great things about you. I'm so glad we finally got to meet."

"Same here. Philip always talks about you and Wayne. It's great to meet the faces behind the names."

Marina nodded. "I know. When Wayne mentioned that..."

She stopped speaking when Angela turned toward Philip and smiled at him with a look of adoration that sent a wave of chills from the base of Marina's neck straight down her spine. She looked at Wayne, telepathically calling for him to look back, but he was in the midst of an animated conversation with Jonathan and so her screams went unheard.

"Please do not put Angela on the stand tonight."

"So," Marina started. Angela was still gazing at Philip. "So," she reiterated, turning up the volume. "You knew Philip in college?"

Angela slowly directed her attention back to Marina.

"Yes, we went to BU together."

The conversation was like pulling teeth and Marina's uneasiness was increasing by the second. It was as though a smoky haze had crept up around Angela, an intangible barrier that kept her insulated within her own universe. Marina couldn't remember having such a problem communicating before and didn't know why it was happening or how to manage it. Again she glanced at Wayne. Nothing.

"I love those two," Marina said, moving her eyes to Philip and Jonathan. "They are the sweetest, most wonderful people in the world. *And,* they've been the perfect couple for about twelve years now. Fate definitely had a hand in the two of them getting together."

Angela, now completely enveloped by the fog, was obviously somewhere Marina couldn't reach. When she finally did reply, Marina wasn't certain if the response was to her previous statement or to a conversation Angela was having in her own head.

"Twelve years," she muttered, unable to move her gaze away from Philip. "That's a long time. How much longer can *that* last? Six months? A year, the most? And now with the baby… things are going to change."

The chill returned, now spreading throughout Marina's entire body. *She didn't just say that. There's no way she just said that.*

"I'm sorry? What did you just say?"

As though someone snapped a finger an inch from her face, Angela's expression changed and her eyes opened wide. She was coming to, returning to the conversation as quickly as she'd left.

"No, *I'm* sorry." Angela laughed, still trying to shake off the daze. "I was just repeating something a friend said to me today when I told her about Philip and Jonathan." She cut one of her beets in half and brought it to her mouth. "She's never had a relationship for more than three months, so I wouldn't listen to a word she says anyway."

Again Marina forced a smile. She took another bite of ceviche and chewed slowly, still not knowing how to respond. Angela might've thought she got herself off the hook, but Marina could hear the truth between her words: that statement hadn't been uttered by a friend; they'd been conjured up by Angela herself and spoken by a woman with a plan.

"Honestly," Marina chortled. She felt her throat tighten up. "Who would say such a thing? Especially when they don't know the people involved. Anyone who knows the two of them knows that no one or no thing could break them apart. They are two of the…"

Angela let her fork drop to her plate loud enough for the rest of the table to stop their conversation. She feigned a grin and looked into Marina's eyes with such force, Marina moved back slightly in her chair.

"I said, *Marina*, that I was repeating something a friend said to me this afternoon." Her voice was barely audible but Marina felt each syllable. "And I *also* said that she doesn't know what she's talking about. Can we leave it at that, please?"

Bitch! Angela's wrath caught Marina off guard and for a few seconds she was speechless. *There's something wrong with this woman. I have to have a talk with Philip and Jonathan.* She looked toward Wayne who returned her glance with an expression holding both confusion and anger.

"What are you two talking about?" asked Philip, obviously attempting to initiate a ceasefire. "Seems pretty intense." Silence. "It's about Jonathan's belt, right?"

Angela threw back her head and cackled like a hen.

"Oh, Philip. You're too much!" She dabbed her lips with her napkin. "We were just talking about my friend, June. Nothing important. It's my hormones, I guess. They have me up all night and then irritable all day long." She turned to Marina and rubbed her arm. "I'm sorry. I knew I shouldn't have come tonight. I'm just not myself."

Marina smiled back at her. "I understand. Not a problem." She looked at Wayne and widened her eyes hoping that he'd see her need to for an immediate pow wow. "Excuse me for just a moment. I need the Ladies' Room."

"Perfect timing!" announced Wayne. "I need the Men's Room." He glanced around the table. "We've been together for so long, we even need to use the restroom at the same time!"

"Wayne... really?" Marina said, embarrassed. She turned to Philip. "He's *your* friend."

Wayne made his way around the table and gently held her elbow to escort her to the restroom. They walked in silence, past the bar and into the foyer until Marina felt sure they were out of earshot.

"I don't like her," she said. "I don't like her at all. There's something up with her. You know I'm usually not like this, Wayne, but I just don't have a good feeling."

Wayne attempted to place his hand on her shoulder but she brushed it away.

"Not that I want to get into this here, Marina," he started, obviously trying to choose his words carefully. "But do you think there might be a little jealousy here? You know, that we've been trying to get pregnant for so long and here Angela is, one try with Jonathan's sperm and…"

"Don't!" She peered back to the table to make sure the three of them were still seated. "I'm not jealous and I'm not envious. And I'm not imagining this or jumping to conclusions. This woman gives me the heebie jeebies. Are you telling me you aren't getting the same vibe?"

Wayne traced Marina's gaze back to the table. He shrugged.

"I really haven't had the chance to talk with her. She *seems* nice. She treats Philip and Jonathan great. What did she say that got you so up in arms like this?"

"Some crap about Philip and Jonny being together for so long that it can't last much longer." She shook her head and rolled her eyes. "And that the baby is going to change their relationship. Then she started in that it was her friend who said it, not her. Nonsense stuff. But she's also strange. It's like she's in her own little world. I don't like it and I…"

"Marina, can you please keep in mind that she's having a baby? Think about all your friends you used to complain about while they were pregnant… their moods, their odd cravings, their irritability. Can you give Angela a break? Try to imagine that she's one of your friends and have the same patience and understanding." He circled his arms around her neck and hugged her close, whispering in her ear. "Can you do that for me? At least just for tonight?"

She rested her head on his chest and sighed.

"If you promise to have a talk with Philip and Jonathan. I need them to know how I feel. I'll talk with them if you want." She backed up and looked directly into Wayne's eyes. "Yes. Definitely. I should talk with them. I won't be mean or catty, I'll just let them know what I'm feeling." Her eyes rolled toward the ceiling as though envisioning the actual conversation.

"Slow down, Babe. Please, let me take care of this. At least for now. It's a delicate situation. We have to think this through. Okay?" Marina didn't answer. "We have to get back to the table. Can we play nice til dinner is over?"

"Wayne, please don't talk to me that way. You know it makes me angry. I should say, 'angrier'."

Wayne kissed her cheek and started to lead her back to the table. "I love it when you're angry. It's *so* hot."

Marina took her last sip of Earl Grey and eyed the remaining piece of bread pudding sitting in the center of the table. *Don't do it. You'll be sorry as soon as you swallow it.*

"I know exactly how you feel," Angela said, taking Marina by surprise. "I'm holding myself back, too. I used to eat entire bread puddings in one sitting."

Wayne had told Marina about Angela's past weight problem but looking at her now, it was hard to believe she was ever as large as Wayne described. If she had been that heavy, she must've had some masterful cosmetic surgery because there was no outward sign of obesity. Sure, she was a bit overweight due to the pregnancy, but nothing like Wayne had made her out to be. Marina was curious but decided to stay away from that topic since they'd gotten along so well since Angela's apology.

"Yes, it looks so good now and probably tastes amazing. But then I ask the question, 'Is it worth it?'. I usually tell myself, 'No'. Unless it's gelato, of course. Now that's a whole different story!"

Angela grunted and rubbed her belly. "Don't I know it. Gelato and I are old lovers. I was very upset when we broke it off, but it was best for both of us."

Marina laughed quietly. *Maybe she's not so bad. She is kinda funny.* But there was still something in the air, something Marina couldn't quite put her finger on.

"When Wayne tells me I have to choose between him and the gelato, I tell him that I'll get back to him."

Angela smiled. "He seems like a great guy. Handsome, smart, charming. You hit the jackpot."

"He's okay," Marina replied. Her own sarcasm brought forth a pang of guilt. "That's not true. He's more than okay, really. I did get very lucky."

Angela turned and looked at Philip, that same expression of adoration from earlier blanketing her face and placing Marina on high alert.

"I'd like to make the final toast of the evening." Wayne said, lifting his Remy-filled snifter high in the air. "To the good health and happiness of all at this table." He gestured toward Angela. "And that includes the little person we can't quite see yet. Marina and I wish only the best of everything for all four of you and are so happy to welcome Angela into our family."

"Salute!" Philip chimed in.

"Salute!" Angela replied, clinking her water glass against everyone else's.

Marina did the same and brought her glass to her lips, offering a smile but refusing to take a sip.

16

The backyard was white with snow, a heavy blanket stretching from the deck and lattice pergola to the border of shrubs that only a few months earlier billowed with pink and blue hydrangeas.

Jonathan sipped his coffee, watching the squirrels leave tracks across the yard and up the maple tree trunks where they swirled over and across the snow covered branches. Brahms played throughout the house, the sound of crackling wood from the fireplace adding a cozy feeling Jonathan rarely gave in to. When he did manage to relax, his mind drifted back to a time when life was simple and happiness was achieved simply by making snow angels.

In his childhood bedroom he stood on the bed, a ten-year old gazing out the window, anticipating a day of igloo building and snowball fights. Soft morning light shrouded the snowy pavement with a purplish hue. His father pushed a metal snow shovel along the driveway, clearing the way for Thanksgiving guests who'd be arriving from all across the state. Dad's breath hung in the frozen air like a ghostly presence hovering above him.

Jonathan smiled, his flannel pajamas keeping him warmer than the baseboard heat set at sixty-five degrees. But Jonathan didn't need heat to keep him warm. That day, at that moment, he felt a warmth from within; heat radiated by the love of his parents, the flannel against his skin, and the snow-covered roof above his head.

Later that night, his parents beamed with pride when he revealed his epiphany: no matter how low the outside temperature dropped, as long as the three of them were together, he'd be warm forever. He would cherish that moment for the rest of his life, because a few days later he and his mother stood in the frosty, overcast afternoon, holding hands beside a newly dug grave. This time, the wispy cloud of breath hovered above his mother's head; crystallized air that, to this day, Jonathan believed was the apparition of his father – dead of a pulmonary embolism at forty five, three days after a Thanksgiving that would fade into memory like a kidnapped child.

When Jonathan felt the warmth of Philip's body behind him, he leaned back, tilting his head so Philip's chin could rest within the arc of his neck. He banished the heavy thoughts from his mind as quickly as they'd entered, letting the peace of Philip's embrace overpower the sense of uneasiness that crept in with the sad memories.

"In like a lion and out like a lamb," said Philip, watching the final flakes of the all-night snowfall spatter on the walkway. "March sucks. I can't wait for spring."

"Me too, but I do like the peaceful view." Jonathan turned and tousled Philip's hair, picking at strands that stood unbent as a tiger's whiskers. "Just like your hair – natural and messy." Looking deep into Philip's eyes, their chins almost touching, Jonathan felt passion rise from the back of his legs into his groin. Through all their years together, this flame had never died; a sexual drive that caught fire the moment they met and only amplified as their love grew.

He brought his lips closer, so the heat of their breath fell onto each other's mouths. Tingling crept up his neck and along the back of his head as he moved his lips closer to Philip's and closed his eyes.

The phone rang and Jonathan's passion descended like a waterfall down the length of his spine.

"Shit," he whispered and kissed Philip's cheek. "If that's Angela again, I swear I'm going to say something." He headed toward the phone. "The baby isn't even born yet and she's driving us crazy."

Philip grabbed his arm and gently turned him around. "Hey, I know it's annoying. But think about it, Jonny. What if she was calling about the baby? What if she was bleeding or something?" He held Jonathan's hand, rubbing his palm. "This is what it's like having a kid."

Jonathan rolled his eyes and tried to ignore the jangling phone. "I know. I know. But she's only four months pregnant and this is at least the sixth time she's called this week. And she's called for stupid reasons, or no reason at all. We do have our own life, you know."

Philip pulled Jonathan close and hugged him. "You've heard everyone say it, Jonny. Once you have a kid, you don't have your own life. Angie's just getting us used to it."

Jonathan withdrew, leaned against the back of the sofa, crossed his arms, and waited for the phone to stop ringing. "I see an ostrich complex coming on. Head in sand, ass up in the clouds."

"Don't go there, Jonny. My head isn't in the sand. I'm just saying our life as we knew it is pretty much over. We discussed all this before making the decision, remember? We knew the quiet solitude would disappear and we'd be asked to do a lot, for both Angela and the baby." He slid his hands into the pockets of his silk lounge pants. "Am I sensing regret?"

Jonathan looked to the floor, shaking his head. "No, there's no regret at all. I just didn't know the constant calling would happen *before* the baby was born. I mean, there's really no good reason for her to call so often. She's either complaining about morning sickness or bellyaching that the hospital keeps reprimanding her for coming in late." Jonathan walked to the fireplace and leaned against the mantle, the fire warming the small patch of exposed abdomen where his shirt came up. "If she called to tell us she was bleeding and needed help, that's one thing. But I don't need to hear about how many times per day she pukes. We'll all have enough things to deal with once the baby is born. This stuff is just ridiculous."

"She's a woman, Jonny," said Philip, ambling toward the telephone. "We both know what that means as far as hormones go. And the chemicals in her body are going haywire. Let's give everything a chance to settle down and then see how she does."

Jonathan rubbed his abdomen, trying to spread the warmth of the fire across his entire stomach. "And once we're done helping her, we'll get back to where we were." He closed his eyes, determined not to allow his neuroses to influence his emotions, especially where Angela was concerned. She'd been kind and sweet since the day they met. He and Philip had already discussed that they would probably be her only friends for a while and needed to accept that responsibility. But in view of her independence and strength over the year they'd gotten to know each other, he expected her to show more self-reliance. Maybe it *was* her hormones and things would get better after they settled down. He crossed his fingers behind his back, hoping regret wasn't going to rear its ugly head before the baby was even born.

"With the way Angela's been acting," he announced, "I bet it's a girl. Two girls in one body can definitely create this kind of havoc."

Philip laughed and moved toward the phone. "We can always find out what the baby's sex is. You sure you want it to be a surprise?"

"I really don't need to know. I don't want to deal with any of my demented preconceptions. Plus keeping it a surprise is cool." He followed Philip to the phone and leaned on the console table. "Anyway, Angela said she'd wait with us to find out. There's no way she'd go behind our backs. I think she's better than that. Now we'll all find out together on the *big day.*"

"Whatever you want, my love." Philip pressed the speakerphone button and speed-dialed Angela. "It's time to call her back."

"Hello?" Angela's voice was almost inaudible. Philip and Jonathan looked at each other, aware of the fact she'd been crying.

"Angie, it's us. What's going on? What's wrong?" Phillip sipped his lukewarm coffee.

"I'm sorry," she said, clearing her throat. She was on speakerphone and they could hear her walking across the hardwood floor. "I know I've been calling a lot. But this snow took me by surprise and I'm not sure what to do. I don't think I even have a shovel. What if I need to leave? What if there's an emergency? How do I get out of here?"

Put off by Angela's tone, Jonathan furrowed his forehead. Her questions sounded more accusatory than fear-induced, as though Philip should have thought of this situation and taken steps to make sure it never reached this point. He looked at Philip, awaiting acknowledgement and silent understanding. . But Philip kept his eyes on the phone.

"No need to worry, Angie. I'll call D'Antonio. They're the guys who remove our snow, but I'll have them come to your house first. Does that work?"

"That would be great, Philip. Thank you so much. Will you and Jonathan be coming, too?"

This time Philip looked at Jonathan and shrugged his shoulders. Obviously Philip had no idea how to answer. Jonathan walked toward the phone.

"Hey, Angie. It's Jonathan," he said, trying to display a bit of sternness without sounding too harsh.

"Hi, Jonny," she whimpered.

An image of Angela's head on a deer's body, staring into headlights flashed through his mind. He tried to shake it. "What else is going on? Is there something you need us to be there for?"

A few seconds of silence, clomping, and then the rustling of the phone against her shoulder. "No."

Jonathan gazed at Philip who stared back, expressionless. It was too early in this relationship with Angela for Jonathan to be overwhelmed with emotion, he knew that, and he also interpreted the lack of expression on Philip's face to mean he was thinking the same thing.

But why was she being so childish? How did this secure, autonomous woman suddenly become so needy? Was it really just hormones? Jonathan felt a wave of suspicion, the same feelings he'd suppressed on the night Angela entered his life.

"Sure, we'll come over," he blurted. "We'll take a nice walk in the snow with you. It'll do us all good."

"That's a great idea!" Angela shouted. "I'm going to get ready right now. When will you be here?"

Before Jonathan could respond, Philip chimed in. "Give us an hour. We have something to take care of first," he half-whispered, the gleam in his eyes and mischievous grin telling Jonathan what that "something" was going to be.

"Okay, but hurry up! And can you bring donuts? The baby and I are starving over here!" She hung up the phone, leaving dead air and another errand for them to run.

"Donuts?" Jonathan shook his head. "What happened to the healthy meal schedule we spent hours going over with her? Remember? 'This baby gets no sugar and no hydrogenated fat.' Those were *her* words."

Philip walked over to Jonathan, took his hand, and gently led him toward the bedroom. "Yeah, and that meal schedule was your idea. Now let it go. It's a snowy Sunday and we're all allowed to splurge." With those words he pushed Jonathan against the bedroom door and brushed his tongue over Jonathan's top lip.

"Now, getting back to where we were..."

By the time they pulled the four-wheeler up to Angela's house, D'Antonio had already cleared the driveway, the walkway leading up to her stoop, and the entire porch. Piles of snow lined the shoveled paths and Jonathan breathed a sigh of relief. Hopefully the cleared trail would help make Angela happy, at least happier than she sounded on the phone.

"We're lucky it didn't snow too much," Jonathan said, placing the styrofoam coffee cups on top of the donut box. "Otherwise we'd be stuck in the warm house in front of a cozy fire, having sex and enjoying the day together."

Philip laughed. "Yeah, we're *so* lucky." He saw a figure standing behind the storm door glass and squinted. "Uh oh, she looks a little pissed off."

"Screw her," said Jonathan. "She's lucky we're here… and with saturated fat, too."

"Well, we *are* an hour late, Jonny." Philip shut off the ignition.

Jonathan removed his glove and raked his fingers through Philip's hair. "That's not my fault. You're the one who kept making me…"

"Okay, okay. It's my fault." He opened the car door and climbed out. "Not that you were fighting back." He slammed the door shut before Jonathan could answer.

With every step Philip took up the walkway, Jonathan watched the white haze of residual snow turn black beneath his boots. His loose jeans were tucked into untied Timberlands, flaunting his sculptured butt and thick legs. Jonathan realized they'd left the house too soon. *We still have unfinished business.*

Angela remained motionless behind the glass storm door, even after Philip walked up the steps and reached the door. From inside the car, Jonathan watched Philip's head and arms moving and felt his muffled voice vibrate against the car window. Still inside the car, he opened the door slightly to hear the conversation.

"But I've been waiting for you for over an hour, Philip. You promised you'd be here." Angela sounded like a spoiled child who didn't get the bicycle she wanted for Christmas.

"I know, Angie. I'm sorry. Like I said, we got held up at the house with all the snow and everything. Cut us a break, okay?"

Jonathan listened carefully. There was no response from Angela and he knew he had to help Philip appease her. *Hormones, my ass. She's nuts.* He jumped out of the SUV and slammed the door behind him, hoping coffee and donuts would help bring her back to earth.

"Hey, look what I have!" Jonathan yelled, trudging up to the door. "I have your coffee just the way you like it and a jelly-filled donut with…"

Stunned by the sight at the door, his initial reflex was to stop talking mid-sentence in order to process what he was seeing. Through the storm door glass stood a woman who resembled Angela, although she was twice the size of the Angela he'd seen only two weeks before. It was as though her face had been widened, stretched side-to-side, along with hips that swelled through the red sweat pants. Her hair was pulled back into a tight ponytail, exposing swollen eyes and a pale, round face that, for the first time since Jonathan had known her, did not have an iota of makeup.

He swallowed hard, uncertain of his next move. He looked down at the coffee and donuts and wondered if he should inflict more calories on someone who'd obviously been satisfying all of her pregnancy cravings. Angela was not going to be one of those women who carried gracefully; an expectant mother who "glowed" through the entire process. If Angela was the size of half a house after only four months of pregnancy, she'd be a full condo complex by the time all was said and done. His first reaction was selfish, embarrassed by the fact that the mother of his child was so big, her lovely face hidden by rolls of flesh. He was also concerned about the health of his child, imagining this high-speed path toward obesity had to result from chocolate, cookies, cake and other saturated fats.

His second reaction was pity; she was becoming the woman she used to be, Philip's corpulent, affected friend from college – the disturbed woman with unruly emotions and an unmanageable appetite. *Did she know this was going to happen? Did she plan on getting fat again? Was getting pregnant an excuse for her to eat like a starving elephant?*

Jonathan looked at Philip, who offered a tiny smile and rolled his eyes. Jonathan forced a smile back. Between the madness of both he and Angela, a sudden fear hit him head on: this child didn't stand a chance.

"I'm sorry," Angela said. "I know I look like crap. I've had a bad morning and didn't remember to put on makeup. Please come in." She held the door open and took a coffee cup from Jonathan as he passed. "Did I hear you say something about jelly?"

Still choked up from the onslaught of unhinged thinking, Jonathan nodded his head and walked toward the dining room table. He scanned the room, appalled by blouses hanging over the back of the sofa, plates of half eaten food, and shoes lying lace-side down as though they'd been thrown off her feet like a five-year old. When he entered the kitchen, his stomach tightened: a stack of dishes teetered in the sink, and a track of more dirty plates and pizza boxes lined the counter.

He closed his eyes. Yes, he was a bit overzealous when it came to cleanliness, maybe a little obsessive. But this house had become a pig sty. It was unimaginable to him that someone like Angela, who seemed so orderly, would allow things to get away from her like this.

Something must have happened. Something's wrong with the baby and she's not telling us.

"What's wrong?" he asked, lightly placing the donuts onto the table and turning toward Angela. "What is it? What's wrong with the baby?"

Angela looked at Jonathan, her swollen eyes widening, getting darker by the second. She turned to Philip.

"What's he talking about?" She zeroed in on the donut box and lifted the cardboard cover. Her eyes scanned the box like a lioness stalking its prey.

"I'm not sure," Philip replied, looking at Jonathan quizzically. "What do you mean, Jonny? Why would there be something wrong with the baby?"

Now he was in trouble, and the less he said the better. "I don't know, just letting my imagination run wild, as it always does. Sorry."

His words didn't matter, because Angela's mouth was buried in a mountain of powdered sugar, surrounded by gushing blobs of red jelly. Judging by the look of pleasure on her face, he realized he could tell her the house was on fire and she'd just close her eyes and smile with delight.

"No worries, Jonny," Philip said, flicking his head toward Angela.

He draped his coat over the dining room chair and rubbed his hands together. "How 'bout we help you clean up a little before we go for our walk?"

Angela grabbed a filthy dishtowel from on the table and brought it to her mouth in an attempt to stop jelly from falling onto her lap. "Thanks, Philip. That would be great." She swallowed hard. "I haven't had a chance to clean." She leaned back and patted her stomach. "This boy's been keeping me up day and night."

With a stack of dishes in his hands, Jonathan stopped in his tracks and jerked his head toward Philip.

Philip, stood completely still. He inhaled deeply, taking in the breath he always used to help compose himself.

"Angela." Philip placed the tips of his fingers on the table and leaned toward her. . "What do you mean 'this boy' has been keeping you up?" He blinked his eyes slowly. "Or are you just making a guess?"

Angela smirked as she licked the powder from her fingertips and gazed at the donut box. "No, it's not a guess. I stopped by Dr. Jarrett's yesterday to talk with her about my morning sickness. I mean, I'm four months already and I don't think I should still be sick every morning. So while I was there I told her I didn't want the sex of the baby to be a surprise anymore. She said morning sickness in the fourth month is normal for some..."

"Did you ask her if women with morning sickness should eat three donuts in less than five minutes?" Jonathan interrupted, hands still full of dishes.

Angela twisted her head in a painstakingly slow movement until her eyes met Jonathan's. Her eyes were on fire and he could feel the pores on the back of his neck draining perspiration. He opened his mouth to say something in his defense, but no sound escaped.

"Jonathan." Philip's soothing voice called from somewhere in the distance. "Jonny!" Jonathan broke his stare with Angela and turned to Philip, whose face held a look of concern.

"Angela," Philip walked around the table and sat in the chair beside her. "Why would you do that? The three of us discussed it and decided to wait until the baby was born. That's not fair."

Angela turned her head away from Jonathan, and as she did so, her demonic expression changed to an angelic smile. She used the dishtowel to wipe away the jelly from her fingers, then touched Philip's cheek with her fingertips.

"Don't look so serious, Philip." She brushed his face with the back of her fingers, leaving a trail of powdered sugar. "It's not such a big deal. And if you think about it, now we can start buying things specifically for a boy. Since we know it's a boy, we can start planning for a boy."

Philip moved his gaze to Jonathan, who was placing dishes back on the table, then he turned back to Angela. "That's not the point, Angie. The point is we're in this together, right?" He waited for Angela's nod. "And if we all decide on something and then one person changes their mind and does something without telling the others, it's not a threesome anymore. It's one person making a decision for all of us." She nodded again. "If you wanted to know the sex of the baby, you should have said so from the beginning. I'm sure we'd have worked with it." He put his hand around hers and brought it down to her lap. "The big deal isn't that you know the baby's a boy, it's that you found out *without* us and then sprang it on us while we were still hoping to keep it a surprise."

Angela clutched Philip's hand and wrapped her other hand around them both.

"I'm sorry," her voice was shaking with emotion. "I screwed up. I know we discussed it and I know we made a decision together. But my hormones are going crazy and I can't take my pills because I'm pregnant and I..." Her breathing had become labored and tears dribbled down her cheeks. "I won't do it again. I promise."

She leaned into Philip, who held her sobbing head in his hands.

"What pills?" asked Jonathan, now standing behind her, arms crossed. "What pills can't you take, Angela?"

She buried her head deeper into Philip's chest. "Lithium," she sobbed. "I can't take my Lithium because I'm pregnant."

Philip took hold of her shoulders and gently pushed her back. Her eyes were almost swollen shut, her lips dry and cracked. "Are you saying you were on a mood-stabilizer and never told us?"

She wiped her eyes with the palms of both hands. Jonathan glared at the back of her head, knowing if he walked to the other side and looked her in the eyes, the devil inside him would appear and ruin any chance of reconciliation.

"I went off it so I could become pregnant." She stood, holding onto the table for support , and walked into the kitchen. She blew her nose into a paper towel and gently rubbed her stomach. "I haven't taken a pill in five months. I stopped before insemination, so there's no need to worry about the baby, he's fine. You've been to all my exams with me, you *know* he's fine."

"Yeah, but you're not," Jonathan said, almost under his breath.

"What?" Angela placed her hands on her hips. "What, Jonathan? If you have something to say, please just spit it out. Whispering to yourself only makes you look crazy."

Jonathan's teeth were clenched and his neck muscles tightened. "I said, you're *not* fine." He extended his arm and moved it around slowly. "This house is a mess and you're a mess. And it's because you're not taking the pills you should be taking. Pills you never told us you needed. You lied to us, again, for Christ's sake."

"Jonathan!" Philip stood and walked toward him. "I know this isn't good, but let's just…"

"Let's just what?" Jonathan grabbed his coat. "You want to sit around and find out what else she's lied to us about? I have to get out of here."

"Jonny, hold on a second. We have to talk this out."

Jonathan zipped his coat and looked at Angela. She stood in the kitchen, staring back at him without expression or excuses. "You asked me about regrets this morning, remember?"

"Yeah, I remember," Philip said with his hands in his pockets.

"Well, now I have it. A regret like I've never felt before, and I have to tell you, it feels *beyond* shitty."

He threw open the door and the biting air slapped him in the face. The temperature had dropped at least ten degrees since they first arrived; dense, gray clouds covered the sun and cold, moist air settled on his face. He eyed their SUV, then looked up and down the block, unsure where he was going or what he had hoped to accomplish by storming out.

For a fleeting moment his anger focused on the words "it's a boy." From the first moment Angela said she was pregnant, he'd wanted a boy. But he never got his hopes up, keeping his primary focus on making sure the baby was healthy and well taken care of. He would've loved a baby girl. She'd be a part of him and he a part of her. But now that the uncertainty was gone, a new kind of electricity ran through him – excitement and paternal pride. As the wind picked up around him, he wasn't sure whether the chills came from excitement or the intense cold.

He kicked the toe of his boot against the ice crystallizing across the porch steps. He had a hissy fit and now he was standing alone, wondering if he'd overreacted: *If the house wasn't in such shambles, would I have reacted this way? If she hadn't also omitted the fact that she's on Lithium, could I have forgiven her for going behind our backs and finding out the sex of the baby?*

Being hit with three bombshells at once was more than he could handle. He liked things predictable and certain; leaving surprises and spontaneity for emergencies. But standing on the icy porch, shivering and alone, Jonathan knew he had to change – and fast. He was about to have a son and overreacting or storming out of the house when his child did something upsetting wasn't going to work. Another bombshell – he was the adult and needed to start acting like one. And now he realized Angela was still a child. No doubt she'd disappointed him and actually lied to them, but he had to dig deeper, to understand her motivation and let her know he was on her side and would do what he could to help. As Philip said, they were all in this together and he had to take the good with the bad.

When he turned to walk back to the door, Philip was leaning against the living room window, smiling, his tongue sticking out and wagging like a puppy waiting for food.

Jonathan ducked his head to hide his laughter. "Great! "I've got three freakin' kids to deal with."

<u>17</u>

Philip's mind was somewhere else, far away from the income statements, balance sheets, and piles of other financial reports stacked up on his desk. His thoughts were in Florida, lying on a lounge chair on the sands of South Beach – a cosmo in one hand and Jonathan's hand in the other, soaking up the blistering Florida sun. In two and a half days they'd leave for a four-day pass: a quick escape from the daily grind and a shot of relaxation before Angela entered her final trimester and would need them around even more than she did now.

Both he and Jonathan needed a few days to get used to the news Angela threw at them the week before. Not only did she hide the fact that she'd been taking Lithium, she also went behind their backs to find out the baby's sex. These "sins of omission" concerned him, although he took them a lot better than Jonathan. What really worried him was the weight she'd gained. When he first saw her standing behind the screen door that day, he flashed back to when they first met and she was ten-times the size of the Angela he'd reacquainted with a year ago. Of course, she hadn't reached that previous weight yet, but who knew what would happen during the remaining three months of pregnancy.

Plus, her recent attitude made the hairs on the back of his neck crawl; spidery sensations reminiscent of the way he felt after they'd had the final argument more than fifteen years ago. He'd spent the night before trying to convince Jonathan not to regret the choice they made, while he was barely able to convince himself.

"What if she's crazy?" Jonathan had asked, pacing the living room and drinking his vodka martini a little too quickly. "What if we got ourselves involved with a nut? We have a baby inside that nut! What are we supposed to do now?"

Philip rolled his eyes and dropped the skewer holding three olives into his martini glass. Closing his eyes, he took a larger-than-normal sip and let the warmth of the liquor seep into his veins. He walked to the loveseat closest to the sliding doors. "Jonny, sit down."

"Philip, don't try to calm me down. We might've really screwed up."

"Jesus Christ!" Philip shouted. "Will you please just sit down?"

Jonathan's expression turned from worry to complete surprise. And Philip knew why: he almost never raised his voice during their discussions. But this time was different because he was afraid that Jonathan's fears made real sense and deep down it made him angry.

"Jonny, can you pull yourself together enough to think through this logically? First of all, she's pregnant. Her hormones are going haywire and she's trying to deal. Second, she's not on her Lithium anymore." He held up his hand, stopping Jonathan who was trying to interrupt. "I know, she never told us she was on Lithium. *I* think it's because she was embarrassed about it. Yeah, it was like a sin of omission. It's not like we asked her if she was taking drugs and she said no. She just never told us. I'm not condoning it, I'm just saying we have to consider she might've been ashamed to mention it."

Jonathan sat on the edge of the loveseat opposite Philip, biting his lip.

"And lastly," Philip held his breath and after a few seconds, exhaled loudly through his nose, "the baby's a boy for Christ's sake! Can't we be happy about it instead of being paranoid that she purposely went behind out backs to find out the baby's sex? She said she was at doctor Jarrett's and just couldn't help herself. The explanation might be that simple." He gently grasped the stem of his martini glass and took a sip. "The way I see it, this all comes down to hormones, shame, and more hormones. Something we'll never really be able to experience."

Jonathan switched from a posture of attack to one of submission, slouching into the corner of the loveseat and gazing at the ceiling. He didn't say a word.

"Maybe I should shout more often," Philip joked.

"Don't even think about that! It's just that you might be right."

Philip grabbed the left side of his chest, feigning a heart attack. "What? Can it be? Did you say I was right? I don't think my heart can take this."

Jonathan smirked. "Cut the shit, Philip. I didn't say you *were* right, I said that you *might* be right. She definitely has a lot of stress, hormones, and all the other crap that goes along with being pregnant. Plus, she's in a new home with a new job. I guess we'll have to cut her some slack."

They sat in silence for a few seconds before Jonathan sat up again. "I guess the weight thing freaked me out the most. I remember how she looked the first time I met her, and even just a few months ago. She was thin, pretty and looked... well... refined. And now, I don't know, she looks so different. Not to mention her house is a pig sty. Our son will not live in a pig sty."

"What did we just finish saying, Jonathan? More likely than not, she'll change again after the baby is born. Once her hormones get back to normal and her Lithium kicks back in, all will be well."

Holding his glass aloft, Jonathan walked over to Philip. He clinked Philip's glass and held his own up in the air as though making a toast. "I hope you're right. I really do." He kissed the side of Philip's head "I did this for us, you know. How many times have we fantasized about you, me, and a little boy we could raise together? It's finally going to happen. And I'll keep that in mind when I'm ready to lose it with Angela."

Philip hugged Jonathan for a few seconds before he felt him tense. "What is it, Jonny? What's wrong?"

Jonathan filled his cheeks with air. Exhaling hard, he said, "Now... how are we going to come up with a name?"

Philip slapped his butt. "Jesus, Jonny. One problem at a time." He closed his eyes and said a quick prayer that Angela would work with them and make it easy for everyone when it came to naming the baby. "One problem at a time."

Gazing from his twenty-first floor office window, Philip watched the northbound traffic on I-95 crawl through the five o'clock jam. He gazed over the Stamford train station in the distance, his eyes moving somewhere deep into the Long Island Sound, where his peripheral vision caught a flicker of light. For a split second he thought came from across the water, from a spot on the North Shore of Long Island, but that was impossible. Although the North Shore was directly across from Stamford, the edge of the Island was too far away to see anything of substance. He figured the flash of light came from a boat cruising into Manhattan. Wherever it came from, the light flash gave him the sensation of distress, a feeling that somewhere out there, someone needed help. The feeling caused a chill that raised the hair on his arms and made him don his suit jacket, something he never did while in his office.

"I hear you're going away for a few days," a voice said from the doorway.

Startled, Philip turned around to see Wayne walking toward him, his hand held out, offering a piece of gum. "No thanks," he said. "And yes, Jonny and I are heading to South Beach for a quick getaway. Actually, it's right by your condo."

Wayne strolled to the small, round meeting table in the corner of the room and sat down on one of the chairs. "Actually, that's why I'm here. I told Marina you guys were going down there and she asked why you're not staying at our place." He popped another stick of gum in his mouth. "I told her 'they never asked.'"

Philip pulled a chair out from the table and sat beside Wayne. "You know us, we don't like to impose. Besides, I'm leaving you here to clean up the aftermath of tax time. I wouldn't ask to stay at your place, too."

Wayne laughed, playing with his gum wrapper. "First of all, you of all people don't leave an aftermath. You're so good at what you do, it's like tax time never happened. Your clients are happy as always, and you're all caught up. Plus, that's what friends are for. We'd ask to stay at your place… if you had a place down there."

"And we'd say yes, of course." Philip slapped the table. "That's what friends are for."

"You're screwing with me." Wayne's smile quickly faded, the wrinkles between his eyebrows deepening. "Speaking of friends, Marina also wanted you, Jonny, and Angela to come over for some tapas and drinks. Well, no drinks for Angela, but, well, you know."

"I know," Philip replied, "But why the hell do you look so serious? Shouldn't an invitation be, well, inviting?"

Wayne leaned back in his chair and gazed out the window behind Philip's desk. "Sorry, it's just that we've only met Angela that once at the restaurant. Marina didn't like the way it went between she and Angela and says she wants to get a better feel about Angela. She wants to get to know her better, or some shit like that." He stood up and walked to the window. "You know Marina, she's all about feeling things and understanding people on an emotional level. Sometimes I think Marina's got a bit... just a *tiny* bit of a chemical imbalance."

"Ha," Philip tapped his fingers on the table. "Funny you should say that."

"Why? Don't tell me *you* have one." Wayne spit his gum into a wrapper and threw it into the wastebasket under Philip's desk. He then put another slice into his mouth.

"No, I don't have one. But why does Marina want to get to know her *now*? If she wants to be friends with Angela or get to know her better, why wait three months to have her over?"

Wayne slid his hands into his pants pocket, leaned his shoulder against the window, and faced Philip. "Yeah, well, that's really my fault. See, Marina wanted to get together sooner, but I said no because I knew she'd only cause trouble."

Philip gestured with his head for Wayne to continue.

"She didn't get such a good vibe from Angela that night... said she was nice enough, but something bothered her – something she couldn't put her finger on. And she wanted to put her finger on it – in order to protect you and Jonathan, of course."

The scene from Angela's house pounded his head like a mallet. *What kind of vibe had Marina gotten from Angela? And why did Wayne wait so long to say something? If he and Marina had issues with Angela, why wouldn't they say anything sooner?*

"By the look on your face, I can see I shouldn't have said anything. That's why I waited so long before asking you all over. I didn't want Marina making a mountain out of a molehill. She can do that sometimes. He placed his hand on Philip's shoulder. "Honestly, I wouldn't listen to her vibe or anything else for that matter. Do you hear me?"

Philip nodded, his mind foggy with negative thoughts he'd been trying to squelch for the past week. "What did *you* think of her, Wayne? Did you get the same vibe?"

Wayne looked out the window, his gaze following the headlights of a car circling down the exit ramp of the train station. "You know me, Philip. I'm about as intuitive as a cement slab. She seemed like a nice, well-intentioned woman to me. I didn't notice anything out of the ordinary. Like I said, you should ignore Marina's vibe. I was just letting you know why we haven't invited you over. I didn't want Marina pressuring Angela – or you guys either. She can be pushy and sometimes act like a private investigator… not stopping until she gets the information she's looking for." He gently poked his index finger into Philip's chest. "I've seen her in action, and it's not a pretty sight."

Philip smiled. "It's okay, Wayne. I totally understand." He stood up, walked to his desk, sat down and leaned back. "Men and women are definitely from different planets... especially when they're pregnant. That's become apparent to me over the last few months"

"Pregnant or not," Wayne said, rubbing the back of his neck, "they're still from a different planet. Is Angela giving you problems?"

Philip paused, afraid if he told the truth his suspicions would become solid matter that would accumulate more negativity until the situation became unmanageable. He had only one choice: turn the negative to positive and just make it work – otherwise, the life he and Jonathan had planned for so long would crumble into pieces.

"No. Everything's fine," he told Wayne. "Like I said, she's a little 'off' right now, but we're doing okay."

"I'm glad to hear it." Wayne walked to the door. "You sure you guys don't want to stay at our place in South Beach? It's empty, just waiting for you."

Philip smiled and gave a slight wave. "Yes, I'm sure. But thank you for the offer. When we get back, we'll set up a date for the tapas. Love to Marina."

Wayne gave Philip a casual salute. "Sounds good. You two have a great time. And do me a favor, relax a little. I think this is the first time I've ever seen stress on your face."

"Yes, sir!" Philip said, straightening out the piles of paper on his desk. "See you when we get back."

He watched Wayne walk out the door and swirled his chair around to look out the window. Stars dotted the sky which was now black as coal, smothering the lights of the Manhattan skyline far out in the distance.

He picked up the telephone and took a deep breath: Time to tell Angela he and Jonathan were going away for a few days. His pulse raced with each number he pressed on the keypad and he closed his eyes, hoping she wouldn't answer. His hopes were quashed when he heard her voice and the familiar sound of crunching echoing in his ear.

"Hey, Angie. It's Philip. Whatcha up to?" He forced himself to sound cheerful.

He heard her swallow, a strange noise from deep down in her throat. "Hey!" she said, taking a few sips of something. "How are you?"

Tightening his grip on the telephone, Philip tried to think of a way to cushion the blow. He felt like a husband afraid to tell his wife he wanted to play golf or go out with the boys for a drink.

He cleared his throat. "I just wanted to make sure everything was okay, that you were feeling good and have everything you need for the next few days." He waited for her response. Nothing. He heard her move, a sloshing sound as though she were repositioning herself on the sofa. *Don't give in.* "You still there, Angie?"

"Mmmm, yeah?" She whispered in a way that let him know she was waiting for more.

"Great, so are you set for the next few days?"

"What do you mean, 'set', Philip?"

He rolled his eyes, the churning in his stomach starting to roll like boiling syrup. *It's now or never.* "It's nothing big. Jonathan and I are going away for a few days. We just want to make sure you don't need anything before we leave. We'll be back on Tuesday."

A few seconds of quiet and Philip could feel a thread of hostility stemming from both ends of the phone and meeting somewhere in the middle. He was done speaking and decided not to say another word; they'd sit in silence until Angela spoke, even if he had to stay in his office all night.

After thirty more seconds of quiet, she moaned and he heard her getting up from the sofa. He pulled his neck forward as though it would help him hear exactly what she was doing.

"Where are you going?" Her voice was monotone.

"Florida," he cleared his throat again. "Just for a few days. We just wanted to get away, catch up on some rest so we can be there for you in full force over the next few months. Plus it's tax time here and I've been working eighteen hour days. I need to decompress and get some good sleep."

"Huh," she said. More silence, then, "I don't think you want to talk to *me* about not being able to sleep, Philip. I have to try to fall asleep sitting up, surrounded by pillows. I feel like the God damn Elephant Man. I'm basically up the entire night, trying to get comfortable. And the doctor won't even give me a sleeping pill. So I'm pretty much screwed until the end of June or July or whenever this baby decides he wants out."

Philip closed his eyes and took in a deep breath. "I know, Angela and I can't imagine what it must be like. But remember that day we were sitting in the living room discussing these exact things before we got pregnant? We talked about how you'd gain weight, how uncomfortable it would be, how your hormones would go haywire. Remember that?"

"Yes, Philip, I remember. But talking about it and living through it are two different things."

He sensed the bitterness on the edge of her tone; resentment that although they'd discussed the potential pitfalls of pregnancy, they could never know the harsh reality of a hypothetical conversation that came to fruition.

He looked at his watch: 7:10. He was tired and felt too weak to have this discussion with a logical and constructive outcome. Time to end it before they both said too much.

"I understand, Angela, and for now…"

"You don't understand, Philip, and that's the fucking problem! You're getting on a plane to go lie on the beach and swim in the ocean while I'm stuck in this shithole with no life. You think you and Jonathan need to get away? Did you ever think I'd like to go away for a few days? Did you ever consider I'd like to crunch my toes in the sand and get some sun on my face? When did you become so selfish, Philip? You never used to be so egocentric. Did Jonathan make you like this?"

Philip's heart was pounding, his hand trembling as he pulled the phone receiver from his ear. *Who the hell was he talking to? What was going on inside her head?*

Even when he and Angela had had their disagreement those many years ago, she'd never spoken to him like this; so full of accusation and hostility, as though he'd done this to her on purpose. For a split second he wasn't certain who was on the other end of the phone – the anger making her voice almost unrecognizable.

His mind shot back to the meeting he and Jonathan had with G many months ago to get her legal take on things. Her words rang in his head, "agreements are great to have… but it's the *people* who will make the difference between a wonderfully civil partnership and a horrific, unsettling one." How right she'd been.

"Angela, I honestly have no response to that, and I'm going to end this conversation before one of us says something that might cause damage to our relationship. There's way too much on the line for disagreements like this. I think we need time to calm ourselves. When we get back, we'll talk this through. We have to make it work – for all of us."

Silence again and Philip still refused to speak first.

"Fine, Philip. That's just fine. You have a nice trip."

Click. She hung up without giving him the opportunity to smooth things out just a little more.

"Bitch!" Philip grunted under his breath. He slammed down the receiver, more distressed by his furious reaction than her audacious provocations. He'd learned long ago how to make sure people didn't get under his skin. Through experience, meditation and an innate spiritual sense, he discovered that allowing others to raise his blood pressure would only cause him harm – both physical and mental. He learned early in life how to command his negative emotions. But this conversation with Angela made him forget everything he'd learned.

He jumped when the phone rang and picked up it immediately, hoping she was calling back to apologize.

"Hey," he said.

"Hey back," Jonathan replied, "How are you?"

"Great," said Philip. "Everything's great."

"You're full of it. What's wrong?"

Philip closed his eyes, trying to think of something to say. Jonathan knew him too well. "It's work… just trying to get out of here. I should be home in about thirty."

"I'll be waiting. Martini in hand, as a precursor to our vacation."

"Nice. I'll try to make it twenty!"

"Drive careful and I'll see you in a few."

Philip gently placed the receiver in its cradle and looked into the dark sky. For now, he wouldn't tell Jonathan about his argument with Angela. Maybe he could get her back on meds before Jonathan had to deal with her again. The idea of hiding something from Jonathan clawed his gut but this was the best way to handle the situation – for now.

He threw the folders from his desk into his leather bag, looped the strap over his shoulder, and walked to the door to shut the office lights. His mind needed a few moments of calm, just a minute or two in the quiet of the room with the fluorescents off and nothing but the lights of the city and shadow of the sky to fill his view.

As he took in the tranquility, he caught a glimpse of a spark of light, the same flicker of distress he'd seen earlier. Squinting, he leaned forward to discover its source, but the light was too far away. He moved slightly to the left, trying to get a better perspective and noticed it disappeared. Moving back to the right, it quickly reappeared.

"Idiot," he whispered to himself, realizing it must be a reflection from inside the office behind him. He turned around, but could see nothing on the wall behind him: no illuminated computer buttons, no fire alarm warning light or anything electrical that could produce this kind of reflection. Turning back around, he listed left to right, watching the light appear then disappear with each movement. The hair on the back of his neck rose from a strong feeling that started to penetrate his skin; a sensation that the signal of distress was for him. He flew to the door and stumbled into the lighted hallway.

"I definitely need a vacation," he muttered, trying to cast off the feeling of dread. His mind was now on one thing: getting home and hugging Jonathan, the one solid thing in his life. He shook his head as he hurried toward the elevator... the mysterious flickering light now another secret to claw at his gut.

18

"Holy shit, Angie, what the hell happened to you?"

Tommy dropped his suitcase next to the mud-stained welcome mat and closed the door behind him. He followed Angela to the sofa, sidestepping to avoid an empty pizza box, and watched her fall onto the grimy cushions.

If he wasn't so bewildered by the sight of her, he would've laughed at the paisley housedress she was wearing – almost identical to the one his obese Gramma wore every single day. Angela moved painstakingly slow, the sofa pillows giving in to her every move, apparently making it impossible for her to get comfortable. He caught glimpses of the huge limbs beneath her dress; folds of skin dangling like a sack of potatoes, heavy with cellulite that looked as painful as it did hideous. Her once slender legs were now thick and mapped with veins that traveled all the way down to the powdery-blue ankle socks covering her swollen feet. Tommy felt sick to his stomach.

She leaned over to grab the television remote, heaving a short grunt with each movement. He hesitated before looking into the short sleeves of her housedress, taking in the sight of the dangling skin beneath her arms, miniature versions of the potato sacks he'd observed swinging below her thighs. He covered his eyes with his hand, using his thumb and forefinger to rub his eyebrows and hoping that when he reopened them, the old, beautiful Angela would be sitting beside him, her slim legs crossed, her perky breasts awaiting his searching hands. But when his eyes parted, a younger version of his Gramma seemed to drape herself over the entire sofa. Once again, his heart dropped like a weight.

He glanced at the door, planning his escape, but his eyes caught Angela's and he saw a vague reflection of the woman he'd fallen in love with; the Angela who always made his heart skip a beat and his groin burn with desire; the woman who could literally drive him away at times, then draw him back with a sensual gaze. Her eyes were as deep and mysterious as they'd always been and for a few seconds her face changed; the jowls gone, the dark circles under her eyes lightening like magic. He fell back into the sofa and wrapped his hand around her foot.

"Angie, what the fuck? What happened?"

She hit the Mute button and threw the remote onto the table. "For God's sake, Tommy, I didn't invite you out here to give me the third degree. I need help." She grabbed an open bag of Ruffles lying on the table, stuffed a few into her mouth, and jammed them down with a swig of Diet Coke. "Can you do that for me? Can you help?"

Tommy squeezed her foot. He wasn't going to be strong-armed by her without a fight. "Yeah, Angie, I can help. I can help you with anything. But I'm not doing a God damn thing until you tell me what happened and why you look like this. If I'm going to help you get your shit together and lose all this weight, I gotta know where it came from... why you let yourself go like this."

She tossed her head back and laughed, clapping her hands as though he'd just told her the funniest joke she'd ever heard. Tears rolled down her round cheeks as she stamped her feet against his thigh and tried to catch her breath.

"Lose weight?" Angela wiped her arm across her eyes to help dry her tears of laughter. "Are you kidding me?" She grabbed both sides of the housedress and pulled down to show Tommy her swollen stomach. "There's more than fat here, Tommy."

Tommy sat motionless, his head spinning.

"You're not..." he started.

"I am." She rubbed her stomach like a genie's lamp. "About five months. Due in July." She continued to massage her belly.

Tommy jumped up and took a deep breath, leaning against the wall and banging the back of his head against it a few times. Strands of hair fell in front of his eyes. "Whose is it?" His tone was vapid, lifeless. She tried to shift around on the cushions and held out her hand.

"Tommy, let's not get into that right now. The thing I need your help with is that..."

"Fuck you!" The force of his voice made her jump back, the words hanging between the two of them like a rabid dog that both of them were too afraid to approach. He swung his arm through the air at nothing. He gathered air into the pit of his stomach so he could increase the force of his voice. "You don't let me visit you for all this time, and then out of nowhere you call me up and ask me to visit." He pointed his open hand to her stomach. "And then you tell me this?"

"Tommy, you have to let me…"

"Holy shit, Angela. I actually thought you were ready to have me live with you… to start a life together like you always said we would. And now you're pregnant with someone else's kid." He held his head with both hands and rattled it back and forth as though he could shake up the pieces inside and make some sense out of them. Tommy knelt beside the sofa, his face only inches from hers. "Whose is it Angela? Who did you fuck to get pregnant?"

"I didn't fuck anyone, Tommy. I swear."

Hearing a tremble in her voice, the knot in his stomach loosened a bit. Maybe he finally had the upper hand with her.

"So now you're Mother Teresa! God got you pregnant?"

Angela closed her eyes and winced. "First of all, it's Mary, not Mother Teresa,"

"I don't care if it's the freakin' Queen of England." He grabbed her by the arm. "Tell me who got you pregnant."

Angela tried to pull away, but he held on tighter. She huffed and fell back.

"I was artificially inseminated."

"By who, Angela?"

"Jonathan," she said under her breath.

He threw her arm onto her stomach and leapt up, almost tripping backward over the coffee table. "You've got to be fucking kidding me, Angela. I'm sitting forty-five minutes away in New York waiting for an invitation, while you're getting knocked up by a God damn fag? None of this makes sense. I don't get it."

As though ice water had been injected into his veins, Tommy's entire body went cold. Here it was again – the irrepressible anger and anxiety that showed up every time he was in an unmanageable situation – overpowering his thoughts and creating bedlam inside his head. With his eyes on fire and his muscles starting to twitch, he ran to his suitcase, unzipped the side compartment, and pulled out his Xanax bottle. He tossed two pills onto his tongue and let them slide to the back of his throat.

Seeing Angela open her mouth, Tommy held up his hand.

"Don't!" His voice quivered, but was strong enough to keep Angela quiet.

Kneeling on the floor beside her, he started banging his palms against the side of his temples, trying to get the cruel thoughts out of his head. This is *Angela. Angela. Angela.*

"Tommy! Stop it! Now!"

From what seemed like a far distance away, he heard the old Angela yelling to him, telling him to stop hitting himself. So he did, letting his fingers crawl down the side of his face and onto his knees. The Xanax started to kick in, bringing warmth back to his veins. He crawled over to Angela, leaned over the sofa, and gently kissed her on the lips. She kissed him back the way she used to, her tongue gliding over his, her hand reaching down the front of his jeans. He pulled himself onto the sofa and slid up against her, her hugeness so new to him he opened his eyes, unsure what to do with his hands.

"It's still me, Tommy," said Angela, pulling him closer.

But it wasn't. He closed his eyes again and laid his face on her chest. The flannel of her housedress rubbed against his cheek, pulling an unvisited part of his mind back to a place he'd been long ago; a time when this same long-familiar sense of comfort had enveloped and given him peace. At first, his memory wouldn't offer up the exact time and place, but the sensation was enough to bring tears to his eyes; the comfort and pain of the surfacing thought at odds with one another. For a brief moment he let go, waiting to see which one would win.

Tommy lightly scratched the lint pills on the arms of the housedress, listening to Gramma's voice as she stroked his hair and twirled his curls around her plump fingers.

"That father of yours will never beat you again," she said softly. "God saw to that by crashing his drunken ass into that tree."

Tommy put his thumb in his mouth, hooking it onto the back of his front teeth. He wanted to respond to Gramma, but couldn't find the words or the energy. It had only been a few hours since the police had pounded on his front door sweeping him into a semi-conscious whirlwind of activity. Still in a sleep-induced fog, he'd followed the sound of incessant knocking, glancing in to his father's room and noticing the night table lamp still burning, the bed unmade. When Tommy opened the door, a woman police officer bent down to greet him.

"Hi dear, is your mother home?" She pulled off her hat and a few strands of auburn hair fell in front of her eyes. She wasn't wearing any makeup, but Tommy saw her beauty right away, as he did any woman who took the time to show him kindness.

Her complexion was as smooth as glass. The lights from behind him gave her cheeks a glow that almost lulled him back to sleep. Through the strings of hair bunched atop her head he could see blue and red lights flashing from the police cars. On the other side of the street stood people he'd known for years, families dressed in bathrobes and pajamas watching the scene play out like a television drama.

"Is your mommy here?" the policewoman repeated. "We need to speak with her." Tommy shook his head, his hands by his sides as he still waited for some sort of news. "Where's my dad?"

The woman shot a look to the balding officer standing by her side and turned back to Tommy. "That's what we need to speak to your mom about, son. Where is she?"

Tommy looked down to his bare feet and curled his toes. "She's dead," he said. "Gone." He returned his gaze to the policewoman. "Where's daddy?"

The officer stood up, tucked her hat under her arm, and led Tommy inside with her hand on top of his head. "You're the only one home?" she asked.

He nodded.

She walked with Tommy into the living room, taking in the sights: beer cans littering the floor, a half-empty bottle of generic vodka sitting atop the television, a chocolate brown carpet discolored by grease, bleach and what looked like dried blood. She gestured for him to sit down on the lumpy sofa and then sat down beside him.

"What's your name?" Her voice was softer now, and she offered Tommy a friendly smile that helped settle his nerves.

"Tommy," he whispered.

"Tommy, my name is Maria. Your father's been in an accident. Is there anyone else in your family we can call? We'd like to speak with them and have them come pick you up so you won't be alone."

"Gramma," he whispered. "But she lives in Queens. She's probably not up, because she sleeps a lot. And she doesn't come here. She's too big."

"That's okay. We'll give her a call," Maria glanced around the room. "Do you know Gramma's telephone number?"

"On the frigerator."

The bald officer headed toward the kitchen. Maria grabbed Tommy under his arms to lift him up. "Let's go get you dressed. I don't think Gramma would want you traveling all the way from Brooklyn to Queens in your pajamas."

"Why do I have to go? What happened to my dad? Where is he?" Tommy was on the verge of crying, a sense of reality finally penetrating the fog of sleep; this wasn't a dream after all.

"He's with your mom," Maria said. "Now let's get you dressed."

Tommy grabbed Maria's hand and followed her upstairs to his room. A tear fell down his face and he wiped it with his forearm. "I don't think Mommy's gonna like that," he said to no one in particular.

It was early morning, maybe five thirty or six, when Tommy rested his head on Gramma's chest as she rocked them both in the giant rocking chair that took up most of her TV room. With his thumb in his mouth and his eyes half open, he gazed through the dirty apartment window, above the roofs of the other apartment buildings, out into the lightening sky, now a grayish-blue from the mixture of morning sun and city smog.

"That father of yours will never beat you again. God saw to that by crashing his drunken ass into that tree." She took a deep breath and Tommy swore he could hear her lungs creak. "And now we'll take care of each other. I'll take care of you and you'll take care of me." She pulled his chin up so he could see her face. "Open your eyes, Tommy."

His eyelids, laden with hundred pound weights, felt numb, but he forced them open so Gramma wouldn't start yelling.

"You hear me? You'll take care of Gramma, won't you?"

Tommy nodded and closed his eyes.

"You promise?" she pulled the thumb from his mouth, causing saliva to drip down his chin and onto her housedress.

"Promise," he said, the sensation of comfort and peace dissipating with each breath Gramma took. He had a feeling the deal he just made was going to be one-sided.

Tommy turned away from Angela and stared at the ceiling.

"I'm gonna help you get back to normal, Angie, I swear I will." He felt her hand on the back of his head, tangling his hair within her fingers. "I just don't understand... why would you have a baby with *them* instead of me? It was Philip, right?" He turned his head around. The anger started to boil in his abdomen again and he clenched his teeth. "He made you do this, didn't he? Two fags can't have a baby so they make *you* do it for them? That's it, isn't it?"

Still lying on the sofa, Angela wriggled onto her side and continued playing with his hair. "Don't worry about that, Tommy. It's really not anyone's fault."

"Why are you sticking up for them?" he shouted. "They're using you like a freakin' oven for their kid. What are *you* getting out of this piece of shit situation?"

"More than you think. And in a few days, a lot more than that."

"What the hell are you talking about?" As usual he was confused by Angela and her cryptic statements.

"That's where I need your help, Tommy. I won't go into the legal details, but when this whole thing started with Philip and Jonathan, we signed an agreement that they'd give me twenty five hundred dollars a month to help take care of things." She took a deep breath and pushed herself upright. Tommy grabbed the blanket from the arm of the sofa and threw it over her legs. "Well, that was when I could work and I had a salary that would also help pay expenses. But look at me for Christ's sake. I *can't* work. And I haven't been working at the hospital long enough to get any kind of severance."

"I'll give you money. Don't worry. I'll help take care of you."

Angela huffed again. "That's nice of you, Tommy, but I won't need your money. I'm going to get more from Philip."

He lifted his head. "More than twenty five hundred a month? How are you going to do that?"

"My lawyer will be doing that. While Philip and Jonathan are lying on the sandy beaches of Florida, drinking pina coladas and dining at fancy restaurants, my attorney will be contacting theirs, asking them to double the monthly payment."

"What? Five grand a month? No way."

"Yes way, Tommy. And I'm going to get it. There's no doubt about it. And you know what else?"

"There's more?" he asked like a wide-eyed five-year old.

"I'm going to *keep* the baby and they're going to pay five grand a month for at *least* the next eighteen years. And that doesn't include college tuition and anything else I can get them for."

"Holy shit, Angela, how you gonna do that?"

Angela smirked and attempted to cross her arms. "My attorney is Fiona Wilder, the number one fertility law attorney in the country. From what I've heard, she can pretty much crush the sperm donor in court every time. You were absolutely right when you said they're using me as an 'oven' and I should be getting something out of the situation. I'm tired of being treated like dirt, and it's time I flex my muscle."

"But are you sure you want to keep the kid? That's a lot of crap to deal with. And if you and I are going to be together, it's gonna be mine too."

Angela closed her eyes. Tommy couldn't tell whether she was getting angry and losing patience with him or happy he'd just offered to act as the father of her child.

"Yes, the baby will be yours too, Tommy. But no one can know that yet. If anyone knows you're involved, Fiona will never be able to get the amount of money we're looking for."

"Got it!" he said, jittery with excitement. "So how can I help? What can I do?"

"First I have a question for you and I don't want you to get upset when I ask it. Promise?"

A pang in his stomach made him flinch but he hid it well.

"I promise."

"Do you have a criminal record?"

"What the hell? Of course not!" He was almost yelling. "A few run ins, but nothing on record. I never did anything *that* bad. You should know that. God, Angela, why would you ask?"

"You promised not to get upset, Tommy!"

He took a deep breath. "Well, why'd you ask if you didn't want me to get upset? Jesus, Angie, that's a loaded question."

"I had to ask. Fiona says if this thing goes to court, I'll need character witnesses. I have some people from my old job, and June of course, but they'll probably want to speak with friends who've known me for a long time. You have a good job, an apartment, a nice, steady income and we know how professional and hot you look when you put on a suit and tie."

Tommy smiled and lowered his head, feigning embarrassment. "Yes, we do know. And I'm glad you remember." He placed his head back down on her lap, waiting for the warmth of her hand to caress his face. When he felt her fingers touch his cheek, he shut his eyes and tried to imagine their future together: Angela, her body once again slender and beautiful; the house clean and tidy, the way she'd kept her old apartment; a child crawling around with a toothless smile, calling him Daddy. Except for the kid, it was a scene he'd imagined for years.

"So you'll vouch for my character?" Angela's voice was high and fluttery.

He'd never heard her sound this weak and vulnerable and it was eating at him, way down deep, as though a wild coyote was chewing on his intestines. No way would he let those fags get away with this; using her like an insignificant vessel; letting her blow up like a whale and leaving her alone to live in squalor just so they could have a child. They were going to pay, one way or another.

"Of course I'll vouch for you. I wouldn't want to spend my life with you if I didn't think you're the greatest, most wonderful person in the world."

Angela lifted his head, studied his face, and swept aside the thin strands of hair that fell in front of his eyes.

"We will spend our lives together, Tommy. I promise. But we can't do it yet. Character witnesses need to be impartial and if we're seen as a couple or if you're living with me, then no one will buy it. You do understand that, right?"

Tommy felt his heart drop into his stomach and his body go limp. She was right, but he wanted to start their new life together right away. He looked into her eyes and started to melt, as always.

"I understand, but I don't like it. By the way, do you know if it's a boy or a girl?"

She turned her face away and looked out the bay window to a place he didn't think he could reach with her. Her attention had suddenly departed, taken an express train to somewhere far away. He hoped it wasn't in Florida with Philip and Jonathan.

"Doesn't matter," Tommy said, trying to interrupt her thoughts, "I'll be a good father no matter what." He jumped up and placed his hands on his hips. "Now, we've got to get this place in shape. If anyone comes here to judge your character, this mess isn't going to help you. Let's start in the kitchen."

Angela turned back to him, slowly returning from wherever she'd gone. A single tear fell down her cheek and she let it drop onto the lace collar of her oversized housedress.

"A boy," she whispered. "It's a boy."

19

It seemed to Jonathan that an invisible wall two miles from shore held back the clouds, opening up an expanse of sapphire sky from one end of the ocean to the other.

Lying on the chaise lounge, both legs dangling off the sides so he could feel warm sand on the soles of his feet, Jonathan felt at peace with the world around him: the hot sunlight on his skin, a ghostly touch soaking into his pores; crashing waves making a soothing, natural rhythm to match his heartbeat; the mixture of pineapple, coconut milk, and light rum in his pina colada granting him the taste of South Florida ambrosia.

"This is amazing." Jonathan peeled off his sunglasses and turned to Philip, whose chaise was only inches from his own.

"It's called relaxation." Philip chuckled, pushing his sunglasses onto his forehead. "You've probably forgotten how it feels."

"Yeah, it's been a while for both of us." After a few minutes of perfect silence, Jonathan asked, "By the way, have you come up with your number-one choice for the baby's name?"

Picking up his glass from the steel table between them, Philip stirred his drink with the straw and gazed at the endless horizon. He took a sip and stirred some more. "Well, it's between…"

"Ahem. We decided only one name each. I don't want to hear any it's between crap. Gimme a name or I throw you in the water."

Philip faked a shiver. "Oooo, I'm shaking in my boots." He took a deep breath and crunched his toes into the hot, white sand. "You might think this is crazy, but... well... it's your sperm and Angela's egg. If I'm going to be a real part of this, maybe he should have my name."

The pang in Jonathan's chest forced him backward. He had no idea Philip felt so removed from the situation. Something in the way Philip said his own name struck a chord that threw all his own name choices out of his head.

"First of all, why didn't you tell me you felt like you weren't a part of things?"

Philip shrugged his shoulders, which raised Jonathan's guilt level another notch. "That is *so* not true. You're just as important as I am, or Angela is. It might be our physical stuff that got him here, but your personality and mental soundness, or whatever you want to call it, will keep him happy and well-balanced. I can tell you right now, you'll be a thousand times better dad than me."

Jonathan sat up and clinked his glass against Philip's.

"Philip it is." he said. "I love the name, I love the sound of it, and I love you."

"You're drunk." Philip slapped Jonathan's knee and stood up, stretching his arms and groaning from the tautness of his sunburned skin. "No decisions while you're drunk."

"I'm not drunk." Jonathan placed his glass on the table and tried to keep his balance as he stood. "As long as we don't call him Little Philip, or Philip Junior, or Phil. I just want to call him Philip, okay?"

The ground started to feel shaky under his feet. Before he had a chance to fall Philip gripped both his arms.

"Holy shit," said Jonathan. "What the hell is this?"

"Sun, plus alcohol." Philip moved to one side and Jonathan leaned against him. "You okay?"

"I'm fine. Just stood up too fast." Jonathan let his arms fall to his side and tried to steady himself.

"Yeah, weenee," Philip said, pretending to talk under his breath. "I mean, Mr. Weenee. Or would you prefer, Ms. Weenee?"

Jonathan feigned laughter and wriggled his arms from Philip's grasp. "If you don't stop, Mrs. Weenee, I'm going to drown you."

Philip dashed toward the water stopping midway to face Jonathan. "C'mon! I'm ready! Drown me Mrs. Weenee!"

Jonathan glanced around to see who might've heard Philip's taunts, but the few people left on the beach were either flat on their stomachs or lounging on their backs, listening to music or the crashing of waves, caring about nothing but the sun on their skin as they enjoyed the sunset.

Jonathan looked toward the ocean where Philip waved for him, his beautiful body glowing in the late afternoon sunlight against the backdrop of cobalt blue water. *Like a postcard*, Jonathan thought, *the perfect picture.* He ambled toward the waterline without taking his eyes off Philip, a sense of overwhelming jubilance coursing through his veins. Maybe he was a little drunk, but this sense of joy and relaxation was something he'd never experienced. He focused only on Philip, wanting to be certain he could remember this perfect picture, this amazing moment, for the rest of his life.

The Blue Moon restaurant was about a mile off Brickell Avenue, a few miles north of downtown Miami where Jonathan and Philip had been shopping for baby clothes all day. With a bay front view only reserved for celebrities or regulars who bought no less than three bottles of the restaurant's highest priced Brunello in one sitting, Jonathan was thrilled Wayne could get them a table on such short notice.

The sun had nearly set, its remaining light disappearing into the hard edge of the ocean. Puffy white clouds with blackened edges hovered above the sea like giant, amorphous starships protecting the earth below.

Ignoring the view, Jonathan dropped the salad fork onto his plate and fell back in his chair.

"She hung up on you? Are you kidding? Why did you wait until now to tell me?"

"She didn't *exactly* hang up. It was really a mutual hang up." He laughed, but Jonathan saw the hollowness in his smile.

"Bullshit! She was pissed because of our trip and she hung up on you." He looked out over the bay, letting himself focus on the warm breeze against his face. He closed his eyes and tried to relax. It didn't work. "She's been this way for weeks and it's only getting worse. We discussed with her from the beginning: that we have our life and she has hers. I swear, Philip, if she keeps up like this after the baby is born, we're up shit's creek."

For a moment, clinking silverware and muffled sound of voices of the other guests was the only sound between them. Philip picked at the lettuce and rolled a cherry tomato around the rim of his plate, picking up as much of the fig balsamic vinaigrette as he could before spearing the tomato with his fork and popping it into his mouth. Jonathan knew Philip's food playing was procrastination in action.

"I'm sorry." Jonathan tapped Philip's foot with the toe of his shoe. "I don't mean to get so upset, and I don't want to ruin our evening. It's perfect." He turned his head toward the setting sun, the faintest glow of burnt-orange sizzling along the horizon. "Well, it *was* perfect, until her name came up. We won't talk about it now, but the three of us definitely have to sit down and set this thing straight once and for all." He now felt a shoe tapping his own.

When he turned back, Philip was staring at him. His sober expression and the impenetrable darkness of his eyes said everything he was thinking.

"Okay, I'm done," Jonathan whispered. "Let's enjoy the night."

As they held their glasses up for a silent toast, the smile on Philip's face disappeared.

"My phone's buzzing," he said, reaching into his shirt pocket. "Who would call us while we're here?" He looked at the phone's screen then back up to Jonathan. "It's G. She knows we're on vacation. She's either calling to see if we're having fun or there's a problem with..."

Shit! Jonathan felt a pang in his abdomen. "You have to answer it."

Philip held the phone up to one ear and covered the other with his hand, trying to cut down the restaurant noise. Jonathan watched him carefully, waiting for some kind of expression that would tell him if he should start worrying or if G was checking in to make sure they were relaxing. But once Philip started rubbing his forehead and shaking his head, Jonathan knew this wasn't a social call.

Another minute passed before Philip spoke. "We're just about to get our entrée, G. Can we call you back when we're done with dinner?"

Jonathan looked over the railing, past the sandy shore to distant lights that sparkled like stars on the other side of the bay. From miles away they winked at him, taunting him, as though they knew what would come next, but refused to let go of their secret. He watched them blink until Philip's voice crept into his head through a back door.

"There's a problem." Philip ended the call, poured himself some more wine, and filled Jonathan's glass halfway.

"I pretty much figured that by the horror-stricken look on your face. I'm just trying to control myself before I even ask you what it's about."

Philip allowed the Brunello to sit on his tongue for a few seconds, then tilted his head back and gazed at the sky.

"No need to get angry, Jonny" he said quietly. "I'm going to take care of everything."

"Take care of what? What's going on? What happened?"

The waiter and two servers suddenly appeared at their table. A short, thin Cuban boy no more than nineteen years old set Philip's plate on the table in front of him. Another Cuban, almost a doppelganger of the first, delivered Jonathan's meal. Anxious for them to leave, Jonathan beat the waiter to the punch.

"Great. Thanks, Stefan – we don't need anything else right now."

Stefan forced a smile, his perfect white teeth a sharp contrast to his dark stubble, and gave them a quick bow before leaving the table in silence. He was either very perceptive or mortally offended. Either way, Jonathan knew he'd be paying for his guilt by over tipping.

"So what did G say? You look as though someone just slapped you."

Philip picked up the knife and began to slice his steak.

"That's probably because someone just *did* slap me. Angela slapped me." Philip put a small piece of filet in his mouth and chewed slowly. "And she slapped you, too."

The temperature by the bay was a balmy seventy degrees, but Jonathan felt a chill through his body. He pushed his dish to the far side of the table and clasped both hands in front of him. He could barely speak, let alone eat. "Go on."

"We have to call G later, but the gist of it is Angela's looking for more money – double what she's getting now. Plus there's some bullshit about a college fund, other household expenses and... I don't know... I didn't get the details. G said she just received papers from a Fiona somebody – some big time fertility lawyer who's now representing Angela." He shook his head and threw his fork down onto his plate. "*Representing Angela!*" Philip shouted. "*I still can't believe it! What the hell did I get us into?*"

Guests from nearby tables turned their heads and glared at him. He didn't notice, his eyes focused on his plate as though the answer to his problem lay somewhere between his steak and the organic mashed potatoes.

Jonathan took Philip's hand and gently squeezed it. "We'll make this work, Philip. Don't go crazy over it. And I don't want you feeling guilty about it either. We made this decision together and now it's something we have to deal with."

"Yeah, but I knew who she was... who she used to be." Philip blinked his eyes trying to suppress tears. "I should've known people can't change. At least not to the degree Angela changed. She's a screwed up mess and now we're a part of that mess."

Jonathan tossed his napkin onto his plate. "Let's get out of here. We'll take a walk along the water before we call G. Okay?"

Philip just nodded. Jonathan had seen Philip in this state only once before, the day his sister Jen succumbed to the non-Hodgkin's lymphoma she'd endured for more than three years. Philip had consistently said he was prepared for her death, but when the time came, he was inconsolable; silent for days with nothing more to eat than the toast and coffee Jonathan practically hand fed him.

Philip was an eternal optimist, believing Jen could find something within herself to defeat the disease. But she never did find it, which made Philip feel more disappointment than grief. And tonight, Jonathan saw the glass wall of optimism Philip spent so many years rebuilding shattered by a woman who deceived them in ways Jonathan had only imagined during fits of paranoia.

The sudden realization that his son was inside of a deceitful, hateful woman made his stomach churn. He quickly stood to stop from vomiting. He waved to Stefan, gestured for the check, and walked around the table to Philip.

"It's going to be okay, babe, I promise." Jonathan lightly combed his fingers through Philip's hair, then bit down hard on his bottom lip, remembering he'd said those exact words to Philip the day they found out his sister had cancer.

They walked side by side along the shoreline, pants rolled halfway up their calves, shoes dangling from their fingers. Light from the restaurants and bars fell onto the sand, creating shadows that resembled a two-dimensional cityscape. Philip and Jonathan stayed within the shade of night, hearing the noise of laughter and clanking plates to their left and the tranquility of the ebbing tide to their right.

They strolled in silence, neither uttering a word since leaving the restaurant. Ready to jump out of his skin, Jonathan tapped Philip's shoulder and waited for a response. Nothing. He did it again.

"What, Jonny?" He sounded annoyed.

"Are we going to talk about this or walk all the way to Boca?"

Philip slowed his pace and faced the ocean before he finally stopped walking.

"Are we *that* gullible, Jonny or is Angela the best actress in the world? I've been trying to figure it out, thinking back for any indication she'd do something like this to us. I can't find one and that makes me feel like an idiot."

Jonathan planted his feet in the wet sand beside Philip and gazed at the miniscule lights blinking on the ocean's dark surface.

"I'll take your second option. I think she's the best actress in the world. You know me, Philip. I admit I'm one of the most paranoid people around – especially when it comes to people like Angela who are so full of goodwill … always so nice and accommodating. I don't think we're idiots. I think we're just too trusting."

Philip flicked sand off his toes and dropped his head back to take in a deep breath. When he opened his eyes, he turned to Jonathan.

"I know you'll think I'm crazy, but I still have to believe somewhere inside that this is her hormones reacting. That she was upset with us for going away and didn't know how to handle her emotions, so she called this lawyer to get even with us. That's why I need to talk with her about it. I need her to understand that she needs to grow up and stop acting like a child."

Jonathan shook his head and looked at the side of Philip's face illuminated by the lights.

"Are you kidding me? You're still giving her the benefit of the doubt? Jesus, Philip, this is going to take more than a slap on the wrist or a lecture on how an adult should act. Are you sure she hadn't planned this all along? Do you think she's asking for five thousand dollars a month simply because we went on vacation for a few days?" He turned toward the ocean, his head pounding with each thump of waves. "My paranoia is back in full force and I don't want that bitch getting away with anything. I say we have G take care of the whole thing. She and her team are top notch and I think we should stay out of it."

"Jonny," Philip said, gently rubbing his arm. "She's carrying your baby. How can you say we should stay out of it? Can you imagine living the rest of our lives through lawyers, courts, restricted visitations, and all the crap that goes along with parents who don't get along? It's not a way for any child to grow up." He grabbed Jonathan's hand. "Why can't we try to nip it in the bud now, in a civil way? And if it doesn't work we'll let G take over."

For a few seconds Jonathan felt dizzy, seasick, as if he wasn't standing on shore but instead was drifting upon the waves crashing only a few feet beside him. His anger about the entire situation was affecting him physically and he knew he'd better get it under control before his feelings started impacting his relationship with Philip. The last thing he wanted was for Angela to cause a rift between them. He suspected nothing would please her more than to have Philip all to herself.

He steadied himself by letting the cool breeze blow through his hair and down the collar of his shirt.

"G is *not* going to like this," Jonathan said, turning around and heading back toward the hotel. "I can hear her voice in my head and she's not sounding happy."

Philip laughed and ran to catch up with him.

"You wanna play good cop, bad cop with her, or would you rather me take care of it myself?"

"We'll start with good cop, bad cop and take it from there. I just hope she lets us get a word in edgewise."

"Don't you worry your sweet little head about it. You know I can pretty much use my charm to make things work my way."

Jonathan picked up his pace.

"You're going to need more than charm for G. When she makes up her mind, it's pretty much locked up."

It was locked tighter than either of them expected.

"I'll say it again, I emphatically oppose that strategy," G's tone was sharp and angry. "I can't let you speak with that woman without counsel present. That would just be asking for trouble – especially with an attorney like Fiona Wilder. Who, by the way, has a last name that fits her to a tee."

Philip and Jonathan sat on the balcony of their Ritz-Carlton hotel room, leaning toward the cell phone on the table beside them. The breeze from the ocean was cool and a bit strong, but not as forceful as the voice emanating from the phone.

"I have to do it, G." Philip said. "I know her, or at least I used to know her. I know where she comes from and what buttons I need to press to knock some sense into her. Sitting down and talking with her is the only way."

Silence from the other end of the phone. Jonathan looked at Philip who shrugged his shoulders.

"G... are you still there?" Philip asked hesitantly.

Jonathan looked out over the balcony wall, catching sight of cruise ship lights floating like ghosts upon an ocean of black ink. He wondered if there was someone standing on the ship's balcony watching the light from their hotel room and questioning, like he was, if there were other people whose lives had just been turned upside down.

"Yes, I'm here. But it's obvious I'm speaking with two brick walls." G sighed. "I'd rather start this in mediation, during which minutes are taken, witnesses are present, and everything is out in the open – well, most everything. I'm sure Fiona will have a few tricks up her sleeve that she won't be sharing, but we'll have some of our own, too. And just so you know, they're requesting a lot more than they know they'll get. It's just another piece of their strategy."

After a few seconds of silence, Philip stood and leaned against the balcony railing. He shook his head at Jonathan, then shrugged.

"Okay G, you know best," he said, sweeping his bare foot along the balcony floor. "We're cutting this vacation short and will be on a 9:50 am flight into LaGuardia. We should land by one-ish. When's the soonest you can meet with us?"

"I'm in court for most of tomorrow, but after that I'm all yours. Call Missy and let her know what day and time work for you and we'll make it happen. I'll have Jason in on the meeting, too. I think he drew up the initial contracts for Angela, right?"

"Yes, he did," Jonathan said. "And I hope the both of you can convince Philip that everything will be okay." He poked Philip's foot with his big toe. "What do you think, G, can you do that?"

G didn't answer immediately and Jonathan moved closer to the phone, thinking he'd missed something. They heard papers shuffling, and then G spoke. "Guys, I'm telling you right now I can't promise anything. As I discussed with you before the decision was made, there are a lot of gray areas in the realms of assisted reproduction and sperm donation. I *can* tell you this firm will do everything humanly and legally possible to insure you're protected and your assets are secure."

She paused and sighed. "Of course, there's a lot more fallout from this than financial. There's the emotional and personal side, visitation rights, etcetera. So many things that might be gray areas now, but we'll be forced to make them black and white for this particular case. It's going to be a game of give and take. Right now I'm suggesting you take the rest of the night to enjoy the Florida air and get some sleep so you can be fresh for your trip tomorrow. Okay?"

"Well, that doesn't sound too reassuring," Jonathan said, forcing a laugh he knew came off as nerves. "But we trust you and know you'll do whatever you can." He looked up at Philip. "Anything else before we hang up?"

Philip shook his head. "Thanks, G. We'll see you on Thursday." His voice was almost a whisper. "Goodnight."

Jonathan hung up the phone and walked to Philip, who was now leaning on the railing staring into the distance.

"I'm going to see her," Philip said. "I have to meet with her at least once, just to make sure she wants to take it this far."

"Philip, you heard G."

"I know what G said, Jonny, but she's a lawyer. You know the way it is. Lawyers think law suits, courts, drama all that crap. We're talking about people... you, me, Angela. And like I said before, we don't want lawyers in the middle of our lives forever." The breeze had picked up a bit and Philip brushed the hair from in front of Jonathan's eyes. He touched Jonathan's cheek with the back of his hand. "I'm going to make this right, Jonny. I got us into this and I'm going to get us out of it."

Jonathan grabbed Philip's hand and held it against his face. "Please stop saying that, Philip. You did not get us into this. *We* got us into this and it's up to *us* to get us out of it. So if you're going to see her, then I need to be there too."

"No way, Jonny. That won't work. She'll feel like we're ganging up on her and that'll kill it right from the start. I need her to be calm, to feel like she's talking to her old college friend, someone who understands and sympathizes with her. I think I can do that, but I have to do it alone. You understand, right?"

"I understand," Jonathan said. "But I don't like it." The whole situation made him feel uneasy. Having Philip confront Angela by himself while he, the father of their child, sat waiting at some Starbucks up the block, sent chills down his spine.

"I don't trust her, Philip." Jonathan shook his head in disbelief. He walked through the French sliders and into the suite, falling onto the loveseat. "And to be honest, I don't trust you. You're too nice, too giving, too compassionate. I can see you calling me from her house tomorrow telling me to pack my stuff because we're moving into her house and she's moving into ours."

Philip leaned over the back of the loveseat and kissed the top of Jonathan's head. "That's why I love you so much. You've got an imagination that pretty much orbits another planetary system. Can you come back down to earth for a minute or two?"

"I don't think you want me down to earth right now." Jonathan slouched in the corner of the sofa and threw his legs over its arm. "Because if I was, I'd be dwelling on the fact that our only real vacation in almost two years has been ruined by a crazy, lying, lazy bitch who wants to suck our finances dry while she refuses to work and eats her way into donut heaven. And if I came back down to earth, I'd also have to come to the realization that my biggest fear has come true: our son's future will be in the hands of a woman we despise. We'll have no say in how he's brought up, she'll take her frustrations with us out on him, she'll make him as obese and unhealthy as she is and…"

"Okay, okay. I get it, Jonny, I get it. And that's why I have to go talk with her tomorrow. I'm going to make sure none of that ever happens."

Jonathan twisted himself around and set his feet on the floor. "And let's also make sure this doesn't screw up you and me. Bad enough she's getting between us and our son; we can't let it affect our relationship." His throat tightened and he found it difficult to swallow. "We promised we'd be together forever, remember?"

Before Jonathan had the chance to stand, Philip crouched before him and leaned his arms on Jonathan's thighs. With their faces only inches apart, he closed his eyes and inhaled deeply as though trying to catch Jonathan's breath with his own. Without saying a word Jonathan watched, waiting until Philip opened his eyes and smiled.

"Now you're with me forever," whispered Philip.

Jonathan kissed Philip gently on the mouth and smiled back, although at that moment all he really wanted to do was cry.

<u>20</u>

Philip was hoping for a sunny day, a good reason to pull open the curtains throughout Angela's house and brighten the atmosphere before getting down to business. But the cold front that had been slowly moving in stalled just north of New England, bringing clouds and drizzle, overcastting the entire tri-state area with a somber mist.

It was almost 3:00 in the afternoon. They'd made good time, the traffic from LaGuardia unusually light, allowing them to stop at the house and drop off their luggage. On their way to Angela's, the SUV was silent except for the sound of the tires eating up the road before them. The occasional squeal of the windshield wipers occupied more of the car than the two men inside, each of them working through their own thoughts. Philip watched the droplets on the window beside him crawl along the glass, the car's sixty seven mile per hour speed keeping the water propelled in a straight line. An odd sense of awe hit him; a realization that once the car slowed down, the droplets would trickle down its side, onto the pavement and then evaporate into thin air, as though they'd never existed. *Just like people,* he thought.

He shook his head, trying to get his mind in a better place.

Placing his hand on the armrest, Philip turned to Jonathan. "Hey, you know this is going to work, right?"

Jonathan nodded and laid his hand on top of Philip's.

"And Jonny, please, when you drop me off, don't sit in the car and wait down the block. Just go to the Starbucks on Blackrock and wait for my call. And don't drink too much coffee or you'll be more wired than you usually are... and we don't want to have to deal with that on top of everything else!"

Jonathan squeezed Philip's hand, hard. "Any more rules before I throw you to the wolves?"

"Ouch!" Philip yelled. "Not so hard!" He pulled his hand away, rubbed it and examined it for wounds. "Yes, there's one more rule. You have to give me *at least* a half hour before you start freaking out and trying to call me. I mean, I'm hoping after about fifteen minutes I can call and invite you to partake in a reunion of the happy trio. But if not, don't be concerned."

He knew his words were going in one ear and out the other. Jonathan was a born worrier and no words would stifle his edginess. He'd hoped that giving Jonathan a timeframe would help ease his nerves, but from Jonathan's expression it was evident that trying to keep his anxiety at bay would be fruitless.

"Whatever you say, boss." Jonathan tapped Philip on the knee. "Whatever you say."

Jonathan got off I-95 and made a left on North Benson, the main route cutting through the center of Fairfield. The clamminess in Philip's palms told him they were getting close and he wiped them on his jeans. The car made a right onto Osborne Hill, which within seconds would turn into Jennings, just one block from Angela's house. As Jonathan slowed down, Philip had the sudden urge to call the whole thing off. For a brief moment he considered waiting until after their appointment with G tomorrow before trying to reason with Angela. But he stopped himself. Like he'd told Jonathan, he needed to try and reason with Angela before things got out of hand. Otherwise, the lawyers would take over and there'd be no turning back.

Before making the left onto Angela's street, Jonathan pulled off the road to the right, halfway into the shallow, gravelly ditch that served as an emergency shoulder. He put the car in park and turned to Philip.

"Are you sure about this, Philip?" He moved his hand up to his face and brushed the hair from Philip's eyes. "You don't have to do this, you know. G is totally on the case and we can have her take care of everything for us."

Philip took Jonathan's hand, kissed it, and held it against his face.

"Yes, I'm sure. I want to make this happen for us. There's some logic somewhere inside Angela's head and I'm going to make her find it."

The drizzle turned into a heavier rain that pelted the car like a thousand pebbles, creating metallic echoes that slammed throughout the car. Philip and Jonathan looked at one another in silence, listening to the rain, trying to think each other's thoughts. Philip smiled, kissed Jonathan's hand again, then placed it on the steering wheel.

"Let's get this over with, Jonny," he said.

Jonathan put the car in drive. "You'll call me if you need *anything*, right?"

"*Anything*," Philip replied.

They made the left onto Angela's block, drove past her house on the left, continued to the dead end, and then made a U-turn so the passenger side door was facing the house. Phillip snapped up the umbrella from the back seat and grabbed the door handle.

"Wish me luck," he said.

"Good luck, Babe. I'll be waiting," replied Jonathan.

Philip was about to reinstruct Jonathan to go to Starbucks and not wait up the block in the car. But he knew it would be futile. "I'll see you in a few!"

Philip got out of the car and slammed the door.

Without opening the umbrella, he ran up the driveway and onto the porch steps. As he reached the top step, droplets of rain fell from the roof's gutter into his collar and trickled down his neck and back. He wasn't sure whether the cold water gave him goose bumps or the strange sense of heaviness he suddenly felt around him. He tried shaking the feeling off, along with the rain that had soaked his hair. Nothing worked. The odd feeling still hung on top of him like viscous rain and his hair was still wet.

He peeked in through the porch window. Angela lay on the sofa with one leg stretched out in front of her and the other falling over the side. The television was blaring and countless bags of snacks were scattered on the coffee table beside her. He shook his head in disbelief. What had become of the woman he met not even a year ago – the beautiful, vibrant, confident woman who swaggered into his home with finesse and refinement to capture their hearts?

He turned to the street, half tempted to call Jonathan back, but the road was empty except for a few puddles lining the curb on the other side of the street. He turned back and rang the bell. A faint smile crossed his lips as he remembered Angela's words on the day she moved in, "Mi casa, es su casa!"

I hope she still means that, he thought, waiting for the door to open. He heard the television noise lower, but the door remained closed. He swung open the screen door and knocked on the wooden door behind it.

"Angela, it's Philip!" he yelled, knocking a few more times. "Can we talk for a minute?"

He pressed his ear against the door. Other than muffled sounds from the television, he couldn't hear a thing. He moved back to the window and peered in. The sofa was empty. Searching the room, he saw no sign of life. Maybe she planned to ignore him. A picture of her hiding in a back bedroom crouched in the corner with a blanket over her head passed through his mind. *I really hope it hasn't come to this.* His hair was still wet and shirt damp from the sweeping rain and the cool breeze now whipping around the porch sent chills throughout his entire body.

"One more try." He walked back to the front door and rang the bell. "This is it, Angela. Your last chance."

Still no answer. He grabbed the phone from his shirt pocket, but before he could dial Jonathan, a shuffling sound came from behind the door, like an old man who could no longer lift his legs to walk. Philip stood motionless, waiting, listening carefully as the scuffling grew louder and then suddenly stopped. When it did, the door opened and Angela stood before him, staring at him through the dirty screen.

She looked much worse than the last time he'd seen her. Her face was as he remembered from their college days: turgid and puffy as though ready to explode from too much fluid; her eyes empty with dark shadows painted beneath them; the corners of her thin lips pointing downward, a permanent frown tattooed above her chin. Her greasy hair was pulled back and held in place by blue rubber bands, the only semblance of color anywhere near her face. She wore an oversized housedress that exposed only her forearms and her legs from the knees down, four limbs the size of winter bark tree trunks, blanched and colorless but for the small tributaries of blue vein lining their surface.

"What is it, Philip? Why are you here?" Her voice was cold, without any sort of inflection.

She sounds like a zombie, Philip thought, forcing a smile and stuffing his hands in his pants pockets. "I thought we could talk, Angie. Just for a few minutes."

Angela didn't move or change her expression. "I don't think my attorney would like that."

The warmth from the house crept through the screen and hit Philip in a way that sent another chill through his core. His muscles tightened and he pushed his fists deeper into his pockets. He was losing his patience and was about to turn around when his eyes caught sight of Angela's stomach. Even rounder than the rest of her body, her belly protruded almost to the screen door. Her palm was flat against its edge, rubbing in full circular motions, her face seemingly unaware of this behavior, as though it was as natural as taking a breath. Jonathan's child was inside that belly, and in that moment his anger receded.

"Please, Angie. I'm just asking for a few minutes. Just us… two friends. Me and you. That's all." The look on her face didn't shift and he thought he was losing the battle until she dragged her feet backward along the wooden floor and opened the door wider for him. "Great. Thanks. It's starting to get cold out there."

Angela didn't respond, but Philip could feel her gaze on him as he strolled past her and into the dining room. The tension was like a thick fog, her silence and unmistakable defiance helping him realize this would be much more difficult than he originally thought.

He looked around the room, surprised at its tidiness. Someone had recently cleaned up and put everything in its place, except for the bags of Cheez Doodles, pretzels and boxes of cookies spread out on the table next to the sofa. He placed the closed umbrella on the counter that passed through the living room and into the kitchen. Although she didn't offer him a seat, he plunked down on the chair next to the sofa, hoping she'd sit on the couch next to him. She slowly closed the door and shuffled to the end of the table, slipping her pudgy hands in the pockets of her housedress. Her body concealed the view of the television, but Philip could hear the faint voices of soap opera actors reciting their lines as if by rote. He couldn't understand how anyone could watch such drivel and had to bite his tongue not to say what he was thinking.

"I really don't think this is a good idea, Philip. My attorney specifically warned me not to speak with you or Jonathan before…"

"Screw the attorneys, Angela. They don't know *us*. They don't know what we've been through together, how we all feel about each other. They have no idea the plans the three of us made and how we only want the best for the baby. To them, it's all about money. And that's why I just want you and I to talk this out." He patted the sofa cushion next to him, gesturing for her to sit down.

"As far as I'm concerned, this is a rough patch we need to get through and I know we can get through it by working together."

She took a step toward him. "Where's *Jonathan?*"

The tone of her voice held such disdain, Philip felt a sudden throbbing inside his head. *Where was this coming from?*

"He's at the Starbucks filling up on caffeine. I thought it best if just you and I spoke first. We have a longer history together, and I think that's important."

He couldn't remember ever feeling this uncomfortable with another human being. Sure, he'd met difficult clients and had disagreements with friends and family, but there always seemed to be an open channel through which they could discuss and solve any problem.

But Angela had completely shut him out. Still, he wasn't going to give up until they patched things up or she kicked him out.

With both hands on her belly, she dragged herself to the couch and plopped down at the end furthest away from him. She caught her breath. "How was Florida?"

Philip wriggled in the chair. *More contempt. Holy shit.*

"It was okay, but we cut it short when we heard from G." Angela responsively looked down and intensified the rubbing of her stomach. Philip realized he'd hit a chord of some sort. *Guilt?* Whatever it was, he knew he had to keep playing off it. "We were shocked, Angela. I mean *really* shocked. If we knew things were bothering you so much, we would've come over here and talked about it with you. But you didn't say a thing."

"I *did* say something, Philip. That night on the phone before you left. You knew something was wrong, but you went on your sunny Florida vacation anyway."

Philip took a deep breath and pursed his lips into a smile. "Angie, you didn't say anything on the phone that night. You just sounded angry and upset. And I guess I was so busy trying to button things up before we left, I didn't ask. I can't read minds, Angie. When something's bothering you, you need to tell us."

Angela turned to look out the window, then slowly started shaking her head. When she finally stopped, she looked at Philip, her eyes filled with fury, her face looking larger.

"I am so sick of all this us and we crap, Philip." She clapped her hands together and began to imitate him. "'If something's bothering you, you need to tell *us. It's always we, us, ours. Like you and Jonathan are one freakin' person. Don't you think it's time you get your own identity?"

Philip leaned forward and placed his elbows on his knees, his only way of moving closer to Angela without getting up and sitting next to her. She was talking nonsense, and they both knew it.

"Oh, my, I didn't know you had such contempt for personal pronouns," Philip said, hoping for a laugh. He didn't get one, not even a smile. "Angie, I say we, us, and our because three of us are involved in this thing. I use those words because it's important for you to know we're *both* here for you. Not just me." He pointed to her belly. "It's Jonathan's baby in there, for God's sake."

She puffed out her cheeks and turned toward the television.

"And I don't think that's what's really bothering you anyway. What's the real issue? Are you mad at us for going away and not taking you?"

She chortled and her eyes rolled far back inside their sockets. "Like I'd be able to get on a plane anyway, Philip. Get real. Are you an idiot?"

From the rippling sensation feeding through his veins, Philip understood for the first time what the expression "blood boiling" meant. He closed his eyes. The rain pattered on the roof and he used the sound to help him wash away the notion that this was a losing battle. It couldn't be. There had to be something he could grab hold of to make her see what she was destroying.

He stood up and approached her, knowing in the back of his mind this was his final opportunity. When she looked up at him, he saw, for the briefest instant, the gorgeous, vivacious Angela staring into his eyes. She was mesmerizing, like the night they'd reacquainted last July, pulling him in with her beauty and charm, allowing him to imagine for a flash of a second that she was open to his words. Then he blinked his eyes and the old Angela was back, leering at him with condemnation and loathing.

"I loved you, you know." Her voice was low and hoarse. She peered into his eyes searching for something, piercing so hard it felt as if she was looking through him. "I knew I couldn't have you, but that was okay. Being part of your family was enough for me. Until you both started treating me like a piece of trash."

Philip ran his hands through his hair and shook his head.

"Treating you like trash? What are you talking about, Angie? We cleaned for you, took you out for meals, shopped with you, watched TV and played video games with you. We went with you to see Dr. Jarrett all those times, and we called to check up on you if not every day, every other day. We treated you just like family. Actually, we treated you *better* than family."

"Until I got fat," she said. "Until I started to show and you didn't want to be around me." Her voice grew louder and her face looked inflamed. She wiggled around the sofa cushion until her arms were in the right place to help lift her up. When she caught her balance, she took a deep breath and dragged her feet toward him. "Just like in college, you didn't want any part of me because I was fat. And now fifteen years later, you do the same fucking thing. Toss me aside like garbage." She was yelling now, heaving after each sentence, trying to catch her breath and find the right words. She pointed to her belly and began to slap it with her hands. "And that's why I was waiting until after the baby was born before telling you the surprise. I wanted to be skinny and pretty again when I told you."

Philip was almost trembling; the moment was unreal, as if he'd been sucked into a movie he was watching.

"When you told me what?" he asked, his voice shaking with panic. "What surprise are you talking about?"

She looked up at him, her mouth forming a sinister smile.

"I lied to you and Jonathan. I was too embarrassed to tell you that…"

"You don't have to tell him *shit*!" A man's voice shouted from the other side of the dark kitchen. Philip squinted his eyes and pulled his neck forward, struggling to see who was there. At first he saw no one. A few seconds later the kitchen light flicked on and a man appeared, his face vaguely familiar, the look in his eyes identical to Angela's.

In disbelief, Philip spun his head around toward Angela, who shifted from foot to foot, rolling her eyes and shaking her head. He thought about calling Jonathan right then, but decided against it, thinking it might create even greater hostility. He tried to remember where he'd seen this guy.

"Tommy, what the fuck? I told you to stay in the bedroom!"

"I know what you told me, Angie. But I don't like the way he's talking to you. And I didn't want to miss meeting Philip again. Philip the fag. That's correct, isn't it Philip? You are a fag, right?"

Philip felt a cold tingle of panic rise up from his feet and spread through every fiber of his body. Once Angela said the name Tommy, he remembered the man from the brief encounter in front of her apartment building.

Now he was standing between two psychopaths, wondering what to do next. *Respond? Fight? Run?* Sweat broke out across the back of his neck and it seemed as though time was slowing down. His limbs felt weighted, his heart heavy, each beat thumping harder than the last. The television noise faded into the background as the ticking of the clock on the dining room wall grew louder. For a moment he swore he could hear Angela breathing on the couch behind him. He blinked his eyes and shook his head, trying to get his thoughts back on track.

Philip decided not to press Angela about her lie, knowing it would further antagonize Tommy. So he forced a smile and looked Tommy in the face, choosing his words carefully.

"I think it's best I go. It was nice to see you again, Tommy." He looked over his shoulder at Angela. "I'll be in touch, Angie."

He started for the door, leaving Tommy laughing from the kitchen.

"Oh, Philip! You forgot something." Tommy held his umbrella aloft.

Shit. Philip came back to the kitchen and reached for the umbrella, but Tommy snatched it away at the last moment.

"We don't want him to get wet out there, do we Angie?"

"Tommy! Cut the shit!" Angela yelled from the living room. "Philip, just go."

Philip took a deep breath and held out his hand. "Either give it to me or don't. I'm not going to beg for an umbrella." Philip looked at his outstretched hand, surprised it wasn't trembling.

Without warning Tommy lunged forward and poked his chest with the tip of the umbrella. Philip smacked it aside, but Tommy jabbed him again, in his chest, his belly, the side of his ribcage. With a quick twist of his wrist, Philip grabbed the center of the umbrella, twisted it back and pulled it from Tommy's hand. He lifted the umbrella above his head as though he were going to thrash Tommy with the handle, but then slowly lowered his arm.

"I don't know what you're problem is, asshole, but I don't want any part of it. You're nuts."

Tommy edged toward him. "*I'm* the asshole? *I'm* the asshole?" Tommy was yelling and his voice clapped hard against the pine cabinets. "You and your fag boyfriend get *my* girlfriend pregnant, then go flying away on vacations and leave her here to rot. You use her like a fucking baby oven and *I'm* the asshole?"

"Tommy!" Angela screamed. Philip could hear tears in her voice and the strain of trying to be heard over the commercial playing on the television. "Stop it! Please!" She pleaded. "Philip, just go. Please!"

Philip half turned to Angela. He gripped the umbrella, unconsciously banging it mercilessly against his thigh. "Your *boyfriend?* Since when do you have a boyfriend, Angela?"

A forceful shove against his shoulder drove Philip sideways into the refrigerator and he grabbed the edge of the counter beside the sink to stop himself from landing on the floor.

"Since she decided she needed a *real* man to take care of her, not some fancy, shmancy faggot from Snob Hill, Connecticut."

Tommy's push caught Philip by surprise and came close to knocking the wind out of him. The moment he regained his breath, he was seized by a frantic rage that forced him to lunge at Tommy and push him backward against the sink's counter. Tommy slid sideways and knocked over the dish rack, sending dishes, bottles, and silverware crashing to the floor.

Once Philip maintained his balance, he turned to rush out of the kitchen, run past Angela, and straight to the door. As he eyed his escape path, he felt movement behind and in an instant he knew Tommy was about to retaliate.

"Tommy! No! No!"

Angela's high-pitched screams echoed in Philip's head as he turned to confront Tommy. A second later, the razor-cold, steel blade of a chef's knife pierced his skin and slid into his groin. Although the pain was excruciating, he was paralyzed. For what seemed like an eternity, he couldn't move a muscle, not even his mouth to scream or his eyes to look away from Tommy's face, now inches from his own. He caught a faint scent of alcohol off Tommy's breath as his legs gave way and he fell to his knees.

His insides were ablaze as if he'd swallowed lighter fluid and someone lit a match in his intestines. He fought to breathe, slowly pulling out the knife and gazing up to Tommy, who stood with his bloody hands in the air and a look of disbelief on his face. Hot liquid surged from his abdomen, soaking his hands as he tried to cover the wound and stop himself from losing too much blood. But he could still feel warm liquid oozing from somewhere deep inside his belly and spreading within his body.

He fell onto his side, his left cheek flat against the cold kitchen floor. This time the fear that paralyzed him was the thought that his last vision on earth would be a one inch square of dirty linoleum floor. The high-pitched screams grew louder as the television noise seemed to move further away. He felt dizzy and nauseated. His head pounded, and with each beat he felt blood escaping and his energy withering. He tried to take a deep breath, but it hurt too much, causing him to choke. Warm liquid flowed from the corner of his mouth and dribbled onto the floor.

His vision blurred, the linoleum tile fading away as quickly as the sounds around him. Finally, he couldn't feel anything and tasted only the distant flavor of iron. Closing his eyes, he tried to speak, but only a gurgled puff of air passed through his lips.

All he had left were his thoughts, and so he filled them with images of Jonathan: his face, his smile, his eyes. This was the only way he could be sure he'd die with a smile on his face.

21

Jonathan placed Philip's coffee in the passenger side cup holder, backed out of the Starbuck's parking space, and pulled onto Blackrock Turnpike. He'd waited in the car up the street from Angela's house for nearly fifteen minutes before deciding to get them both a coffee and Philip's favorite: a pecan danish, which he placed in the glove compartment to keep as a surprise. On his way back to the house, he decided he'd pull onto the driveway, call Philip's cell, and ask him to come out. If things weren't settled by now, another few minutes were not going to make any difference.

When he made the turn onto Jennings Street, the flash of police car lights cut through the misty fog of his rear window. He slowed down and pulled over, letting them pass at the gravelly section of shoulder where he and Philip stopped only twenty minutes before. Two cop cars flew by, one right after the other, hurling gravel and mud into the air as they veered to the left and turned onto Angela's block.

Icy fear overcame him, and for a few seconds Jonathan couldn't move. His hands felt glued to the steering wheel, his legs heavy as tree limbs. Angela's house was on a cul-de-sac with no outlet, which meant something was happening on her block.

Jonathan forced himself to move, guiding the SUV back into the street. He stepped harder on the gas, almost missing the left turn onto Angela's street, twisting the car so sharply it went up the curb and onto the grass apron lining the sidewalk. He came close to losing control of the vehicle before he stopped, took a moment to get hold of himself, and then backed off the curb. Along the street people stood in front of their homes, gaping at the flashing lights and yellow tape at the end of the cul-de-sac – directly in front of Angela's house.

Jonathan rammed on the brakes, stalling only inches from a police officer who stood in the street with his arm raised. His eyes filling with water, Jonathan turned off the engine, tore open the door and ran up to the cop.

"I have to get in there!" He tried to keep his voice from quivering. "I have to get in there!" He moved toward the house.

The officer held up both his arms, his giant hands holding back Jonathan without touching him. "Not possible. This is a crime scene, Sir. I must ask you to stand back and stay on the other side of the tape."

The rain had turned to an annoying drizzle that coated Jonathan's face with tiny beads of water. Ahead of him in the driveway, police swarmed the porch like bees to a hive. *What the hell happened? Oh my God, Philip, what the hell happened?* Once again, he tried to walk around the policeman, but enormous hands grasped his arm and pulled him backward.

"Sir! This is a crime scene! Get back into your car, turn around and..."

"My partner is in there!" The officer crunched his eyes and cocked his head. "My *partner*," he repeated. "My lover... my boyfriend. Philip Stone. Is he in there? What the hell happened? I need to see him!"

The officer reached for the mobile transceiver strapped to his shoulder. "Please stay where you are for a moment, Sir." Turning away from Jonathan, he pressed a button and spoke into the radio as he walked to his patrol car. Every few seconds he twisted his head around and look back over his shoulder, giving Jonathan a poker-faced glare.

Jonathan paced the sidewalk. He couldn't imagine what would create this kind of scene. Philip had too much common sense and experience to let the conversation get out of hand. More confounding was the fact that Philip hadn't called him. Did the police take his phone? Did Angela smash it on the floor when he tried to leave?

He peered at the open front door, trying to see through the dirty screen. People moved around inside, but he couldn't tell what was going on. The screen door opened and three men stepped out of the house – two police officers escorting a man whose hands were cuffed behind his back. Jonathan's heart leapt as he took a few steps forward to get a better view.

He turned to the officer who was still talking on his radio. "For Christ's sake! What the hell is *he* doing here?"

The officer turned to Jonathan and released the button on the radio. "You know him?"

"I met him once," Jonathan answered with a voice that sounded as though it came from another galaxy. He was lost in thought, trying to fit the pieces together. "In front of Angela's apartment in the city. He's her friend. I think his name's Tommy."

"This guy might know something," the officer muttered into his radio. "Should I bring him up?"

A garbled response sent a chill through Jonathan. He used all his strength to hold back his tears and not allow the twisted knot in his stomach to strangle his insides. He reached for his phone to call Philip. *Enough is enough.*

"You can go up there now," the officer said, lifting the yellow tape. "Detective Lancer will meet you at the front door."

Jonathan slipped the phone back into his pocket and walked up the driveway toward the house. He glanced at Tommy, now leaning against a police car parked in the driveway. Tommy stared back, his face pallid and drawn, his eyes empty.

A tremor ran through Jonathan's body. *What did you do? What the fuck did you do? If you hurt him, I swear I'll kill you, you son of a bitch.* About to scream his thoughts aloud, he stopped short as a gentle hand fell on his shoulder.

"I'm Detective Lancer," a distant voice said.

Jonathan turned to face the detective, who immediately reminded him of their friend Max: salt and pepper hair cut close to his head, fine lines on a perpetually tanned face, and stubble way past five o'clock. Jonathan moved closer to the detective, his eyes not leaving the screen door.

"My partner's in there and I need to know why he hasn't come out here to see me. What happened, and where's Angela? What the hell is going on in there?" His own voice sounded strange, aloof, as though coming from someone beside him.

"What's your name?" asked the detective.

"Jonathan Beckett."

Detective Lancer pointed in Tommy's direction. "Jonathan, do you know that man?"

Jonathan clenched his teeth and pressed his anger down deep in his gut. "Detective, I don't give a shit about that asshole. I want to go inside and see Philip. If you let me in there, I'll tell you anything you want to know. Just let me in there, please, I have to see him."

The detective turned toward the front door. He flipped open and closed the memo pad in his hands. A smear of blood marked one of the pages. Jonathan took a deep breath and looked up to the clearing sky, blinking back tears.

"Jonathan, this is a crime scene and we need to make sure it remains uncontaminated until all evidence is gathered. It should only be another few minutes, I promise."

Jonathan looked to the ground. The grass, dormant from the long winter was now beginning to gain color and strength; the first sign of spring, the time of year he and Philip treasured the most.

"Philip," he said. "Where is Philip?" He started to dig up the soggy grass with the toe of his sneaker, penetrating the top layer and working his way into the mud. The dirt stuck to his sneaker and when he hit the wettest part of the soil, it splattered up the bottom half of his pant leg.

"Jonathan," Detective Lancer said softly, "I think you know what happened in there."

Jonathan shook his head on the verge of losing control.

"Tell me what's going on. Where's Philip? I need to get in there!" He attempted to convey force in his voice, but his words sounded shaky. Other than having the ability to shake his head, he felt paralyzed.

Lancer swung an arm around Jonathan's shoulder and led him to the porch steps. He paused and called to the officers guarding Tommy. "Get him out of here. Lock him up at the station."

After helping Jonathan sit down on the middle porch step, Lancer squatted in front of him. He picked off the thin pieces of mud stuck to the top of his black, lace-up shoes, allowing the silence between them to sink in.

"Is there someone I can call for you... someone you want to call?"

Jonathan cleared his throat. "You're not getting it," he said, holding his head in his hands. He stared at the peeling paint chips on the step below him. "I don't know what happened, for Christ's sake. I don't know where Philip is. If I called someone, what would I tell them? Huh? What the fuck would I tell them?"

The voices from inside the house were background noise, the wings of a thousand bees vibrating inside Jonathan's head.

"Do you know the woman who lives in this house?"

"Yes, Angela. I know her."

"Well, according to Angela, it appears she and Philip were having a disagreement. Her boyfriend, Thomas Flynn, was in a back bedroom where Angela asked him to stay. When the conversation between Angela and Philip got loud, Thomas entered the kitchen, under the influence of alcohol and apparently drugs of some kind. He confronted Philip and then became enraged. There was a struggle between the two men." Lancer paused and stopped picking the mud from his shoes. He looked at Jonathan and waited until their eyes met. "He stabbed Philip in the abdomen and evidently hit an artery. Your friend lost too much blood too quickly. He was dead within minutes."

Jonathan squeezed his head and took a deep breath. *Minutes. Minutes. What was Philip thinking during those minutes?* Jonathan winced, pain tearing through his gut, opening his insides like he'd been stabbed himself. The worst part, he suddenly realized, was that he'd live through it.

"How long have you and Philip been together?" Lancer asked, getting to his feet.

"Twelve years." Jonathan choked on his words.

"I'm very sorry for your loss, Jonathan. I really am. Who can I call for you?"

Jonathan reached for the phone in his pocket, his movements robotic, his energy coming from some unknown source.

"I'm calling our lawyer. She's also our friend." Jonathan fumbled the phone and it fell to the ground. Detective Lancer grabbed it from the mud and wiped it on his pants before handing it back to Jonathan.

"I'll wait by the door. By the time you're done, it should be okay for you to come in."

Struggling to see through his tears, Jonathan pressed G's cell phone number and waited through what felt like an endless repetition of rings. Finally they stopped.

"Mr. Beckett! So nice to see your name pop up on my Caller ID. How are you? I just happened to get out of court early and was about to call the two of you. Can you swing by the office today?"

Jonathan tried to speak but his throat was too constricted. He pushed again. Only air escaped.

"Jonathan? Are you there?"

"G…" was all he could get out.

"Jonathan. What is it? What's wrong? Where are you?"

"Philip…" His voice sounded strangled. "Philip…"

"Jesus, Jonathan. What happened? Tell me where you are."

He took a deep breath and leaned back on the steps trying to get air into his lungs.

"Angela's. I'm at Angela's. We need you."

"Jonathan, where's Philip? Is he with you?"

He pressed the phone to his ear unable to say the words. It was all too unreal. He closed his eyes and began to silently pray that this was one of his lucid dreams from which he'd awake sweating and panting. He'd then lean over and rub Philip's back, thanking God or whoever was running the Universe, that life was still as it should be.

But when he opened his eyes, his sneakers were still muddy and the buzzing from inside his head persisted. Through the buzz, he heard G's voice and a click on the other end of the phone. He wasn't sure what she said, but he knew she was on her way.

As Jonathan passed through the living room, Angela huddled on the couch sobbing, a tissue in one hand, a female officer holding her other hand. For a few seconds they stared at one another, neither saying a word until he moved toward the kitchen.

"Oh, Jonathan!" She cried out, her blubbering creating more sympathy from the woman beside her. "Philip!" Her bellowing filled the room and everyone stopped what they were doing to look at her. "Our baby! Oh, Jonathan."

Jonathan seethed, the tightening of his gut pushing his anger to the surface. The obvious falsity and overacting of her cries made him despise her in ways he never thought possible. It was as though a storm swept through him, leaving shards of glass and debris in every corner of his being.

"This is your fault!" He looked askance at Detective Lancer, then turned back to Angela. "You killed him."

From the corner of his eye he saw Philip's hiking boots. They were still on his feet, lying on their side, the rest of his body hidden by the kitchen's entrance wall. He walked toward the kitchen, ignoring Angela's sobs and pathetic moaning. When he turned the corner, Philip lay on the floor, the left side of his face flat against the tile, his hands curled beneath his chin as though he was merely sleeping. He almost would've thought Philip was sleeping, except for the pool of maroon colored blood on the kitchen floor.

The buzzing in his head ceased, leaving him with a quiet that circulated throughout his body. He sank onto his hands and knees and touched Philip's boots, his jeans, gently squeezed his calves.

Trying to stay clear of the blood, he crawled further up Philip's body, rubbing his face along Philip's arm, up to his neck, breathing in the scent of his hair. He pressed his lips against Philip's face. It was cold, like when they'd come in from shoveling snow and he'd warm Philip's cheeks with kisses. He waited for Philip to move, to turn his head, to whisper something, anything. *Please.*

"Jonathan," the voice was soft, almost maternal. "Jonathan," she said.

He looked up to see G standing only a few feet away from Philip's head. Still on his hands and knees, he crawled toward G, but before he reached her, he sat on the floor and began combing Philip's hair with his fingers.

G crouched next to him and brushed the back of her hand against his cheek. Still twirling Philip's hair between his fingers, he leaned into her as a strange sense of calmness took hold of him. It was as though the anxiety he'd felt his entire life had vanished; the invisible fear that followed him day in and day out had vaporized into thin air. The reason, he knew, was simple: the one thing he'd feared the most had happened. He'd lost what he lived for and without it, he had no reason to be scared of anything ever again.

22

He slouched in the center of the sofa, his thoughts as blurred as his watery-eyed vision. The buzzing in his head had returned, the result of people milling about his house, keeping their voices low as they tried to make sense of the tragic loss that led them to where they were today.

Jonathan refused to have a funeral or wake of any kind. Many years ago, both he and Philip decided that if one of them died before the other, the person left behind would do three things.

"Do you want me to have G put it in our wills?" Jonathan had asked, puffing up his pillow and turning on his side to get a better view of Philip.

"Are you kidding me, Jonny?" Philip stuck a bookmark into the book he was reading and placed it on the nightstand beside the bed. He then imitated Jonathan's actions by puffing up his pillow and lying on his side so he could peer at Jonathan straight on. "It's just three things we have to do. And they're personal, between us. Why would we put them in a will?"

Jonathan shrugged. "So we'll remember?"

"We'll remember," Philip assured him. "Just remember the three C's. Cremate. Celebrate. Circulate."

Jonathan hugged his pillow, awaiting an explanation, but none came.

"I get the cremate part, but what's the celebrate and circulate all about?"

"Celebrate the life. No depressing funeral or wake. Just a celebration."

"Got it," Jonathan agreed. "And circulate?"

"Spread the ashes, babe. Circulate. Take Max's boat straight out to the ocean, right off Montauk Point. Open the urn and let it fly!"

Jonathan smiled and swept Philip's hair from his forehead. "Just don't celebrate too hard or I'll have to come back and haunt your ass."

Philip turned onto his back, closed his eyes, and released a breath through puckered lips. "You're not going anywhere. If anyone's going to do any haunting, it'll be me. Now let's get some sleep. I've got a shitload of reports due tomorrow."

Jonathan propped himself up on his elbow, leaned over, and kissed Philip softly on the mouth. "You wouldn't leave me, would you?"

Philip kissed him back and whispered, "Only if you don't let me sleep."

"Promise me," Jonathan insisted, "or you don't get to sleep."

"I promise," Philip said, turning on his side. "I promise."

But the promise was broken, and to even the score Jonathan decided there'd be no celebration. He couldn't execute their agreement even if he wanted to. He just didn't have the energy. He felt as though his veins had dried up, his heart beat slowed to half its normal pace, sending only a minimal amount of blood to his body. His limbs were always cold, his head would not stop hurting and he hadn't slept more than six hours during the week since that horrible day at Angela's house.

"You look like shit." Max took a seat beside him on the sofa, placed his arm around Jonathan, and gently squeezed his shoulder. "Not that I can blame you, for God's sake."

Jonathan laid the back of his hand on his own forehead and held it there.

"What is it, Jonathan? Are you sick? Do you have a fever?"

"I don't know. I feel hot. Then I feel cold. I feel sick, then I feel okay. I can't figure it out."

Max tightened his embrace. "It's okay Jonathan. You're not supposed to know how you feel right now."

Jonathan remained as tight as a drumhead, his fists clenched. "Thank you for doing this. The food, the invites, the cleaning crew. I really appreciate it." He looked around the room at all the familiar faces. He might have greeted them, but he couldn't be certain. It was possible he had thanked them for coming, but that could've been on another day. Everything was a blur and the murmuring and soft cries were only making it worse. "But maybe it was a mistake. I know this should be a celebration of Philip's life, but I can't get there yet and I'm not sure I ever will."

"Please, no apologies, my dear friend. We'll consider this little get together an *acknowledgement* of Philip's life. And once you're up for it, next month or next year, we'll have a celebration. How's that?"

Jonathan nodded and let his gaze fall back to his lap.

"By the way, Jonathan, I was thinking it would be nice for people to feel as though Philip was here with us somehow." Max moved uncomfortably on the sofa, unsure which way to sit. "I was wondering... where's the urn?"

Jonathan stiffened and pulled away. "It's in the bedroom, why?"

"Well, I was thinking if it was out here, the guests could..."

"Could what?" Jonathan's voice grew louder. "Stare at it? Talk to it? Cry on it? What could they do with it, Max?"

Max squirmed and started to rise. "It's okay, Jonathan."

"Forget it!" he shouted. "It stays in my room with me!"

Before Max had the opportunity to try to reason with him, G appeared and gave Max a kiss on the cheek.

"Hi, Max, how are you?" She looked at Jonathan then back to Max. "Is everything okay over here?"

"As well as can be, I guess," he replied with a shrug of his shoulders. He bit his bottom lip and looked at Jonathan. "I'll be in the kitchen if you need me."

Jonathan nodded and turned to G, who now sat beside him. She took his hand in both of hers and brought it to her lips. "There are no words, Jonathan. No words to tell how much I hurt for you. I can't begin to imagine what you're going through and I won't pretend I can. Please just know that I'm here for you no matter what you need or when you need it."

He pulled her hands to him and kissed them back.

"You're the best, G," he said, letting go of her hand. "What's the latest with Flynn? Please tell me he's going to get a lethal injection."

Suddenly the room grew quiet and G looked around at the faces gazing in her direction. She grabbed Jonathan's hand, stood up, and drew him towards her.

"Let's talk in the study, okay?" She pulled him gently, but with enough force that he remained only inches behind her.

When they reached the study, Jonathan walked in first and sat on the sofa. He watched G softly close the door and then walk toward the chair behind the desk – Philip's chair, the Herman Miller they'd bought when Dr. Jesup prescribed it for his back pain. Within days the pain disappeared, never to return. Philip had been so excited, he'd sent the doctor flowers along with a note promising free investment consultation for life.

G looked at Jonathan, stopped mid-track, walked back around the side of the desk, and made her way to the sofa. She fell back into the plush cushioned chaise and dangled her legs off the side.

"As far as Flynn goes, I have two of my guys working with the DA's office to make sure nothing falls through the cracks. They're going to try and convict him for first degree murder, but right now we can't say whether that's going to stick. He might plead guilty, go for second degree, and try to get life. It will be a long time before this trial goes to court, Jonathan. So it's good to be prepared for that. In the meantime, he's on suicide watch."

Almost in slow motion, Jonathan shook his head.

"Suicide watch? Why bother watching? Let the shithole kill himself and get it over with. He's a waste of life. He doesn't deserve to breathe." Jonathan kept his voice down by breathing through clenched teeth.

G nodded and twisted the rings on her fingers.

"And what about that bitch, Angela? She's guilty too. Can't she be tried for being an accessory or something?"

G's bottom lip disappeared inside her mouth. She shook her head. "Unfortunately, no. The evidence at the crime scene along with Flynn's confession and the fact that both her and Flynn's story match in every detail basically proves she had no part in what happened."

"Bitch," he whispered. Deep down he'd known she couldn't be charged, but he couldn't help fantasize about her living out life in a prison cell. In the smallest of ways it made him feel better.

"By the way, she's in Bridgeport Hospital… also on suicide watch."

Jonathan laughed softly. "We should be so lucky," he said, gazing at the painting on the wall behind G.

It was a vividly colorful abstract of the Grand Canyon he and Philip discovered in Taos a few years back. At first he didn't like it, arguing it didn't go with the room's décor. But Philip fell in love at first sight and talked him into it. Within a few weeks of its delivery, Jonathan was glad he'd been convinced. The painting brought life to an otherwise muted color palette, adding such energy to the room that it became a conversation piece.

"Jonathan," G gasped. "She's carrying your child, for God's sake. I know you're hurting and I know you have to grieve. But there's your baby to think about."

"My baby?" he feigned a smile. "Are you sure? She's been screwing Flynn behind our backs for God knows how long. Another one of her endless lies. How do we know it's not his?"

G leaned forward. "Do you remember the chorionic villus sampling we did back in January? It proved your paternity,

Jonathan. We can do another one if you'd like, but I don't think we'd get a different result. It's totally up to you."

He did remember the sampling and vividly recalled the day G phoned with the results. He was driving to a client meeting when his cell phone rang. He switched on the Bluetooth and listened to her shout through the car speakers: "Congratulations, Daddy!"

Until a week ago, he'd thought that was the scariest moment of his life.

"I remember. And no, we don't need to do it again."

He looked at G then back to his hands, fiddling with his fingers as he struggled to find the right words.

"I'm not a bad person, G. You know that, right?"

She leaned over and rubbed his knee. "Of course I know that. You're one of the best people I know on this planet. You and Philip have always been…"

"Let me finish, G, please." He picked the raw skin around his fingernails and took a deep breath as he forced back tears. "I want you to know that I don't give a shit. I don't give a shit about Angela and I don't give a shit about the baby. I want them both out of my life – like neither one ever existed."

G removed her hand from his knee and slowly reclined against the chaise. The ticking of the pendulum wall clock was the only sound in the room.

"I'm not sure I understand, Jonathan." G crossed her arms, the blue silk fabric of her shirt scrunched beneath them. "For just a moment, let's forget we're in the midst of child support proceedings. You've helped to create a life that in less than three months will be brought into this world. It's something you can't decide to ignore like an annoying relative or nutty friend. This is your baby, Jonathan. Your son."

Jonathan stopped picking at his fingers and sat motionless. He looked at G and a sudden sadness seized him when he realized the limit to her empathy. But he didn't blame her; there was really no way she could understand. She wasn't the one crying and pacing the floors all hours of the night; she didn't hear noises in the house and wonder, for a split second, if it was Philip walking into the room to comfort him; she hadn't stayed in bed every morning searching for a reason to get up, unable to find one. Her sympathy, he knew, was endless. But her empathy, like everyone else's, could only go so far.

"It was *our* baby, G. Philip's and mine. It might've been my sperm, but it was the two of us who fantasized about it, planned for it, and talked about it every night. If I'd lost Philip under different circumstances and Angela wasn't the monster she is, I might not feel this way. But this is the way it's turned out and that's how I feel."

"Of course it's the way you feel, Jonathan." Her voice held compassion in every word. "But please know your feelings will change. You'll always have that sadness and emptiness inside, but please don't take it out on your son. Don't allow him to grow up without knowing the wonderful person you are. It wouldn't be fair to either of you."

Jonathan attempted to smile, but couldn't find the will. "G, I could sit here all day and try to explain things to you. How I blame Angela for everything that's happened and everything I've lost. I'm sure once she's out of the hospital, she'll be back stronger than ever fighting to get the money she thinks she deserves. That's just how she is. There's absolutely no doubt in my mind anymore that she planned this whole thing from the beginning. She first targeted Philip and then manipulated the two of us with lies and deceit to get exactly what she wanted. I don't think she wanted Philip dead. That was an unfortunate occurrence that sidelined her goal for a few weeks."

G tightened the grip around her arms. Her eyes filled with tears and she tried to blink them away.

"Think about it, G. How can I look at this baby and not see her? What about when he starts to talk like her or look like her? When he tells me how he and mommy went shopping or saw a great movie?" He shook his head and started to pick at his fingers again. "I'm not like most people. You know that. The parent-child bond isn't as strong for me as for others. The initial desire to have a child was as much Philip's as it was mine. Sometimes I think he wanted this baby more than I did. Either way, any desire I once had to have a child died with Philip."

G sat up and scooted to the end of the sofa. Leaning her elbows on her knees, she wiped away a tear and clasped her hands.

"And what about the child support battle? Fiona Wilder called me yesterday and…"

"I don't want a battle," Jonathan interrupted. "Give her what she wants. Like I said before, I don't care."

"I will not do that, Jonathan." She stood up and walked to the desk. "I know I'm your attorney, but I'm also your friend and I refuse to let her have what she's asking for. Especially after everything that's happened."

"G, listen to me. I don't want the drama. I really don't think I could go through it. No mediation sessions, no courthouses and all the other shit I'd need to do in order to fight this. I just don't have it in me. I'll be getting insurance money and I make a decent living. Please strike a deal that's as fair as possible but keeps me out of it so I never have to see that evil bitch again. And while you're at it, please see how much it'll cost me to get her to move out of Connecticut and never come back here again."

G leaned back against the desk and hooked her fingers onto its rim until her knuckles turned white. She looked to the floor, then back at Jonathan.

"I really can't believe I'm hearing this, Jonathan. You'd actually give her Philip's insurance money just so you don't have to go to court? Yes, there's child support you have to pay. But why give her extra money if you don't have to?" She walked over to him, knelt down, and took his hand in hers. "Off the record, I want this bitch to suffer and I don't want you paying one more penny than you have to. And I especially don't want her to have any of the money Philip left for you."

He squeezed her hand and rubbed it against his cheek.

"I know it's hard for you to understand, G, but I'm asking you to do this for me. Believe it or not, I'm thinking about the future and honestly, this money is to help assuage my guilt. Right now I feel nothing but contempt and hatred toward Angela. But there might come a time, way down the road, when I feel bad for a little boy who has a fuck up for a mother and a father who never wanted to see him. Knowing I'm helping this kid live more comfortably will ease my conscience."

G shook her head and was about to speak when Jonathan tightened his grip around her hand.

"G, if you can't do this because you're too close a friend, I completely understand. But please let me know now so I can have someone else take care of it."

G closed her eyes and pushed her forehead down onto his hand. He could feel her struggle, but would not buckle under.

The knock on the door made them both jump.

"Come in," Jonathan slowly stood as he let go of G's hand.

Wayne opened the door, Marina by his side, the black smudges of mascara encircling her eyes matching her Christian Dior day dress. She flew across the room and wrapped her arms around Jonathan's neck. With her face against his chest, she could barely catch her breath as sobs broke her words.

"I am... so... sorry... Jonathan... I..." She tried to complete the sentence, but her weeping wouldn't allow it.

Jonathan returned the hug and gently patted Marina's back. He looked at G, anticipating her decision. He hoped she'd be able to abide by his wishes because there was no one he trusted more.

"Can you give me until tomorrow?" She stood by the door, wiping away a tear with the back of her hand.

Jonathan nodded and offered her a faint smile.

Outside the door, a group of people had gathered. Jonathan closed his eyes and collected all the strength he could find.

The dreaded procession had begun.

23

The baby gurgled and smiled, squirming on its back atop the changing table. June smiled back as she wrapped the diaper around his legs and blew bursts of air on the bottom of his flailing feet.

"I can't believe how quiet he is. I've been here two days and haven't heard him make more than a squeak."

"He doesn't take after his mother, that's for sure!" Angela shouted from the bedroom.

June finished taping the diaper closed and lifted the baby up to her chest. Gently bobbing him up and down, she looked around the living room at the boxes and plastic-wrapped furniture, packed and ready for the moving company. It seemed only yesterday she was helping Angela move in as she started a life in Connecticut. But it wasn't yesterday; it was almost a year ago to the day and so much had happened since then; too much to think about without bringing tears to her eyes.

The call had come during her shift on the medical unit, just past 6:00 PM. She'd already finished taking vitals and was updating charts when the phone vibrated against her hip. She hesitated when the telephone number on the display read PRIVATE, but something in her gut told her to flip open the phone.

"Is this June Stokes?" The voice was gruff, as if the man on the other end of the phone was getting over a bout with laryngitis.

"Yes." She fingered the stethoscope hanging from her neck.

"Do you know an Angela Shelton?"

"Yes," she said again, shuffling toward the supply closet where she could be alone. "Who is this?"

"This is Officer Juarez," he said, his tone a bit friendlier and exhibiting a subtle Spanish accent when saying his name. "Your friend Angela asked me to call and tell you to come as soon as you can."

June stuck her index finger into her other ear to shut out the hospital noise. "Oh my God, what happened? Is she okay?"

"Yes, she's okay physically. Though at the moment she's very emotional. That's why she asked me to call. I can't get into the details, Ms. Stokes, but I do advise you to get here as soon as possible. We wanted to bring her to the hospital for routine tests, but she won't leave the house until you get here."

June leaned against the supply closet door and held back what felt like a freight train of tears. "Is the baby okay?"

"Yes. As I said, she's fine physically. She just needs a friend with her. I know you're in New York, could you be here by nine o'clock?"

June glanced at her watch and took a deep breath. She'd have to find someone to finish her shift, go home, pack a bag, get to Grand Central, and hope for an express train to the Fairfield station.

"I'll try my best, Officer." She could hear Angela trying to speak through sobs. "Have you called her friends Philip and Jonathan? They live closer and can get there a lot sooner than I can."

June heard the static of a hand covering the cell phone's microphone. After about ten seconds, she heard breathing. "That's not possible, Ms. Stokes." An uncomfortable silence fell between them. "That's why it's best you get here as soon as you can."

Before June had the chance to ask more questions, he'd hung up. She flipped the phone closed and shut her eyes. What the hell happened? Police? Hospital? And why wouldn't they call Philip and Jonathan?

Officer Juarez's response to contacting Philip and Jonathan played in her head: "That's not possible Ms. Stokes." She felt her insides tighten.

Should she call Philip herself? She flipped open her phone and scrolled down to his number. But just as something told her to answer the phone minutes before, something insisted she flip it closed and focus on getting to Angela's house. She slid the phone into the top pocket of her scrubs and headed toward Maria's office – the head nurse who would find her replacement for tonight and however long it took to get Angela through the mess she'd gotten herself into.

When the cab pulled up to the house, two policemen stood out front, silhouetted by the porch light. June paid the driver and bolted toward the porch steps.

"Ms. Stokes?" one of the officers walked down the steps to meet her. The sound of his voice told her this was Office Juarez, and she was surprised at how wrongly she'd imagined him.

The shorter of the two officers, he had a slim frame and his uniform could've used tailoring. From what she could tell in the dim light, he had a kind face, big eyes, and the shadow of a goatee that helped him appear older than the twenty five years he was. He held out his hand and smiled.

She nodded, shook his hand, and smiled back shyly.

"She's doing better now," he said. "The paramedic who was here earlier gave her something to calm her down, so she slept a little. But she's been waiting for you."

June pulled the tote strap further up her shoulder and peered at the doorway. Yellow light from inside the house seeped onto the porch floor, encircling Angela's welcome mat. June felt a slight tremble deep inside her abdomen. She wanted to get to Angela as soon as possible, but found herself hesitating to climb the steps. It didn't occur to her until that moment: whatever happened must have been tragic. It showed on the face of Officer Juarez and hung in the air outside the house. She couldn't bring herself to move.

"Can I help you up the steps?" Juarez gently took her elbow.

"I'm sorry," June said, her legs moving on their own, her feet somehow finding their way to the steps. "Can you tell me anything, Officer, just so I'm prepared?"

Juarez helped her up the steps and stopped when they reached the front door.

"I'm sorry, but I need to leave right now. There's a situation a few miles away I need to get to." He used his thumb to point to the officer standing beside him. "This is Officer Reilly. He'll be watching things tonight. We understand Ms. Shelton's not a flight risk, but it's protocol to have an officer keep an eye on things after an incident like the one today. Plus we'll need her to come to the station for questioning tomorrow. Officer Reilly will bring the both of you."

"Questioning?" June's confusion peaked to the point of anger. "I don't understand. You're acting as if I know what went on here. Please tell me something!"

Juarez reached into his shirt pocket and handed her a small card. "I'm sorry, Ms. Stokes. I'm not at liberty to offer details. Your friend will explain everything to you, I'm sure. This card has my cell number on it. Please call if you need to." He gazed into her eyes and tightened his lips. "Officer Reilly will be on the porch or in his patrol car if you need him for anything. Goodnight, Ms. Stokes."

She almost begged him to stay; to come inside and help her deal with what was waiting. Instead she swallowed hard, forced a smile and watched him walk to his car.

"June, is that you? June?"

June recognized Angela's voice and shook her head. She had no idea what she was in for, what lay on the other side of the door. She tried to ignore the pounding in her chest while her legs, as if working separately from her brain, led her through the doorway and into the house.

The first thing she noticed was the smell of industrial cleaner, similar to the disinfectant used in hospital rooms. Strangely, everything seemed in order, clean and in its place. Very atypical of Angela's house.

She scanned the room for clues. At first glance she saw nothing, other than Angela spread out on the sofa, her eyes closed with a pillow propped up behind her head and a damp dishtowel lying across her forehead. Her arm was extended, her hand gesturing as though searching for something in the dark.

"June?" Angela whispered, her eyes fluttering open. "Is that you?"

June walked to the sofa and let the carryall slide down her arm and onto the floor. She sat on the coffee table and took Angela's outstretched hand.

"Yes, it's me, Angela. I'm here."

Angela tightened her grip around June's hand.

"Thank God," she said. "Are the police still here?" Her voice seemed to be getting stronger.

"One officer's outside, keeping guard or something. Everyone else is gone. Now please, can you tell me what happened?"

June barely finished getting the words out before Angela grabbed the towel from her forehead and threw it onto the floor. Her eyes were wide open and raking the room. She clutched the back of the sofa and tried pulling herself up. June watched, paralyzed, not only by the sudden change in Angela's behavior, but also by her size. They hadn't seen each other for six weeks, and she figured the huffing and puffing she heard from Angela during their phone conversations was due to the baby getting larger. She never imagined Angela could gain so much weight. Her swollen face looked painful; her fingers and toes, ready to explode. And her legs, like fleshy tree trunks, were mapped with the largest varicose veins June had ever seen.

"Are you going to help me or what?" Angela bit her bottom lip as she continued her attempt to lift herself up. June broke from her spell.

"Yes. Yes. What do you need me to do?"

Angela grabbed June's knee for more leverage, then pulled and twisted her body until her legs slid down the front of the sofa.

When her feet hit the floor, she let out a sigh as though she'd just finished the Boston Marathon.

"What a fucking day," she panted. "I want to forget it ever happened."

"Jesus Angie, what *did* happen? Why do the police want you for questioning?" Angela looked toward the kitchen and let her gaze fall to the floor. "What Angie? What happened?"

"Philip's dead."

June gasped, the words hitting her like a shovel to the stomach.

"Tommy killed him," Angela continued, a tear now falling down her cheek.

Unable to speak, June covered her mouth with her hand. Her eyelids burned, the tears aching to break through. But she forced them back. She couldn't be weak, she was here to take care of Angela. Thank God she'd taken a Klonopin in the cab.

"How did it happen, Angie?" Her voice trembled. This didn't make any sense.

"When I saw Philip at the door, I told Tommy to stay in the bedroom. He'd been drinking all morning and increased his Zoloft dosage. I begged him over and over to find another med. The Zoloft always made him angry and aggressive. He promised he would, but never did." She shook her head harder. "Fucking asshole."

Still sitting on the coffee table beside Angela, June clasped her hands and rested her chin on them. "What happened, Angela? What happened to Philip?"

Angela wiped the tear stain from her cheek.

"Tommy promised to stay in the bedroom. He swore to me!" She took a deep breath and looked June in the eye. "But then he came out. Philip tried to leave, but Tommy wouldn't let him. I yelled at him to stop, to let Philip go, but it was like he couldn't hear me, like he couldn't hear *anyone*." She squirmed into the sofa cushion, then leaned forward and placed her hand on June's leg. "I could see the hatred in his face, June," Angela whispered as though trying to keep a secret. "Even as I yelled and begged him to stop, I knew deep down he was going to do what he did. I could see it in his eyes."

June tried to prepare herself, knowing the worst of the story was about to come. Even more alarming was how calm Angela appeared. Officer Juarez made it sound like she was on the brink of a breakdown and now here she was, lucid, composed, and too tranquil as far as June was concerned. Had she put on an act for the police? Or maybe she was hiding her true feelings; possibly in denial. June hoped that was the case, because if it wasn't that meant her fear had come true: Angela was a completely heartless human being. She didn't say a word and Angela continued.

"They were in the kitchen. I couldn't get up fast enough to see how it started, but they were pushing each other, struggling. I heard things falling and dishes breaking. I was yelling for them to stop. By the time I got to the kitchen, the sounds had stopped and Philip was on his knees. Tommy stood with his bloody hands in the air, looking at them like they weren't even part of his body." Angela placed her hands over her face and shook her head. A slight whimper escaped her mouth. "I still can't believe it, June. It's like a dream, like I'm still not sure it actually happened."

June shivered as the warmth of her own tears ran down her neck. She turned her head slowly toward the kitchen, scared of what she might see. The floor was spotless. Someone must've been called to clean up. She wiped the tears on her shirt and turned back to Angela.

"Where's Tommy now?"

"The cops took him away. They're going to put him away forever, that's for sure." She let out a huge sigh. "And just my luck, I'm the number one witness."

June rubbed the pads of her fingers across her face, trying to erase the mascara staining her face. She swallowed hard and pushed down the lump in her throat.

"And what about Jonathan?"

Angela fell back into the sofa cushion, letting her bare feet dangle a few inches above the floor. Her face was blank, empty, as though someone had vacuumed her emotions away.

"He blames me," she said.

June reached for her hand. "Oh, Angie, that's not true. Why would you say something like that?"

Angela gave a sarcastic chuckle. "Because he said so, right to my face. He came here after it happened and the cops let him in. 'This is *your* fault!' Those were his exact words."

"Angie, he was probably in shock. I'm sure he was saying things he didn't mean."

"Bullshit, June. Jonathan never really liked me. He was nice to me just to make Philip happy. And now, with Philip gone, he's going to treat me like shit, just like he always wanted to."

June forced herself to stand, then walked to the bay window and looked out. The porch light threw a hazy shadow across the front lawn and into the street where Officer Reilly leaned against his patrol car smoking a cigarette. She swiveled around on the ball of her foot and faced Angela.

"You need to give Jonathan some time, Angela. I'm sure he likes you. I mean, he gave you his sperm for God's sake. You're having his child! I doubt he would've done all of that just to make Philip happy. I think he's a little smarter than that."

Angela rubbed her swollen belly. "Screw Jonathan. He's the least of my problems right now. I just need to make sure the cops understand I had nothing to do with this. They need to know that Tommy's psychotic and I had absolutely nothing to do with Philip's death."

"Is that true?" The words escaped June's mouth before she had the chance to hold them back.

Angela's face looked ready to explode. Her eyes bulged and her cheeks puffed up like a blowfish.

"You *bitch*!" She stifled her yell, keeping an eye on the front door. She grabbed the thick glass vase sitting on table and raised it over her head. "If that cop wasn't out there I'd throw this at your head! How could you ask me that?"

June couldn't breathe. The house was incredibly warm, the heat getting more oppressive by the second. She unlatched the casement window on each side of the bay window and cranked them open. Taking a deep breath, she closed her eyes and tried to imagine her lungs filling with oxygen. She felt herself start to settle down until she was startled by a sound coming from the porch steps. When she opened her eyes, she saw Officer Reilly sitting on the top step looking back at her.

"Everything okay?" he asked, taking off his cap to wipe his forehead.

"Yes, fine. Everything's fine," she answered.

She backed up from the window and would've fallen over the coffee table if Angela hadn't yelled her name. When she turned around, the vase was back on the table and Angela once again lay on the sofa. Her inflamed expression had disappeared and her voice was once again trembling and mournful.

"I loved him, you know," Angela said, her gaze moving between June and the window. "I wanted us to be a family. Just the three of us." She rolled her eyes. "And Jonathan, of course. I swear, I would never do anything to hurt him. And I did everything I could to stop Tommy from doing what he did."

June half believed her. She was so tired and confounded by the evening's events, she couldn't find the strength to attempt making sense of anything. Images of the evening at Philip and Jonathan's home rolled through her mind like a slideshow – how politely they treated her; the subtle looks of understanding they'd give one another throughout the night; their compassion toward Angela, trying to make her feel comfortable. Her heart hurt, imagining what Jonathan was going through.

"There's no need to convince me, Angie. It's the police you'll have to convince tomorrow. Let's get you to bed so you can rest." She leaned over, grabbed Angela's hand, and pulled. When Angela was finally sitting up straight, she tried to release the hand, but Angela held on.

"Yes, June. I *do* need to convince you. I want you to know how I felt about Philip. How much I loved him and cared about him. It means a lot that you believe me."

June sighed and looked at Angela's face. So pitiful, like a pit bull after attacking and ravaging all its friends, now trying to hang on to the lone survivor. "Yes, I believe you, Angie. I really do. Now let's get you to bed."

"I'm glad, especially because you're my baby's godmother. Philip was happy about that, you know? He really liked you. And I know you liked him, right?"

"Of course I did, Angela. He and Jonathan were two of the nicest men I ever met. I'm heartbroken, for both of them. I liked Philip very much."

Angela smiled, tightened her grip around June's hand, and raised herself about a foot off the sofa. "I'm glad. And that's why I knew you'd be happy when I told you I'm naming the baby Philip."

June let go of Angela's hand and watched her fall backward.

"What did Jonathan say about that?"

Angela scooted up to the edge of the cushion and held her hand out for June to take.

"I don't care what he has to say. Now please help me up."

June shook her head, cursing herself for reliving that awful night. She and Angela promised themselves not to dwell on Philip's death – and more importantly, they made a vow to never bring it up in front of the baby. It only produced negative vibes, Angela said, and she didn't want any negativity around him. She told June that when he was ready, she'd tell him about Philip and what Tommy had done. But for now they would to pretend as though nothing had happened.

She tossed the dirty diaper into the pail and nested the baby's head beneath her chin. The sound of heavy footsteps from the hallway made her turn around in time to see Angela stop and lean against the wall. Grasping papers in one hand and wiping beads of sweat from her forehead with the other, she tried to catch her breath.

Who was this woman? How did the once beautiful, vivacious vixen who used to run up the stairs to her apartment like a teenager, turn into this heap of blubbery flesh stuffed into a tent dress?

June felt sorry for Angela. Like a pauper who'd won the lottery and lived the high life until the money ran out, Angela made herself skinny and played her beauty and sensuality to the hilt until she got herself pregnant and ate her way back into obesity. A sad situation and no matter how often she wanted to, June never rubbed Angela's face in it.

She often felt an odd sense of delight from Angela's weight gain, a pleasure in knowing they were now on a level playing field. Angela's obesity lowered her status to match June's, and that meant she no longer had to knuckle under to Angela's disrespect. Especially since June had been drug-free for the past six months. The withdrawal process was as painful as it was eye opening, showing her she had the strength to do whatever she put her mind to.

When she announced she was drug-free, Angela gave and expressed her congratulations, almost like an automaton. But June didn't buy it. There was hollowness in her tone, something that told June her best friend was a little distressed by no longer having anything to hold over her head. June ignored her reaction – she was going to be Little Philip's godmother, and that easily crushed any anger she felt toward Angela's resentment.

"This is it," Angela said, clomping toward the kitchen and waving the documents. "Once I sign these, I'll never have to deal with Jonathan Beckett again. Except to cash his checks, of course."

She pulled a dining room chair away from the table and carefully lowered herself onto it. June watched its legs wobble and she tensed up with every creak from the wood. When Angela finally got comfortable, June walked to the table with the baby.

"What do you mean you'll never have to deal with Jonathan again? What about visitation, holidays, and birthdays?"

Angela snorted. "June, tell me. Are you so involved with that Mexican cop boyfriend of yours that you've lost your ability to think? Have you not noticed there's been no sign of Jonathan since Little Philip was born? It's been four months, for God's sake. Do you *ever* think past your nose?"

June moved the baby to her other arm and let his face fall onto the burp cloth covering her shoulder. "No need to get testy, Angela. First of all, Office Juarez is not Mexican. His family is from Puerto Rico. And... if you remember correctly, every time I asked you why Jonathan hasn't come around, you just shrug your shoulders.

Now you're flapping these papers around and not telling me what they say. How am I to know *what* to think?"

Angela threw the pile of papers onto the dining room table and leaned back in the chair. "June, if you ever want to get this guy in the sack, you might want to stop calling him Officer Juarez." She laughed at her wit, picked up the papers, and fanned herself with them. "The long and short of it is that Jonathan wants nothing to do with me or Little Philip. He'll pay hefty support payments every month until Philip turns eighteen. He even kicked in another fifteen hundred a month if we moved out of Connecticut and promised never to return. Hence, we're moving back to the city."

A pang of sorrow punched June in the stomach. She caressed the baby's head, trying to cover his ears as though he could understand what Angela was saying.

"I don't believe it. He wants *nothing* to do with Little Philip? It's his son, Angela. I just can't imagine him not wanting to be part of his life. And to have you both move away?" She patted the back of Philip's head. "It's just unthinkable."

Although June spoke the words, she didn't mean them. In the back of her mind she sympathized with Jonathan. Angela and Little Philip would only be tragic reminders of the lover he'd lost and the life he'd never reclaim. She yearned to speak with Jonathan; to tell him how horribly she felt, how she would watch over his son and make sure he was always taken care of. But she knew he wouldn't want to see her.

"Yeah, unthinkable," Angela mumbled, still fanning herself with the documents. "What's *really* unthinkable is that I'm going to have to keep coming back here for Tommy's trial. I don't understand it. He confessed and my account supports his confession. Why the hell do they need to have a trial? It's a waste of time and money for everyone."

"It's the American way." June placed Little Philip in his stroller. He grabbed the rattle hanging from the crossbar and surprised her by examining it rather than shaking it. She smiled at his inquisitiveness. "Have you visited Tommy?" She could barely say his name without gagging.

"No. And I will never visit, no matter how many phone calls or letters I get from him. Seeing him in court is going to be bad enough. After the trial's over, I never want to see him again. He ruined my life."

June walked behind Angela so she couldn't see her face. "He ruined more than just your life, Angela."

Angela's cell phone rang and June let go a sigh of relief.

As Angela reached into the pocket of her housedress to answer the phone, she turned around and glared at June with eyes that shot invisible flames. She looked at the phone number on the caller ID.

"Shit, I have to take this." She covered the mouthpiece with her hand and used her head to gesture toward the bedroom in back. "Can you give me some privacy, June?"

"Sure." June sauntered down the hallway, but stopped before she reached the bedroom and stood completely still, trying not to make a sound. She extended her neck forward in an effort to hear Angela's voice.

"I can't talk now," Angela said in a stage whisper. "I have to call you from the road." After about a minute of silence, she spoke again. "I have the papers right here. You'll get it every month." More silence. "Enough, Dee. I said I'll call you from the car. I'm in the middle of moving, for Jesus's sake. I have to go."

June waited, unmoving, for what seemed like an hour. Who was Dee? She'd never heard Angela mention that name. . She kicked it around in her head trying to find some recognition. Nothing. She started to inch back into the living room.

"Are you off the phone? Can I come in now?"

"Yeah, I'm done."

"Who was that?" June asked, trying to seem as disinterested as possible as she shook the rattle in front of Little Philip.

"A pain in the ass is who it was." Angela put both palms flat on the table and pushed to lift herself up. "And where the hell are the movers? They said they'd be here by now."

At that moment, the beeping from a truck backing up into the driveway stopped Angela mid-sentence. June ran to the window and pulled aside the curtain.

"They're here!" She looked at Angela and then to Little Philip who smiled and blinked his long lashes over perfectly round, chocolate-colored eyes. "They're coming to take us away!" she said to him in a playful voice.

She looked around the room, her gaze stopping when she reached the kitchen floor. *They're coming to take us away.* Was leaving Connecticut a good thing for Little Philip? Only time would tell. In the meantime, she'd finish packing boxes and help load the truck that would take him away from a house filled with sadness, a sordid past he never chose to be a part of, and a father he'd probably never know.

<u>24</u>

"Hello, Jonathan." The woman moved toward the bed.

He recognized her at once: plain face, straw-like hair, and big teeth. Other than her deep wrinkles and sagging jowls, she'd looked the same thirty years ago. Not knowing what else to do, he clenched his fists and looked out the window. He didn't hate her. He barely knew her. His initial reaction was to have Katy throw her out, but he kept his mouth closed. What did he have to lose at this point?

"This is June Juarez," Katy said. "Do you remember her?"

June took a few steps closer to the bed. "I was June Stokes back then."

He wanted to look at her, but couldn't make himself do it. He stared out the window, where the sky was now blue and a hawk circled in the distance.

"I know who you are," he whispered.

"Would you like me to leave?" Her voice was weak, shaky, as if she were about to start weeping. "I know this must be difficult for you."

He didn't answer, just shrugged his shoulders and watched the birds disappear behind a giant maple. A snapshot of the night Angela and June came to their house shot into his head and his body twitched. It was the night of conception, a memory he'd driven from his thoughts for over thirty years and was now forced to face head on.

A sudden noise came from the doorway and he turned to see Katy lifting the open-armed visitor's chair and placing it beside the bed. June nodded her appreciation and sat down, her movements slow, her frail, inflexible body hard to bend. She laid her pocketbook on her lap and used both hands to sweep brittle strands of hair to each side of her face.

"Jonathan, I'll be right outside if you need me." Katy tapped June's shoulder and smiled at them both before walking out the door and closing it halfway.

Still unable to look June in the eyes, Jonathan watched her trembling hands.

"Angela's dead," June announced.

Jonathan couldn't move. His entire body went cold, numb. These were the words he'd longed to hear for three decades, yet now he felt nothing.

"Supposedly a brain tumor, but I don't know the details. Angela and I hadn't spoken for over twenty five years."

Jonathan slowly moved his gaze up her body until he reached her eyes – hazy and gray, the same as his own.

"Why are you here?" Jonathan clasped his hands so tightly his knuckles were white. "After all these years, why are you here?"

June grabbed her pocketbook with both hands and squeezed it. Tears filled her eyes. She took a deep breath and leaned back in the chair. "I'm not sure you know this, but I was Little Philip's godmother."

Hearing the name made his legs jerk with such force he feared he was losing control of his muscles. The last time he'd heard the name Little Philip was in G's office while signing the child support documents.

"Do you want to know what she named him?" G had carefully watched his expression as she slid the documents across the table.

Jonathan shrugged. Unable to understand the legal jargon, he scanned the pages for a place to sign. He trusted G. She'd fought as hard as she could to minimize his payments to Angela, but as she told him over and over again, without his participation in the proceedings her hands were tied. He didn't care. His only wish was never to see or hear from Angela or the child again and he'd sell his soul in order to make that happen.

"Little Philip," G said softly. "I thought you should know, because I remember that was the name you and Philip decided on."

Jonathan threw the pen onto the table. "G, please stop."

She looked down at the table and shook her head. "I'm sorry, Jonathan. I'm so sorry. I know I shouldn't bring it up, but I can't help it. For God's sake, it's your son. I just can't believe you, of all people, could act as if he doesn't exist. I don't doubt for one second that Philip would want you to be a part of your child's life."

Jonathan jumped up and walked to the window, trying to calm the intense trembling deep inside his stomach. He didn't want to let his anger loose on G, he needed at least one friend to help get him through this. But if she didn't stop talking nonsense, he'd have to let her go like all the others.

"G, please, stop." He leaned his back against the wall and looked deep into her eyes. "First, don't ever assume to tell me what Philip would have wanted. Only Philip knows what he would have wanted. And second, I'm in the midst of building my wall." He smiled at her bewildered expression. "I don't expect you to understand. Maybe because you're a mother and have mother instincts, or maybe it's because we're just totally different people. But I need to build a mental barrier between myself and the child. It's the only way I can get through this."

G tilted her head and looked up at him, her expression pleading for him to reconsider.

"When I think of everything that's happened – Angela, , the insemination, Philip's death, the baby, it feels like a nightmare; like a bunch of unspeakable events that took place with me on the outside looking in. Everyday I'm learning how to package those events and distance myself from them so I don't have to feel the pain and fear that's goes along with every memory." He shook his head and looked out the window again. "I know it sounds crazy, G, but if I want to live any kind of life, this is the only way I can manage."

"Okay, okay," G said. "I'll give in on that. If that's the way you want to live, or think you have to live, then so be it. But Jonathan, to give this selfish bitch five thousand dollars a month for eighteen years? That's over a million dollars. You know that, right? One million eighty thousand dollars to be exact. It's excessive, for *any* child support arrangement." She stood, walked around the table, and leaned against the back of a chair so her face was only inches from Jonathan's. "I know you're getting your insurance claim and I know you make a good living, but I'll say it again: It kills me to think that she'll be living off Philip's memory and your hard-earned money. The only good thing is your son will be provided for. Other than that, I think the whole arrangement sucks." She kissed his cheek. "And that's my professional, legal opinion."

He kissed her back and gave her a tense hug, the only kind of affection he'd been able to display since Philip's death. Touching others had become more of a task than pleasure. He felt more alone every day, pulling away from friends and family in a way that felt dangerous, but unavoidable. In time he'd return to his old self, or somewhat close to it. At least that's what he told himself day after day, year after year, until surrendering to the irrefutable truth that the life he was meant to live had been stolen.

And now, here he was, a shadow of the man he used to be, wondering what this woman sitting beside his bed was up to. Why, after all these years, had she decided to stir up memories he'd buried so well?

"Are you okay, Jonathan? Can I get you something?" June grabbed the bed railing and tried to lift herself.

"No. I'm fine. Now please, June, just tell me why you're here."

Once again June squeezed her pocketbook as though holding on for dear life. "I'm sorry. I've thought this through a hundred times, but now that I'm finally here I can't seem to get it out." She took a breath and pushed it out through her teeth. "It was two days before Little Philip's fourth birthday. The phone rang at one o'clock in the morning and woke me from a deep sleep. When I saw Angela's number on the Caller ID I panicked, figuring something was wrong at the apartment. But there wasn't." Her voice weakened. She opened the pocketbook and rummaged through the contents desperately searching for something. When her hands finally surfaced, they held a bundle of tissues.

"She called to tell me I was no longer Little Philip's godmother. No warning. No reason. Nothing. Just that I was no longer going to be a part of her life – or his." Jonathan watched in awe as she wiped the tears with the wadded up tissues. She acted as though she'd heard this news only days before rather than decades ago. "I asked her why. I begged for an answer. But in her obnoxious, selfish way she just said, 'This is just the way it is, June. You'll have to deal with it.' And then she gave me the worst news of all. They were moving to another state and she wouldn't tell me where."

"That sounds like her," he muttered. "Rotten to the core."

June pulled at the tissues and nodded her head wearily. Jonathan scrunched his eyes to see her better and realized she was lost in thought. Or maybe she had Alzheimers and didn't know where she was. He cleared his throat to get her attention, but didn't get a response. He cleared it again, this time much louder, shaking her from her fog and bringing her back from wherever she'd gone.

"I did everything for that boy. Bathed him, sat for him, took care of him when he was sick. I was the one who potty trained him for God's sake. He was such a sweet child. And then bam! She takes him away from me like it meant nothing." She wiped her eyes with the shredded ends of tissue. "For the first few days I left ten to twenty messages a day. I'd go by her building, but the doorman wouldn't let me in. I even stood outside the building one day in the freezing cold, waiting for them to come out. When they finally did, I ran up to her. She stood in front of Little Philip's stroller so I couldn't see him. Then she said she didn't care if my husband *was* on the police force, if I didn't stop harassing them she'd call the cops and press charges. In the end it didn't matter. Less than a week later when I tried calling her again, the phone had been disconnected. She'd taken Little Philip and moved away."

Unable to look her in the face, Jonathan stared at her hands.

"Was she still big?" His voice was barely audible.

"As a house," June said, covering her smile with her hand. "At least she was the last time I saw her. But that was almost thirty five years ago."

A ray of sun slid past the blind slats and through the crystal Katy had stuck on the window a few days before, painting June's face with spots of color.

"I'll ask it again, June. Why are you here?" He struck the mattress with the side of his fist. "I'm tired." He looked into her eyes. "I'm just so tired."

She placed her hand on his with such lightness he could barely feel it. Even so, his body jerked. "About three weeks ago, I received a call from Little Philip." She smiled and tightened her grip on his hand. "I should say Philip, not Little Philip. He *is* thirty five years old, though it's still hard for me to believe. He told me Angela had died. When he met with her lawyer to review the will, he saw something odd at the bottom: there was a heading that read, 'For Answers' and beneath it was my name and someone called Dee Previn, along with our telephone numbers. The phone number next to my name was old, from before I married Jesse and we moved to the Village. But Philip did some research and found me. I couldn't believe he recalled so well the things we did together. He was only four at the time, but he remembered. We talked for over an hour." She smiled and turned toward the window. "I cried for half of the conversation. Just hearing his voice and the fact that I was part of his memories filled my heart with joy."

Jonathan let her fingers slide into his closed fist as he fought back tears and tried to swallow the painful lump in his throat. Something was coming. He could feel it in the air and in her touch. He felt it in the sun that brightened the room with its midday glow and warmed the side of his pallid face. He'd ask no more questions. He'd just let her speak.

"Philip said the phone number Angela left for Dee Previn now belonged to someone else. He tried every way to discover who or where she was, but had only reached dead ends. I told him my husband Jesse was an ex-police officer and had detective friends who could probably find something. So Philip and I set up a date to meet and I promised him by that day I'd have more information about Dee Previn."

June held onto the bed rails and struggled to pull herself up. Once she was standing, she hobbled to the end of the bed, placed her pocketbook gently on the mattress beside Jonathan's feet, and looked directly at him.

"The week before Philip and I were to meet, my husband's contact found information about Dee Previn. She died about ten years ago in a car accident on Route 91 while on her way from New York City to Boston for a family reunion. At that time she was the Senior Lab Director at Spectrum Diagnostics in Manhattan, one of the top DNA testing labs in the country. She'd worked there for almost thirty years." June leaned forward, keeping her eyes on Jonathan's. "Jesse's contact dug further and discovered that for ten years Dee had received a check for one thousand dollars from Angela every month. The payments started right around the time Little Philip was born and continued until he turned eleven." She glanced toward the door, then back to Jonathan. "It didn't all come together until I met with Philip last week and saw his face and his eyes. When I saw his beautiful smile and his kind-hearted expression, it all clicked."

June stopped talking for a moment and walked to the door. Jonathan placed his hand over his heart, its pounding so strong he thought it would beat out of his chest.

"I should have known when she took Little Philip and ran away to another state she was up to something. She didn't want me to see him grow up because if I did, I'd know the truth – that she paid this Dee Previn woman to manipulate the results of your paternity test. It became obvious when I thought about the night of the insemination, how she kept me out of the bathroom while filling the syringe. She didn't need your sperm. She already had what she needed, frozen from fifteen years before when she volunteered at the cryo sperm bank in Boston."

Jonathan watched June step into the hallway and gesture for someone to come closer. When the man entered the room, Jonathan moaned as if someone was squeezing his chest and wouldn't let go.

What he saw seemed impossible. The man standing before him was Philip, looking exactly as he did thirty five years ago. This had to be a vision; some sort of delusion brought upon by extreme anxiety. But when he saw June and Katy standing behind the man, both wiping tears from their cheeks, he knew this vision was real.

"Philip?" Jonathan groaned, reaching out his hand. He tried to say more, but no sound came out.

The man picked up the chair beside the bed and moved it closer to Jonathan. He sat down and took Jonathan's hand.

"Hello, Jonathan. Yes, I'm Philip." He squeezed Jonathan's hand and glanced at June. "And as June informed me, I'm also Philip's son."

Even his voice was the same. Jonathan moaned again, the emotion coming in such waves and with such force he could barely catch his breath. His hand shook as he softly touched Philip's face with the back of his fingers, tracing across the eyelids of his deep brown eyes, down the length of his perfectly straight nose. He used his fingertips to brush Philip's cheek, to gently press his lips. He touched him as he'd touched his Philip a thousand times before, decades and decades ago in another lifetime.

With his free hand, Philip fished around his pocket and took out an old photograph. Jonathan could hardly pull his gaze from Philip's face to look at it, but when he did, he gasped and felt the warm tears rolling down the side of his face. It was a photo Angela had taken of them in front of her apartment building on that cold, fall day.

"I found this photo while going through my mother's stuff a few weeks ago. I'd never seen a picture of my father before, but I knew right away which of the two men he was. I mean, I look just like him. My mother always told me he died in a car crash before I was born. She said he was the love of her life since college and that's why he'd left us money, so we'd be taken care of. It wasn't until last week, when I met June, that I learned the truth – the *whole* story, including how you were the one who took care of us for all those years."

He squeezed Jonathan's hand, his eyes filling with tears. "I am so sorry, Jonathan. For everything. For what my mother did. For how my father died. For waiting so long to thank you for your generosity. And for never getting to meet you until today."

He let his head fall upon their clasped hands. Jonathan struggled to see through his tears and bit down on his bottom lip when he saw how Philip's feathery blond hair fell over his face, just like his father's used to do. He lifted Philip's face by his chin and brushed the hair from his eyes.

"Philip. don't. You have nothing to be sorry for." He took a labored breath. A chill passed through his entire body forcing him to shiver and squeeze Philip's hand tighter. "You're with me now, and that's all that matters."

The cold continued to flow through him until it stopped suddenly in his chest and pierced his heart like an icicle. Jonathan flinched. He held onto Philip's hand as another sharp pain pinched his heart and enormous pressure crushed his chest.

Katy gently pushed June aside and was about to press the emergency button behind the bed but stopped when Jonathan looked up at her and shook his head.

"No," Jonathan said with a faint smile. "Please, no."

He closed his eyes and let the numbness sweep over him. "Your father's here," he whispered. "He's been waiting for me."

He couldn't be sure if Mozart's Symphony #39 came from inside his head or radiated from somewhere within the brilliantly lit distance; the warm, enveloping expanse from which Philip approached. The only thing he knew for certain was that for the first time in his life, or his death, he was where he should be.

Made in the USA
Las Vegas, NV
15 December 2023

82841551R10193